PRAISE FOR THE NOVELS
OF SAMANTHA YOUNG

Fall from I...

"Everything I expect . . . angst, sw... mance story."

"Fans of romance and bad boys will dump their book boyfriends for Marco, who steals the show in this unforgettable love story. The author's voice can be heard loud and clear through the characters' personalities and true-to-life emotions." —*RT Book Reviews*

"One of those books that grabs hold of you and won't let you go till it takes you along that rocky road to their happy ever after." —Book Mood Reviews

"Complex characters and compelling twists. . . . The tale was hot, gave me the feels, and had me up late finishing this tale." —Caffeinated Book Reviewer

"A winning combination of romance, heartbreak, drama, and great characters." —One More Page (UK)

"This is one of those books that has you cursing by the end of it. Cursing that it's finished." —Serendipity Reviews

Before Jamaica Lane

"Truly enjoyable . . . a really satisfying love story." —Dear Author

continued . . .

"Samantha Young's winning streak continues with *Before Jamaica Lane*. . . . Her enchanting couples and delicious romances make her books an autobuy."
—Smexy Books

"Hot, bittersweet, intense . . . sensual, with witty banter, angst, heartbreaking moments, and a love story you cannot help but embrace."
—Caffeinated Book Reviewer

"Young's third book in the *On Dublin Street* series will entice readers in every way possible. It's flirty, romantic, and passionate. . . . The perfect mix of giddiness along with that dizzying feeling one experiences during the first stages of love [is] exact and ever so sweet."
—*RT Book Reviews*

"Wonderfully written, very upbeat, and easy to read. Samantha Young continues to be one of my favorite contemporary romance authors."
—Under the Covers

"*Before Jamaica Lane* is a delicious morsel waiting to be savored. . . . Samantha Young has done it again!"
—That's What I'm Talking About

Down London Road

"Ridiculously incendiary chemistry."
—Dear Author

"Passion, romance, angst, LUST, major heat, mistakes, personal growth, and the power of love all combine perfectly in *Down London Road*."
—Bookish Temptations

"*Down London Road* delivers on all fronts—charismatic characters, witty dialogue, blazing-hot sex scenes, and real-life issues make this book an easy one to devour. Samantha Young is not an author you should miss out on!"   —Fresh Fiction

"Another flirty, modern, and sexy story. . . . Thanks to the characters' special connection and snappy dialogue, readers will feel the pull of Young's story from the get-go and root for a happy ending."

—*RT Book Reviews*

On Dublin Street

"This book had some funny dialogue, some amazingly hot sex scenes, and emotional drama. Did I mention the amazing sex scenes?"

—Dear Author

"This is a really sexy book and I loved the heroine's journey to find herself and grow strong. Highly recommend this one."—*USA Today*

"Every page sizzles when these two get together, but this book is so much more than a hot romp. This book has heart—and lots of it. . . . *If* you want a book that will lure you in, grab you by the scruff of the neck, and never let you go until you finish reading the last page, then *On Dublin Street* is the book for you."   —TotallyBookedBlog

"This book has it all . . . romance, fabulously written heat, family, friendship, heartbreak, longing, hope, and an ending that is completely satisfying."   —Bookish Temptations

"Lots of heart makes this book an absolute page-turner."

—*RT Book Reviews*

ALSO BY SAMANTHA YOUNG

On Dublin Street
Down London Road
Before Jamaica Lane
Fall from India Place
Until Fountain Bridge (Penguin digital special)
Castle Hill (Penguin digital special)

ECHOES OF SCOTLAND STREET

An On Dublin Street Novel

SAMANTHA YOUNG

NEW AMERICAN LIBRARY

New American Library
Published by the Penguin Group
Penguin Group (USA) LLC, 375 Hudson Street,
New York, New York 10014

USA | Canada | UK | Ireland | Australia | New Zealand | India | South Africa | China
penguin.com
A Penguin Random House Company

First published by New American Library,
a division of Penguin Group (USA) LLC

First Printing, October 2014

 REGISTERED TRADEMARK—MARCA REGISTRADA

ISBN 978-0-451-47169-7

LIBRARY OF CONGRESS CATALOGING-IN-PUBLICATION DATA IS AVAILABLE.

Printed in the United States of America
1   3   5   7   9   10   8   6   4   2

Set in Garamond

For all the everyday warriors

Echoes of
Scotland Street

PROLOGUE

I think I'd worn Gran out with my music and my yapping on and on about Ewan. Her eyes kept fluttering closed and popping open and she'd mutter, "Oh dear," every once in a while. My boyfriend, the aforementioned Ewan, would be in Edinburgh soon to pick me up, so I saw no harm in waiting out on Gran's front stoop and letting her take a much-needed nap.

When I kissed her papery cheek and said good-bye, Gran offered me a warm smile, her lids already drooping. Letting myself out of the large house, I hesitated a moment in the spacious hallway. Her house hadn't seemed so big when Granddad was alive, but ever since he'd passed away three years ago, the house magically grew bigger and colder. Whenever I could, as I had done last night, I'd travel from my parents' house in our small town to stay with Gran for the night, sometimes even the whole weekend. Since Gran's house had always felt more like home than my parents' did, I took any opportunity I could to stay with her.

However, I couldn't stay the whole weekend because Ewan's band was playing a gig tonight and he wanted me there. He was the band's bassist. I was really excited to see him play, although I wasn't much looking forward to girls trying to chat him up after the show, like my friend Caro warned me would probably happen.

Shutting Gran's door, I turned and walked down a few steps to stand near the bottom of the stoop so Ewan could see me. He was seventeen, a few years older than me, and had just gotten his driver's license. He liked any old excuse to drive his wee, banged-up Punto, so I didn't feel bad about dragging his arse all the way to Edinburgh to come get me.

Digging through my bag for my phone and headphones so I could pass the time listening to music, I heard what sounded like a foot sliding along concrete behind me and I jerked around in surprise.

My eyes instantly collided with those of a boy.

He stood on the stoop of the house next door, a few steps farther up than me, and he was regarding me with something akin to shock. As I took him in, I felt my heart rate start to pick up.

His strawberry blond hair was slightly too long and disheveled, but he worked it because . . . I sucked in a breath, suddenly feeling a flutter of nerves in my stomach. The boy was utterly gorgeous. They didn't grow them like him at my school. As he stepped slowly down the stoop, the startlingly light green color of his eyes became clearer. They were "wow" eyes that I felt like I could drown in, and it occurred to me that perhaps I just might. When our eye contact finally broke, it was only because he was distracted by my hair.

Self-conscious, I tucked a strand behind my ear. The boy's eyes followed the movement. I'd been mocked for my hair for a long time

2

when I was little, but as I got older I started to get compliments on it. This meant I was really unsure about other people's reaction to my hair, but I refused to change it. I'd inherited my hair from my mum. It was like the one thing we had in common.

It hung down to just above my bottom in soft waves and natural ringlets. Not ginger, not strawberry blond. It was closer to auburn, but even then it was just a hint too red to be auburn. When the sun or artificial light hit my hair, Gran said it was like a halo of fire around my head.

The boy's eyes returned to mine.

A really awkward length of time passed as we continued to stare at each other, and I could feel myself begin to squirm under the surprising tension that had sprung up between this stranger and me.

Searching for a way out, I dropped my gaze to his black T-shirt. It was a The Airborne Toxic Event shirt and I felt my lips curling into a pleased smile. TATE was one of my favorite bands. "Have you seen them live?" I asked more than a little enviously.

The boy glanced down at his shirt as though he'd forgotten what he was wearing. When he looked back at me, his mouth kicked up at the corner. "I wish."

I felt a rush of excitement at the sound of his voice and unconsciously stepped a little closer to the wrought-iron fence that separated us from each other's stoop. "I'd love to see them live."

He moved closer and I tilted my head back. He was tall. I was a small five foot three and the boy was almost a foot taller than me. My gaze wandered, no longer under my control, taking in his broad shoulders, down his lean, muscular arms to the big hand he had wrapped around one of the wrought-iron spearheads that embellished the fence. I felt a flip in my belly at the thought of being touched by one of those hands. They were masculine but graceful and long-fingered.

I flushed, thinking about what Ewan had done to me last week, except suddenly imagining this boy in his place. Guiltily, I chewed on my lower lip as I looked back up at the boy.

He didn't seem to notice that my thoughts had meandered into the indecent. "You're a fan of TATE?"

I nodded, feeling suddenly shy of this person who had elicited such a strong reaction in me.

"They're my favorite band." He gave me a small grin and I instantly wanted to know what he looked like when he laughed.

"One of mine too."

"Yeah?" He leaned in a little closer, his eyes searching my face as though I was the most interesting thing he'd ever seen. "What other bands do you like?"

The thrill of having his attention broke through the uncharacteristic shyness and I rattled off all the bands I could think of that I'd been listening to lately.

When I was done he rewarded me with a smile, and that smile winded me it was so good. There was something flirtatious there but at the same time boyish, charmingly boyish and utterly endearing. It was a great smile. A really, really great smile.

I sighed inwardly and leaned farther into the fence.

"What's your name?" he asked me, his voice low because we were so close now we could whisper and we'd hear each other. I could actually feel the heat from his body, and realizing we were standing quite intimately made me hugely aware of my own body as well as his. I flushed inwardly again, thankful I wasn't a typical redhead with blush-prone skin.

"Shannon," I replied, sure there was a hush in the air between us and afraid to break whatever it was by being too loud. "Yours?"

"Cole," he said. "Cole Walker."

That made me smile. It fit him perfectly. "You sound like a hero."

Cole grinned. "A hero?"

"Yeah. Like if there was a zombie apocalypse, the hero who tries to save everyone would have a name like Cole Walker."

His chuckle warmed me through and through, as did the way his eyes brightened with amusement. "Zombie apocalypse?"

"It could happen," I insisted because I never liked to rule out any eventuality in life.

"You don't seem all that worried that it could."

That was because I wasn't. I shrugged. "I've just never understood why people are afraid of zombies. They move really slowly and are brain-dead."

Cole snorted. "Two very fair points."

I smiled. "So, are you a hero, Cole Walker?"

He scratched the side of his chin, looking off into the distance. "What is a hero, really?"

Surprised by the deep and apparently serious question, I shrugged. "I suppose it's someone that saves people."

His eyes flicked back to me. "Yeah, I suppose it is."

Trying to lighten the mood, I gave him a flirty smile. "So, do you save people?"

Cole laughed. "I'm only fifteen. Give me a chance."

We were the same age, then. I was surprised. He could pass for eighteen. "You are really tall for fifteen."

His eyes drifted over me, a small smile playing on his lips. "A lot of people must seem tall to you."

"Are you calling me short?"

"Are you saying you're not short?"

I wrinkled my nose. "I'm not delusional. It's just not polite to comment on a girl's shortness. For all you know I'm really mad at the world because I'm vertically challenged."

"Maybe I'm really mad at the world because I'm tall."

I gave him a look that said *as if* and he burst out laughing.

"Okay, I'm not mad at being tall. But you shouldn't be mad about your height."

"I'm not," I hurried to assure him. "I was just making a point."

"A pointless point."

I giggled, thinking over our bizarre conversation. "Yeah."

Cole smiled, and I felt myself go all hot inside again at the way he was looking at me. "I doubt anyone notices your height anyway. You've got all that great hair and those amazing eyes to distract them." As soon as he said it he flushed and ran a hand through his own hair, as if embarrassed he'd complimented me out loud.

My cheeks burned with pleasure. "You've got amazing eyes too."

His momentary shyness instantly disappeared at my compliment. Cole leaned forward over the fence. "Please tell me you live here."

Before I could answer, a loud honk shattered the intensity between us and I jerked my head up to see Ewan approaching in his old Punto. Reality came crashing back down around me, and for some reason I felt a weird sense of loss when I looked back at Cole. "I live in Glasgow," I told him regretfully. I gestured to the car. "My boyfriend's here to pick me up."

Disappointment flashed in Cole's eyes. "Boyfriend?" His gaze flew toward the car and I watched his face fall.

My heart sank in my chest. "Sorry," I whispered, not really sure what I was apologizing for.

"Me too," he murmured.

Ewan honked the horn again and I blanched, moving down the steps, my eyes still on Cole. We held each other's gaze as I walked over to the car and slowly, reluctantly, got into it.

"Hey, baby," Ewan said, finally causing me to break my connection with Cole.

I gave my boyfriend a tremulous smile. "Hi."

He leaned over and kissed me before settling back into his seat to drive away.

Panicked, I turned back to my window to find Cole, but the stoop where he'd stood was now empty. A heavy feeling settled over me.

"Who was that?" Ewan asked.

"Who?"

"The guy on the stairs."

"I don't know." *But I hope I get to find out.*

Ewan started chattering on about the band, not bothering to ask me how my night had been or how Gran had seemed even though I'd told him I was worried about her. As the old car took me away from Scotland Street amid his incessant chatter, I felt like fate had just handed me two cups and I'd stupidly drunk from the wrong one.

CHAPTER 1

Edinburgh
Nine years later

INKARNATE.

I stared up at the sign above the tattoo studio on Leith Walk, worrying my lip between my teeth. There was nothing for it. I had to open the doors and step inside.

I blew out a deep breath until my lips formed a disgruntled pout. The sign for INKarnate was painted in bold font across a long panel of glass above its door. The two large panels of glass on either side of the glossy black door were covered in pictures of tattooed limbs, artwork, and bold red-and-purple signs that screamed TATTOOS, PIERCINGS, TATTOO REMOVALS at the passing public. In the center of the panel farthest away from me were two large white signs that proclaimed proudly SCOTLAND'S #1 TATTOO STUDIO and MULTI-AWARD WINNER.

Even I, who had no tattoos to speak of, had heard of INKarnate.

Okay, true, I'd dated quite a few blokes with tattoos, but that wasn't the reason I'd heard of Stu Motherwell's tattoo studio. I'd heard of it because his signs didn't lie and he'd even been on television a few times over the past few years. Stu had owned INKarnate for about thirty years now. He was an extremely talented and ambitious artist and was purported to only hire fantastic artists to work alongside him.

You'd think I'd be absolutely over-the-moon to get an interview for the admin assistant/reception position they needed to fill. However, INKarnate embodied everything I was running from at the moment. Everything that was bad for me.

I'd only applied for the job because admin jobs were scarce.

Ironic that this should be the only application that had produced a response.

What could I do, though? I crossed my arms over my chest, my eyes glued to the sign TATTOOS. I'd had to get away from Glasgow, and I had nowhere to go—Edinburgh was the only place I knew well enough to feel comfortable moving to, and it was expensive as heck. The hotel I was staying in was really a hostel and I couldn't afford to stay even there that much longer. Although I had enough in my savings for two months' rent on a really crappy flat, I wouldn't get a lease until I found a job.

I needed to eat and I needed a roof over my head.

As Gran used to say, beggars can't be choosers.

Letting my hands fall to my sides (defensive posture wasn't really a good way to start an interview), I waited for a woman with her pram to pass by the studio before striding up to the door and pushing inside. An old-fashioned bell at odds with the rest of the decor jingled above the door as I entered.

My low-heeled boots sounded loud on the expensive-looking white-tiled flooring. It was shot through with chips of silver mosaic pieces and was more elegant than I would have expected for a tattoo studio.

For a few moments I eyed the rest of the interior. It was like a typical tattoo studio but less . . . grungy. The main room was large and spacious. A small curved black marble counter sat to my left, and on it was a shiny iMac I would have given my eyeteeth for. Behind the counter was a massive closet I couldn't miss because its door was open, revealing a chaotic mass of files on the shelves inside. Opposite the counter on the other side of the room was a huge, well-worn black leather L-shaped sofa that looked really comfy. A glass coffee table was positioned in front of it, with a scatter of magazines on it and what looked like a bowl of shiny-wrapped toffees. Directly ahead of me was a mini gallery of sorts. The walls were white and nearly every inch of them was covered in tattoo concepts. The only walls that had been left bare were the partition walls placed here and there throughout the space. On them were television screens where indie and rock music played softly as a sound track to snapshots and video footage of the artists' portfolios.

It was all about art here.

But where were the artists?

I stared around at the emptiness, my eyes eventually coming to a stop on a door near the back left-hand corner. I could hear the buzz of a tattoo needle. The workshops must be back there.

Should I venture in?

I hesitated only to be shuffled forward by someone attempting to open the entrance door. Moving out of the way, I gave the young man an apologetic smile.

"All right?" He nodded at me in greeting before swaggering over to the counter. He hit an old-fashioned bell a few times.

Oh. Okay.

A few seconds later a figure appeared in the doorway at the back. A huge, hulking beast of a figure. I stared openmouthed as he moved toward us, and slowly recognition hit me.

The graying beard and long wiry hair, the jolly grin and crinkles around the blue eyes. No, not Santa Claus.

Stu Motherwell.

He approached the counter in slow, measured steps and I noted that the black motorcycle boots he was wearing had definitely seen their best day a long, long time ago. The buzz of a tattoo needle continued from the room beyond, so I guessed there was at least one other tattooist back there.

"Hi, son," he greeted the young man. "How can I help?"

"I've got an appointment for a tattoo removal in ten minutes."

"Name?"

"Darren Drysdale."

Stu bent over to look at the computer screen, clicking the mouse a few times. "Drysdale. Take a wee seat. Rae will be ready for you in a bit. I'd offer you a coffee, but my last assistant bought that fucking contraption and none of us know how to use it."

The customer snorted. "No bother, mate." He nodded at him and turned around, wandering over to the sofa to wait.

I then found myself under the scrutiny of Stu's bright blue eyes. He seemed to take stock of me for a moment and then he gave me a massive grin. "And what can I do for you, wee fairy?"

Wee fairy? That was new. If he wasn't my interviewer, I might reply that this "wee fairy" would ram her wee but effectual foot up his arse if he "wee fairied" me again.

It was possible I was a little angry these days.

But also desperate . . . so . . . "I'm Shannon MacLeod." I stepped forward and held out my hand. "I'm here for the interview for the ad-min position."

"Thank fuck," Stu pronounced jovially, striding around the counter to enfold my hand in his huge one. He shook it, shaking my whole body with the motion. "At least you look normal. The last one looked like she hadn't seen a human being in forty years."

"Oh?" How was I supposed to reply to a comment like that?

"Aye. She didn't even know what an apadravya or an ampallang was."

I winced just at the thought of those genital piercings. A brave man, was all I'd say, a brave man indeed who sucked it up and got ei-ther one of those. "You do those here?"

"Simon is our piercings guy. He does it all." Stu grinned. "I take it from that wee flinch you know what they are."

I nodded, not really comfortable discussing penis piercings with my possible boss—although I guessed if I got the job, that might very well become normal conversation between us. "Surely, you don't get a lot of requests for those, though, right?"

"I'm sure women the world over would prefer more than we do get." Stu chuckled at his own joke and started walking toward the back room, gesturing for me to follow him. "My office is through here. Let's chat."

We passed through the back door, entering a long narrow hallway where light from three doors streamed through. The buzzing noise was coming from the middle room. Stu pointed at them. "Three work-rooms." He pointed to the one nearest us. "I share that one with my manager. He's our main tattooist and our finest artist, so he usually does the big projects, unless I take a particular interest. Fridays are his day off, so unfortunately you won't meet him today. The middle room is Rae's. She's finishing up a small tattoo at the moment. She does our tattoo removals as well. The last one is Simon's. He's a tattooist, but you'll find most of his appointments are for piercings." Stu nodded toward the closed door at the end of the hall. "My office."

We passed by the workrooms and I sneaked a peek inside the middle one. I saw the back of a skinny, purple-haired woman I guessed was Rae. She was tattooing what looked like a butterfly on the lower back of the curvy girl braced over a chair.

I peeked inside the last door, meeting the eyes of a nice-looking, tattooed bald guy. He had a customer, but he gave me a little wave as I passed. I returned it, thinking he had kind eyes.

"In we go, wee fairy," Stu boomed heartily as he opened his office and swept an arm in a gesture for me to enter before him. He frowned as I moved past him. "What did I say?"

I realized I must not have been able to keep my irritation off my face. Oh well, he'd caught me, so I might as well be honest. "Wee fairy? Not really sure how to take that."

"Well, I don't mean anything bad by it, lass." Stu strode into the room, passing me to take the big leather seat behind his cluttered desk. He waved a hand at the chair in front of me, so I quickly took it. "It's just with that hair and those eyes and the fact that you are in fact 'wee,' you remind me of a wee fairy."

Despite myself, I found I was fighting a smile. This big bruiser of a man seemed perturbed and worried that he might have upset me. "It's okay. I'm just a bit nervous about the interview."

"Och, don't be nervous." He shook his head. "We're just going to go over your work experience and then I'll introduce you to Rae and Simon. If you get the job you'll be working mostly with them, so I like to get their feel for a person."

From there we chatted for about fifteen minutes or so about my previous work in the administrative world. He was mostly interested in my experience as a receptionist for a tattoo studio in Glasgow. I'd worked there until I was twenty. I'd been dating a local biker at the time who was almost ten years my senior (yeah, my family had loved him), and his best mate owned a studio. The job lasted as long as the relationship, which was roughly eighteen months. It was charming really—he cheated on me with a skanky biker babe and I was the one that got fired. "Downsizing," my boss had called it. Yeah, more like his mate found it too awkward to have me around after I walked in on him screwing another woman.

I'd soon discover that was just one of the many joys of dating an honest-to-goodness bad boy.

"That all sounds great." Stu gave me a huge endearing grin that made me smile despite myself. He'd really made me feel at ease during the interview, and I'd begun to think that working at INKarnate might not be such a bad thing after all. "Let's go meet Rae and Simon."

Simon's room was empty, but we found him hovering in the doorway of Rae's, watching her work as she talked with the young man who was there for what appeared to be his first session for a tattoo removal. The young guy blinked up at the doorway in alarm when Stu and I appeared.

Rae frowned at his abrupt change in demeanor before following his gaze. She smirked. "Don't worry. They're not all here to watch. Right, Stu?"

Rae's purple-and-black hair was cut choppy and short around her long, narrow face. She had a sharp nose and a thin mouth. A tiny jet stud sparkled on her nose, and a small silver hoop pierced the left side of her lower lip. Huge dark eyes and enviously long black lashes saved her face from being too severe. The more I gazed at her, the more I realized she was striking even without the hair and the piercings and the sleeve of black rose tattoos down her right arm. A skinny Harley-Davidson tank top and black jeans showcased her long-limbed figure.

"Who's Red?" She nodded her chin at me.

"This is Shannon. Shannon, these are my artists, Rae and Simon." Stu gestured to the tall, bald artist.

Simon grinned at me and I felt my warning flag start to fly. He had dimples, very, very charming dimples, glittering hazel eyes, and nicely developed muscles underneath his gray Biffy Clyro shirt. Tattoos covered every inch of both his arms. Black tunnels pierced his ears.

He was a problem.

Perhaps a job at INKarnate wasn't going to work out after all.

"You should hire her," Simon said to Stu without taking those pretty eyes off me. "She's hot. She'll attract interest."

Nope. Definitely not going to work out.

A snort erupted from Rae as she perceptively read the expression on my face. "Don't worry, Red. He prefers dicks. Like, actual dicks."

I blinked in surprise not just at her crassness, and in front of a customer no less, but at the implication. Simon was gay? He caught my look of surprise and laughed. "Yes, I'm gay."

I hated to admit it to myself, but the revelation made me relax instantly, the disappointment I'd felt only moments before disappearing. I grinned at Simon now. "If you're single I'll pass out with disbelief."

He laughed at that, seeming pleased. "I'm not. My boyfriend is called Tony. He's Italian."

"Oh, don't get him started on Tony," Rae groaned, rolling her eyes. "I love the guy, but if I have to hear one more tale of Tony's talented mouth and generous heart I'm going to vomit all over myself."

My eyes betrayed my shock and Simon patted my shoulder. "Don't worry. It's just Rae's way. She loves me really."

She harrumphed at that and turned purposefully back to her client, who'd been watching us with something akin to boredom on his face. "Hire her, Stu. You know I love shocking the fuck out of people, and Red here looks like she'll make that fun for me."

"I take that as a challenge," I said, feeling indignant at the accusation that I was somehow thin-skinned. "I've been around and heard a lot worse, I promise you."

Her mouth quirked up at the corner. "I'll take *that* as a challenge."

"You've done it now." Simon sighed.

"You're hired," Stu announced.

I looked up at him, feeling an overwhelming rush of relief. "Seriously?"

He smiled. "Aye, I like you."

That didn't sound very professional. "You're hiring me because you like me?"

"People have no idea how important that is to a successfully run business. If everyone gets along, if the atmosphere in here is great, people will recommend us."

"Oh yes, because my affable fucking nature, *not* my immense ability with a tattoo needle, is what brings in all the recommendations," Rae drawled.

Stu grunted. "It's not your affable fucking nature or your ability with a tattoo needle that brings in the recommendations. It's—"

"Cole," she finished for him, throwing him a grin. "But I'm not bad either."

Stu couldn't help smiling at that. "Aye, you're not bad either."

"Right." Simon turned toward us and shooed us with his hands. "Let Rae work." He smiled at me as we walked out into the hallway. "So, are you accepting?"

I thought about it as I wandered after Stu into the main room. A customer waited at the counter and Simon hurried over to greet him while Stu stared at me expectantly.

So Rae had a mouth on her and I was guessing no filter between said mouth and her brain, but underneath the prickly demeanor I sensed a real affection for her employer and her colleague. Stu was loud and blunt but easygoing and laid-back. And Simon seemed just as easygoing and nice.

It couldn't be the worst place to work.

Who was I kidding? They could be horrible and I'd still be accepting this job. I stuck out my hand. "Thank you. I'd be pleased to accept."

Stu beamed, shaking my hand and with it my whole body again. "Brilliant. How does Monday sound?"

"Brilliant," I echoed, smiling hugely for the first time in days, weeks even. I was relieved to finally be moving forward with my life.

Stu looked over his shoulder at Simon. "She said aye!"

Simon laughed. "Good news. Cole will love her."

"Oh, aye." Stu chuckled in a way that made me feel suddenly nervous. Who was Cole? Stu's eyes twinkled. "I'm actually semiretired. I'm not around a lot, so I leave the running of the place to my manager, Cole. He'll go over everything you need to know on Monday."

I smiled weakly in response.

I suddenly had a very bad feeling in the pit of my stomach.

The room was cold and narrow, but at least it was a place to rest my head for now. Although that didn't make the surroundings any less depressing. Not to mention I hated having to share the communal bathroom with the five other guests who were staying at the "hotel."

I'd finished filling out the employee details form Stu had given me before leaving INKarnate. On the one hand I felt incredibly lucky to have secured a job so quickly, and on the other I was absolutely dread-ing meeting my new manager. I had to hope that he was just like Stu or even Simon. Not a bad boy.

Grumbling under my breath about the miscommunication that had landed me in this situation, I pushed away the form and picked up my phone. No messages. As if I really expected there to be any—I hadn't been entirely visible back in Glasgow to my family, but at least I'd existed. Now it was like I'd been wiped from all recollection.

Ignoring the burn of anger in my gut, I got up and crossed the small room to where I'd piled my suitcases and five boxes with my belongings. I'd thrown most of my stuff out before moving. I thought it might help to purge myself of those memories in order to start over.

Searching through the boxes, I found the one I was looking for. The one box I'd kept from high school was the one with all my old sketch pads and art materials. Sketching always relaxed me—it took me out of myself for a little while. I seemed to need that a lot lately.

When I was packing up, I hadn't had enough time to go through all my old drawings, but tonight I had nothing but time and four grim walls. I needed something to take my mind off my family problems, and I didn't have money to buy any new books.

Hauling the box over to the bed, I wiped away the dust that had collected on the top of the sketch pads with an old T-shirt and curled up on the bed to look through them. Some of the older drawings made me smile. Drawing wasn't something that had come particularly easy to me at first. I'd loved to do it but was never able to make a sketch come alive. Until a boy in my first-year class (one I happened to have a massive crush on) in high school showed me how to hold a sketch pencil correctly and how to stroke against the paper, not draw in hard, unbending lines.

From there I caught on quickly and I was hooked.

The art lasted. The first crush didn't.

A sheet of paper fell out from the third sketch pad I'd picked up and suddenly I was reminded of another boy. A year ago I would have been able to look at the sketch and feel nothing but a prickle of pain— a ghostly reminder rather than the real thing.

Now, however, looking down at the drawing of my ex-boyfriend Nick, I felt bitterness well up in me. That bitterness was becoming a familiar part of me and I hated it. I just didn't know how to fight it.

But I leaned against my pillow, my fingers crinkling the sketch of the gorgeous Nick Briar. I'd gone out with Nick nine months after my first boyfriend, Ewan, had dumped me out of the blue. For a time Nick soothed the hurt Ewan had left me with. In my immaturity, I actually felt like I had won something over Ewan when I began dating Nick. He was nineteen and gorgeous and the lead singer in a rival rock band.

Nick had been the first of my bad boys . . .

The small club was dingy and smoky and much too hot. But I was filled with giddy excitement as I watched Nick sing onstage with his band, Allied Criminals. I thought their name was stupid and I wasn't a huge fan of their music, but I loved Nick's voice and his passion and how excited people were by them. I felt proud standing in the crowd as his girlfriend, and I promised myself I would always support him, no matter what.

Nick played up his brooding persona onstage, but in reality he was such a sweet guy. The night before, when I told him I wouldn't be able to make it to this performance because of a family thing, he'd been really cool about it. He was disappointed, but he didn't make a big deal about it like Ewan would have. And he made me feel special in a way that Ewan never had. Nick was always telling me how beautiful I was, how funny and interesting. I'd felt ordinary until I met him. I was completely falling for him, which was probably why I'd had sex for the first time with him a few weeks ago.

My friends were acting all immature about it and jealous, which was ridiculous. They thought it was a mistake for me to give it up to him and were really being unsupportive and ignorant about the whole thing. Lucky I had Nick in my life so I didn't have to put up with their silly naïveté all the time.

After Nick was so cool the night before, whispering sweet nothings in my ear while he made love to me, I decided I'd get out of my aunt's birthday party to come and see him play. I couldn't wait to see the look of surprise on Nick's face.

The band finished up and I hurried toward the door that would lead to backstage. A bouncer tried to push me back, but after I explained who I was he disappeared backstage and returned with the band's "manager." In reality he was Nick's older cousin, Justin, and I wasn't really sure what it was that qualified him to be their manager. I didn't really care just then. Justin recognized me and got me backstage only to disappear before I could ask which way I was going. I wandered in the opposite direction and came upon the band sitting around a randomly placed and barren pool table. They were drinking beer and talking loudly among each other with a couple of guys and girls I didn't recognize.

Nick was nowhere to be seen.

Alan, the lead guitarist, glanced up and stiffened when he saw me, his eyes flickering beyond me nervously before they snapped back to me. "Shannon." He stood up abruptly and the guys all looked at me in much the same way. "I didn't think you were coming tonight."

I smiled back, but my lips trembled. The tension my appearance had caused had alarm bells ringing in my head. "I wanted to surprise Nick. Where is he?"

"Uh, I don't know." Digby, the drummer, shrugged, looking at the other guys with a faked nonchalance that they returned.

Not Alan, though. His lips pinched together as he watched them, and when his eyes swung back to mine I stared into them stubbornly. My directness made him flinch. Alan and I got on pretty well. In fact, I sometimes got the impression he liked me. He flirted with me all the time and was always so considerate of me. I'd always brushed it off because I was mad about Nick and no one else could come close to how I felt about him.

"Where is he, Alan?"

Alan's eyes softened with regret. "He's in the cloakroom, Shannon." He nodded in the direction behind me as the others shifted uneasily.

Feeling my heart bang away in my chest, I turned on my low-booted heels and strode with more confidence than I was feeling down a narrow, dark walkway. I came to a stop in front of a black-painted door with the word CLOAKROOM *in peeling white paint across it.*

I heard the gasps and grunts coming from inside and I knew what I was going to find, but I just had to see it for myself.

With a shaking hand I turned the door handle and threw it open.

In the small, dimly lit room that was no bigger than a large closet, I saw Nick with his jeans down around his ankles, thrusting into the blonde he had pinned against the wall.

Nausea and pain like I'd never felt before welled up in me as they both jerked their heads around in surprise at the intrusion. Nick's eyes widened when he saw me and suddenly the blonde was forgotten as he called out my name in horror and let her go. She stumbled to the floor when Nick bent down to pick up his jeans.

I ran out of there, ignoring Alan and Nick shouting my name as they chased after me. I lost them in the crowds of the dirty bar and I hurried all the way to the bus stop. I didn't go home. Instead I found myself knocking on my friend Caro's house. She let me in and I sobbed all over her, apologizing for assuming she was naive, when in the end I was the only one who could be faulted for that . . .

. . .

Nick was an important lesson. Yet somehow it took another man cheating on me before I learned from it. Eventually I got wise to his type. However, I later got caught up in a different kind of bad boy: the kind who didn't cheat but still found a way to wreck my life.

But no more.

I tore up the sketch of Nick into a hundred little pieces.

Never again.

CHAPTER 2

I'd found it hard to sleep the night before I started my new job, but-terflies fluttering around like wild things in my belly as I worried about the next day. When I managed to drift to sleep, it was with the hope that my manager would be very much a younger version of Stu. I could deal with a Stu.

So it was with more than the usual amount of first-day jitters that I stepped into INKarnate on Monday, which was probably why I al-most tripped over my own feet at the sight before me.

Simon was standing in front of the marble reception desk talking quietly to a very tall guy who had his back to me. I got a brief glimpse of strong, broad shoulders and long legs before he turned and my eyes collided with his bright green ones.

Holy . . .

My stomach plummeted.

Dread filled me.

Please, no, no, no. Be a customer. Please be a customer.

Those eyes crinkled attractively at the corners as their gorgeous owner threw me a friendly, boyish smile that penetrated my anti-bad-boy force field. The eyes and smile would have brought me low on their own, but unfortunately those eyes and that smile were enhanced by sexy scruff on the stranger's jaw, and the messy, unkempt strawberry blond hair that framed his attractive face. If that wasn't enough to affect a woman, the tall, handsome stranger had a fit body. A very fit body by the look of things. His navy T-shirt did nothing to hide the perfect V of his torso or his lean, muscular arms. And those arms were covered in elaborate, hot tattoos.

"Shannon," Simon greeted me, yanking my gaze away from the stunning disaster in front of me. "This is Cole, our manager."

Was fate really this heartless?

Cole grinned at me again, and familiarity punched me in the chest along with dismay as he took a few steps toward me and held out his hand. "Cole Walker. It's nice to meet you, Shannon."

I reluctantly stepped forward and took his hand in mine.

I instantly regretted it.

His strong, slightly callused hand with the chunky silver ring on its middle finger felt really nice. It engulfed my small one and I felt surrounded by him.

Dammit!

I ripped my hand away, unable to meet my new manager's gaze. My eyes dropped to the loosely laced black engineer boots his dark jeans were tucked into.

"Shannon?" Cole said my name like a question and I had to unglue my eyes from his feet to meet his gaze. Up close the familiarity I'd felt moments ago only strengthened in feeling as he narrowed his eyes on me. He took in my hair for a few long seconds.

Recognition slammed through me.

No.

No way.

"So, are you a hero, Cole Walker?"

"What is a hero, really?"

Months, even years, after our meeting outside my gran's house all those years ago, I'd often thought of the good-looking boy I'd connected with after only a few minutes of conversation.

Cole Walker.

Cole freaking Walker.

All grown-up.

And he was my new manager.

I was so screwed. I'd be less screwed, though, if he didn't remember me, which I was pretty sure he wouldn't. A guy like him—he was bound to have flirty conversations with women every day. No way would he remember a random conversation with a short, pale redhead nine years ago.

"I know you." Cole stepped back, tilting his head as he scrutinized me with a small smile on his lips. He looked charmed by me, which immediately sent my force field back up at full power. "Shannon." Unbelievably, recognition lit up his beautiful eyes. "We've met." He grinned back at a smiling Simon before returning his attention to me. His eyes were filled with pleased surprise. "On Scotland Street. Years ago."

He waited for me to respond.

I could tell him I remembered him, but surely that would only encourage the flirtiness I saw glittering in his gaze. I remembered he liked my hair and my eyes. Who was to say he didn't *still* like my hair and my eyes, and moreover would like a chance to see said hair spilled across his pillow as he screwed me? A screwing that he would most likely promptly follow up with screwing me *over.*

Keeping my face perfectly blank, I shook my head. "Sorry. I don't remember."

Disappointment caused his smile to wilt. "Really? We talked about bands and zombies and stuff. Your boyfriend picked you up. You're from Glasgow."

Christ, did he have a photographic memory?

I only just managed to stop myself from wrinkling my nose in annoyance. "I am from Glasgow," I answered calmly, not unfriendly but not friendly either. "And my gran lived on Scotland Street, but I don't remember you. Sorry."

Simon tried to muffle a snort of laughter behind Cole.

Cole shot him a displeased look over his shoulder and Simon turned around with an innocent whistle and casually walked into the back.

Sighing, my new manager turned to me with a frown puckering his brow. "You really don't remember me?"

"Sorry." I shrugged apathetically, which only caused his frown to deepen.

"Long time ago, I suppose." He continued to stare at me in an assessing way and I began to squirm uncomfortably. The more he stared, the more I stared, and the more I stared, the more I noticed how deliciously lickable he was.

The tattoos only made him more so.

I blamed the artist in me for my weakness for a man with great tattoos. There was what looked like initials worked into a tribal design tattooed on the left side of his neck. On his left arm was a sleeve tattoo in black ink of a wolf standing on a rocky precipice. It sketched upward into his biceps, and the upper body of a woman in profile appeared to transform out of the top of the wolf's head—her face was upturned; her hair billowed in the wind and disappeared under the fabric of his T-shirt. On his right arm in a reddish brown and black ink was a flying eagle, the tips of its wings disappearing under his T-shirt too. Dangling from the eagle's talons was an old-fashioned pocket watch, but I couldn't make out what time was set on it.

"You like what you see?"

I blinked at the innuendo in Cole's voice, dragging my eyes from his tattoos to his face. He was wearing this sexy little smirk that would have worked like a charm on me a few months ago.

But a lot had happened since then. I raised an eyebrow. "Do you flirt with all your new employees?" I said, unamused and pretending to be unimpressed.

Cole's smirk turned into a grin as his eyes roamed over my hair. "I've never had one like you before," he murmured.

"Efficient, smart, responsible, reliable?" I said through gritted teeth.

Laughter danced in his eyes. "Well, I hope you're all those things too." Clearly pleased with himself, he chuckled and turned around to head toward the reception desk. "Good hair, by the way," he shot over his shoulder.

For the first time in years I cursed my bloody hair.

"I'm thinking about dyeing it pink," I lied as I followed him behind the desk.

Clicking the mouse on the computer, Cole muttered, "And I'm really a tattooist by day and a time-traveling immortal highlander by night."

Before I could respond, he threw me a wry smile and gestured to the computer with a nod of his head. "Desktop." The mouse moved over the screen as he showed me the digital appointment book, the spreadsheet on which they kept their supplies updated, a list of their suppliers' contact details, and a folder with information on regular clients.

"Now." He sighed and threw me an apologetic look. "We have an issue with filing." He turned around, his arm brushing mine as he did so, and unfortunately I couldn't stop my body from reacting to the touch. The hairs on my arms stood on end, and the blood heated in my cheeks. Cole didn't seem to notice as he waved an arm at the huge closet in front of us—the one with the masses of paper files. "Our last assistant was completely inept—"

"And a fucking homophobe," Simon's voice snarled in my ear, and I jumped in fright to discover he was standing at my shoulder.

"Which was why our last assistant was canned," Cole informed me. When I looked back at him he was studying me warily. "You're not a homophobe, are you, Shannon?"

I barely registered the question. He had a lovely accent—it was refined and lilting and it did gorgeous things to the sound of my name.

Realizing they were both now tensely waiting on an answer, I hurried to assure Simon, "Definitely not. Love's just love, right?"

Simon relaxed and smiled at me. "Love's just love, sweetheart," he agreed.

I smiled back at him, but when my gaze returned to Cole, my smile wilted. He had been staring at me with this disarming look in his eyes, a soft look that made me feel things I had no right feeling. At the sudden change in my demeanor, Cole frowned, clearly confused by my reaction to him.

"So, the files . . . ?" I urged.

Cole blinked. "Files? Oh, right, files." He cleared his throat and gestured back to the closet. "These are Stu's files before he went digital. We don't need them—they date back to when the studio first opened—

but Stu wants to keep them. Our boss can be a bit stubborn some-times." He said it with such affection I knew Stu's stubbornness didn't bother Cole in the least. "The files were moved when a pipe burst in Stu's office, but the assistant who moved them turned them into a dis-organized mess. Accounting files have been mixed up with art files and they're all out of chronological order. I'd like you to reorganize it when-ever you're not needed on reception."

I took a step toward the mess. "Why don't I digitize them instead? It'll free up the space in here. The mess doesn't exactly give the greatest impression to your customers."

Cole seemed to consider it. "It'll take you longer . . ."

I shrugged. "I like to keep busy."

His eyes moved over the top of my head to Simon. "Can it be? We finally hired a receptionist who knows what she's doing and actually wants to work?"

"Bigger miracles have occurred," Simon said, a smile in his voice.

Feeling immediately flustered, I pretended otherwise by turning to the reception desk. "Where's the printer?"

"It's in Stu's office. I'll get it and bring it here for you." Cole strode toward the back rooms and disappeared down the corridor. My eyes followed him against my will.

"Don't worry," Simon said.

"Worry about what?"

He gave a huff of laughter. "About getting your knickers in a twist over Cole. He has a tendency to have that affect on people. Believe me, I've never wished harder for someone to miraculously wake up gay one morning."

Despite being annoyed that Simon had somehow guessed my im-mediate attraction to our boss, I couldn't help giggling. "What about Tony?"

Simon waved my question off. "We both have fantasy lists of people we're allowed to fuck if they ever turned gay. Channing Tatum is on his. Cole's on mine."

"Does Cole know you fancy him?"

"He's seen my whole list. Tony printed them for evidence of our pact in case fantasy ever becomes reality."

I was still stuck on the fact that Cole knew Simon fancied him and yet seemed perfectly at ease with him. "Doesn't it bother Cole that you fancy him?"

Simon grunted. "Why would it?"

"Some men, particularly men like Cole, are weird about that stuff. The idiots think it threatens their manhood."

"Speaking from experience, are you?"

I made a face at the thought of my ex. "I once knew a guy who beat the shit out of a bloke who came on to him in a bar. It was one of the ugliest things I've ever seen." Blinking away the memories, I discovered Simon staring at me with an arrested look on his face. It was as though he sensed it wasn't the only ugly thing I'd ever seen, and wanted to know why. The thought of anyone in my new life knowing what I'd been through caused a wall to shoot up inside me, its impenetrableness must have been reflected in my suddenly blank expression.

Sensing the change, Simon stepped back. "Cole isn't like that. He's not like that at all."

It didn't matter what kind of man Cole Walker was. I had no intention of ever finding out.

I heard Cole's rumbling tones nearing the door to the main reception room as he led his client out. Instantly I tensed over the printer he'd set up on the reception desk. For the last few hours I'd immersed myself in creating chronological digital folders to organize all the scanned material. The files contained receipts and client information, and many of them had photographs of the tattoo work. I was with Cole—the stuff dated back years, and with the exception of the accounting, most of it really didn't need to be kept. Stu, it appeared, was a bit of a hoarder. However, as I'd told Cole, I was happy to digitize it all if it meant keeping me busy and out of my new manager's way.

He'd had a guy called Ross Mead in all morning. They were doing work on a massive tattoo that would eventually cover Ross's back. I knew Cole had three more appointments this afternoon and I had to wonder if his hand ever cramped up. In fact, after receiving a couple of calls this morning from people looking to book tattoo appointments, I discovered the studio was fully booked at weekends for the next six weeks. Appointments were available during the week, which was a more difficult time for people with nine-to-five jobs, but it was clear some of them were willing to take time off work rather than wait to get in Cole Walker's chair.

"Same care as before," I heard Cole say as he and Ross stepped out into the room. "And I'll see you back here in three weeks."

Although I wanted to go on pretending I wasn't aware of Cole, my job involved taking payment from the customer, so I had to look up as they approached. Ross looked a little peaked as Cole led him to me.

"Are you okay?" I said.

Ross threw me a shaky, dry smile. "Want the tattoo, don't particularly like the way I feel during and afterwards."

"I've got something"—I bent down to rummage around in my handbag—"that might help. Aha!" I curled my hand triumphantly around the bar of chocolate and tugged it out. "Here." I broke off a few squares and handed them to him. "Sugar."

He grinned gratefully. "Thanks. How much do I owe you?" He chewed on a piece of chocolate as my eyes flicked over the price list on the desk.

I could have asked Cole, but again that meant looking at him. "Four hours . . . that's two hundred and forty pounds."

As I took Ross's credit card and popped it into the card reader, I expected Cole to vamoose back into his workroom, but he stayed there, chatting to Ross about the Lowlight gig they'd both been to a few months ago in Glasgow. Usually I would have jumped right into the conversation, but, again, I was avoiding interaction with my boss. Moreover, I was supposed to have been at that gig. I didn't want to think about the reason why I hadn't gone.

Once Ross had paid he gestured with his last piece of chocolate in thanks to me and departed the studio. Leaving me alone with Cole.

I could feel his stare burning into me.

After a while it became impossible to withstand the intensity. I looked at him in question without saying anything.

Unfortunately he was bestowing upon me that boyish grin that led to dirty thoughts. "Can I have a piece?"

Outraged, I sucked in a breath. "Excuse me?"

His lips twitched with amusement. "Of chocolate," he clarified. "A piece of chocolate."

Embarrassed that I'd misunderstood, I thrust the bar of chocolate at him, ignoring his chuckle as he took it. To avoid him I stuffed the last square in my mouth and turned back to scanning the files.

"When's my next client in?"

"In an hour and a half," I said without looking up or at the appointment book. I'd already memorized Cole's schedule for the day.

A twenty-pound note slid toward me on the desk. "Can you go out and grab something for our lunch? Better get Rae something too.

She'll be in soon and she's usually starving. If we feed her right away, it mellows her a little. But only a little."

Glancing up as I took the money, I found him smiling at me. "What would you like?"

Cole's grin turned positively wolfish. "If I answered that honestly you'd likely find me very unprofessional."

I stiffened at the flirtation but tried to remain polite. "Then perhaps you shouldn't answer honestly."

With an exaggerated, beleaguered sigh, Cole crossed his arms on the other side of the desk and leaned toward me. My breath hitched at the heat in his expression as he stared down at me. "I pride myself on being straightforward."

Willing my body to stop reacting to him, I stepped back from the desk and turned around to grab my jacket off the coat hook behind me. As I shrugged into it, I very deliberately met Cole's still glittering gaze. "I pride myself on being professional."

The door to the studio blew open, stalling whatever Cole's response would be, and distracting us from the crackling tension between us. Rae stomped inside and slammed the door shut with a grunt.

Cole's body language changed as he took in her red face and blazing eyes. His back straightened and his hands fisted at his side. "What happened?"

"My roommate just fucked off! I woke up and she'd fucking packed every fucking thing she owned and fucked off with that fucking Malaysian dude she met a month ago! Fuck!" She stomped her foot, her chest rising and falling rapidly. "How the fuck am I going to pay the rent?"

Despite the voice screaming in my head that it was a very, *very* bad idea, I found myself saying, "I'm looking for a place."

Rae rolled her eyes. "I don't think so."

34

Ouch. "Well, why not?" I crossed my arms over my chest, annoyed by the immediate dismissal.

"I can't be worrying about walking on eggshells in my own place. Shit pours out of my mouth before I can stop it, and I need to be around people that can hack the fucking awesomeness that is me."

I heard Cole laugh but refused to look at him as I made my case. "I never said I wanted to move in with you. I just said I'm looking for a place. Where is your flat? How much is rent?"

She gave me a look that suggested she was merely humoring me. "King Street. Literally just around the corner." She told me what rent and council tax was each month excluding half of the utilities. It was quite a lot. "It's a nice flat," she said, taking in my dubious expression.

It was a little more than I'd been hoping to pay, but it *was* just around the corner from work. Although I had to wonder if living with Rae would balance out the positive aspects. Then again, it would be a while before any letting agent would allow me to sign a lease—I had to prove I'd been in work for three months. The thought of staying in that pokey wee hotel for three months . . .

"I cook. I clean. I keep to myself."

Rae considered me for a second and then threw her hands up in the air in exasperation. "Fuck, I've no fucking choice! Fine! You can have the fucking room."

Blinking rapidly at the overuse of profanity spilling from her mouth, I said, "I'd like to see it first."

Her face turned red again. "It's a nice fucking flat with a double room. Don't you trust me?"

Feeling Cole's eyes burning into me, I flicked a look at him and then turned my focus back to Rae. "I don't trust anyone," I answered coolly.

Rae stared at me for a few seconds before the red in her face disappeared. She grinned at me, her eyes alight with humor now. "I like you," she announced as though she were a queen granting a great honor. "You're moving in."

"But—"

"Tonight. No faffing about. Rent's due at the end of the month. Oh." She ran her eyes over me warily. "No clown paraphernalia."

My mouth fell open. "Eh?"

"Clowns are evil." She strode through the studio toward the back room. "Someone get me something to eat. I've had a fucking awful morning."

My eyes met Cole's. His were laughing. Mine were not. "What just happened?"

He grinned. "I think Rae just adopted you."

"I'm not sure that's a good thing."

"It's not so bad. It's like living with your own personal Rottweiler."

I made a face. "Except Rottweilers are friendly."

Cole snorted. "This one isn't."

"This is everything?" Rae stared at the boxes piled around my feet.

I was standing outside her door in her apartment building on King Street. By the time I'd gotten everything together and into a taxi I couldn't really afford, night had fallen. Now Rae stood in her doorway wearing pajama shorts and a Nine Inch Nails T-shirt that had seen better days.

"I don't need a lot." I tried to peek into the flat. My reservations over moving in with this seemingly crazy woman were abated somewhat by the parquet flooring I could see beyond her.

Rae seemed to contemplate this for a moment and I suddenly found myself uncomfortable with the fact that I had very little in the way of possessions. It didn't occur to me until now that that might invite questions as to why. Most people had loads of crap to their name.

"Okay." Rae shrugged and bent down to pick up a box. "Let's get this shit inside before my nipples freeze off."

Charming.

I huffed out air between my lips and followed her inside.

My new colleague and now flatmate hadn't been lying. The flat was nice. It had a decent-sized modern kitchen, a small but cozy sitting room with a balcony off it, and two good-sized double rooms. We shared a bathroom, but it was almost as big as the kitchen, so I wasn't complaining. After dumping my boxes in my room, Rae left me to unpack.

Once I'd unpacked my measly amount of clothing into a wardrobe from IKEA, I began unpacking my sketch pads, pencils, and charcoals. Not wanting anyone, as in Rae, to see my work, I shoved it under the bed. I was standing there holding my current sketch pad when the door to my bedroom flew open. Heart in my throat, I dropped to my knees and slid the pad under the bed before Rae could see it.

I looked up to find Rae frozen in my doorway carrying a cup that had steam rising out of the top of it. She took in the sight of me on my knees and grinned. "No need to worry about hiding your vibrators, Shannon. You'll probably hear mine through the wall. I have the Rabbit. It's a classic for a reason you know." She thrust the cup out at me. "Tea. I guessed milk and two sugars."

Still flustered and a little stunned, I stood up and reached for the tea she'd made just how I liked it. "Thanks," I mumbled, feeling like an idiot.

Rae smirked and left the room, closing the door behind her.

My shoulders slumped as I turned to stare at my hidden artwork. I felt my throat close with emotion, mostly frustration, that I'd been reduced to acting like a bumbling fool in order to hide my art from people. I never used to hide. I never used to act like this.

Not until . . .

"Why do you bother with that crap? It's not like you're any good at it."

"And what do you know about art?"

"Enough to know you've not got any talent, babe."

The memories flooded me, zapping my energy, and I stumbled to the bed. Staring at the blank wall in front of me, I tried to fight them back, the hand not holding the hot cup of tea curled so tight into a fist my fingernails bit into my skin.

Once I got my emotions under control, I finished packing and decided to get acquainted with my new flatmate. I didn't want Rae to think I was antisocial, although perhaps she would prefer it if I was. I'd find out soon enough.

Instead of Rae, I found Cole in the sitting room. I almost tripped over my feet at the sight of him on the armchair near the balcony, his right ankle hooked over his left knee. My eyes drank in his long-limbed body before I could stop myself. When they eventually traveled upward, Cole was staring at me with this knowing, cocky little grin on his lips.

His very, very kissable lips.

Man, he was annoying.

"Thought you might want to join a few of us for a drink to celebrate the job and the flat."

Processing how comfortable and at ease Cole seemed in Rae's flat, I felt my eyes narrowing as they scanned the room. They stopped on a large black digital photo frame. Every few seconds the picture would change and in among pictures of Rae with people I had never met were lots of pictures of Rae, Cole, Simon, and some Italian-looking bloke I could only assume was Tony.

Bugger.

Rae and Cole weren't just colleagues; they were friends. All of them were *good* friends. This meant I not only had to dodge Cole at work but I had to bloody well dodge him in my own home.

He was *beyond* annoying.

"I'm kind of tired," I said, looking anywhere but at him.

"Rubbish!"

This came from Rae. I turned around as she strode into the sitting room now dressed in jeans, a Celine Dion T-shirt that seemed incongruous to her personality, and a black leather jacket. "Get your shoes on," she said. "You're bloody well coming with us."

"I don't think—"

"Bollocks to whatever you're going to say."

Assessing her authoritative tone and demeanor, I didn't take long to surmise that I was not getting out of this. Instead of glaring at Rae, I shot a glower at Cole. "You knew exactly what I was getting into and didn't do a thing to stop me." I stomped out of the room, ignoring the delicious sound of Cole's laughter.

I was introduced to identical twins Grant and Patrick and Grant's girlfriend, Karen. They were Cole's friends from art school and Rae had adopted them too. Grant and Karen owned a small gallery and a professional photography business. Patrick was working toward qualifying as an architect. They were all very friendly and welcoming, but the uneasiness I felt as we joined them in Rae's local pub, the Walk, wouldn't dissipate. I felt I had no one to blame but Cole.

As soon as we sat down, Cole somehow finagled it so he was sitting next to me in the booth that curved around the table. Almost immediately he pressed his thigh against mine. With Rae squashed in on my other side, there was nowhere to go and no way to remove myself from physical contact with Cole.

Heat burned into my jeans where we touched and I tried—oh, how I tried—to ignore his presence and listen to his friends talk about work and the odd things people said in galleries.

"You have the best hair I've ever seen," Karen suddenly said to me.

Everyone laughed at the random comment.

"She does, though," Karen insisted. "I'd love to photograph you."

"Me?" I was bemused by the notion.

"Yes, you." Karen smiled. "You'd make a great subject."

"I don't think so."

"Oh, I fucking knew it." Rae groaned.

I looked at her in question and she frowned in response.

"You're one of those."

"One of what?"

"A pretty girl who doesn't know she's pretty. Pisses me off."

If I were prone to blushing, I'd be a tomato.

"I think it's great," Cole said.

Without thinking about it, I turned my head to look up at him.

He smiled that soft, boyish smile of his and reached out to touch my hair. "Nothing sexier than a woman who doesn't know she's gorgeous."

I hated the way my stomach fluttered at his attention, at his compliments. I'd been paid those kinds of compliments before, and my reaction to them had brought me nothing but trouble. Turning away, I was thankful for Rae breaking the sudden tension with "Bollocks! Nothing sexier than a man or woman who knows that they are sexy as fuck." She looked down at me, seeming to brim with years of experience despite the fact that she was only twenty-eight and thus only a few years older than me. "Your lack of height makes you cute mixed with stunning. Own it. Rock that fucking hair and those fucking eyes. Then you'll be sexy." She grinned and preened. "Like me."

Patrick nodded, smiling at Rae in appreciation. "I have to admit that *was* sexy."

She threw him a flirtatious grin. "Down, boy. I'm already spoken for."

Surprised, I was about to ask Rae who she was dating when I felt the lightest touch on my lower back. I tensed.

Cole was touching me.

I glanced up at him.

With his thigh pressed to mine, his fingertips on my back, and his gaze boring into mine, words deserted me. The noise in the pub seemed muffled all of a sudden, like an invisible wall had encircled Cole and me.

His fingers pressed deeper and my body began to tingle.

The sound of a glass shattering loudly broke the spell between us and I jerked back, bumping into Rae. Something like annoyance flickered in Cole's eyes, but I adamantly turned away, shifting closer to Rae, who was too busy mocking Patrick about getting his eyebrows waxed to notice I was trying to crawl my way into her lap to escape the sexual tension between me and our boss.

I'd never been so thankful to get away from someone in my life. Sure, there were times I'd been stuck in conversation with people that bored me or offended me, and that was never fun. However, being stuck in close proximity with the ultimate daydream-worthy bad boy whose clothes you wanted to rip off despite the fact that you knew he wasn't right for you was worse. A lot worse.

In fact, it was downright upsetting.

I berated myself the whole way back to the flat, wondering what the hell was wrong with me that after everything I'd been through I could still be attracted to the likes of Cole Walker.

Inside the flat, I kicked off my shoes in a tantrum with myself.

Rae snorted as she shrugged off her jacket. "You've certainly caught Walker's eye."

I flinched. So it was that obvious? Channeling the depths of my dislike of the bad-boy species into my expression, I lifted my gaze to Rae's and stated firmly, "I'm not interested."

Rae jerked back at my tone and quickly her surprise melted away. She looked . . . impressed? "I actually believe that. A woman that hasn't fallen at Cole's feet. Will wonders never cease?" She grinned. "I knew I liked you."

I laughed softly, tiredly, and bade Rae good night. I was almost at my bedroom door when she called out my name. "Yeah?"

She strolled toward the door next to mine with a swagger in her slender hips. "My boyfriend, Mike, works back shift tonight—he's a nurse. He usually comes over late and we like to fuck loudly. There are a pack of earplugs in the sideboard drawer in the hall."

A few hours later I was awakened by squealing. It didn't take me long to work out that the squealing, followed by male grunts, was Rae and her man having sex. Loudly. Just as promised.

Slightly mortified I hadn't taken Rae at her word (and now knew way more about her than I'd ever wanted to), I quietly hurried out into the hall, snatched up the earplugs, and hurried back to bed. To my everlasting relief, the earplugs muffled the noise enough I could drift back to sleep. But I did so on the thought that I had never met anyone like Rae. I didn't quite know yet whether that was a good or a bad thing.

The dog—I think it was a Welsh terrier—was tied to the lamppost on the opposite side of the street. He'd been there for the last three hours since his master had tied him there and wandered into the pub. My chest ached with how miserable he looked as the spring temperature dipped when the clouds obscured the sun.

He shivered and I cursed his master to hell for leaving him there for that length of time.

My anger had begun simmering two hours ago and showed no sign of losing heat.

"You all right?"

I jerked around at Cole's voice. He stood on the opposite side of the reception desk, his eyebrows puckered in concern.

I gestured to the dog outside our window, visible through the street traffic. I couldn't help the sadness in my voice as I said, "Some people shouldn't be allowed to own a dog."

Cole seemed confused.

"He's been there all morning," I explained.

The confusion melted from his expression only to be replaced by that soft look that was a hundred times worse than his smoldering one. "Gives my clients chocolate when they're feeling faint, can handle Rae better than most people, feels sorry for strange dogs, is gorgeous but doesn't know it, and has shit hot taste in music." His voice lowered to an unbelievably sexy rumble. "Are you perfect, Shannon MacLeod?"

My pulse started to race. Shuttering my expression, I looked down at the file I'd been in the middle of scanning. I'd worked at INKarnate for three days and had barely made a dent in the files. "I'd really like you to stop flirting with me," I said primly.

The sound of movement brought my head up, and my eyes widened at the sight of Cole rounding the desk. I leaned back as he deliberately crowded me in against it, his hands coming to rest on the desk at either side of me. My breathing stuttered as the air thickened. Heat danced from his body to mine, and no matter how hard I tried I couldn't stop the tingling between my legs or the swelling in my breasts as he stared down at me with blatant sexual intention.

He lowered his head and I braced myself. Instead of kissing me, though, he murmured against my mouth, "That might be a problem for me."

The sound of the front door opening drew Cole back from me, and I gratefully gulped in some air. I felt like a total idiot.

"Tamara," Cole said, surprise in his voice. Catching sight of the pleased smile on his face, I whirled around to have a look at this Tamara person.

I frowned.

A tall, curvy brunette was walking across the studio toward Cole with a huge smile on her pretty face. She enveloped him in a hug, so tall in her high-heeled boots that they were the same height.

They fit perfectly together.

Something I was determined not to admit was a wave of jealousy slashed in a fiery pain across my chest.

"What are you doing here?" Cole asked as they stepped back from their embrace.

Tamara shrugged with an excited smile. "I'm here on a talent scout and was hoping you might be able to fit me in. I know it's last minute and you're a very busy boy."

Fit her in? Busy boy?

My stomach dropped.

Finally, here was evidence of Cole the player. I had no right to feel disillusioned and disappointed. None. So I didn't.

Really. I didn't.

No, siree, not me.

I waited nosily to see if Cole did have time in his man-whore schedule for her but looked down at my work as though I didn't care.

"Shannon, I'm free for the next hour, right?"

"Two," I said without looking up, "if you count lunch break."

"Is it just a small tat? Two hours enough?"

"More than."

My hands stilled on the scanner button. They were talking tattoos . . . not a sexual hookup? I bit my lip, hating that the jealous burn in my chest was already disappearing. Glancing up at them from under my lashes, I saw Tamara watching me carefully.

Cole noticed her appraisal of me. "Tamara, this is our new receptionist and Rae's flatmate, Shannon. Shannon, this is Tamara. She's an A-and-R executive for Tower Records in Glasgow. We went to Edinburgh College of Art together—Tamara is a graduate of the Reid School of Music there."

Bloody hell. She was gorgeous, accomplished, smart, and successful. She scouted talent for a living while I . . . scanned stuff.

"Hi," I said.

What else was there to say?

Tamara gave me a nod in acknowledgment, a small smirk playing on her lips as she drank me in. She turned to Cole after scrutinizing me. "You never change."

Cole stiffened.

What the heck did that mean?

Whatever look Cole gave his friend, she shrugged unapologetically. He sighed and turned to lead her across the studio, and thankfully I got to ignore his departure because a customer walked in.

The young woman was looking to have her ear cuff pierced. After I alerted Simon, who was on his lunch break, he came out into the main studio. He talked quietly to the girl in the waiting area and gestured for her to go into the back room. He stopped by my desk before following her. "You met Tamara?"

Warily I nodded.

"Gorgeous girl," Simon said. "Not *the* girl, though." And with that rather enigmatic statement and a cheeky wink, he disappeared after his customer.

Not for once I cursed fate's twisted sense of humor for handing me a good job in the worst possible setting. I was in bad-boy heaven. Or hell. Whichever it was, it was the wrong place for me.

Beggars can't be choosers, Gran had always said.

Sighing, I looked back out the window, my annoyance level increasing when I saw the shivering dog's owner approach to untie him. The dog jumped up at the man, his tail wagging pitifully. All attempts to greet his master were ignored, his owner shooing him down before leading him away. The dog might as well have been invisible on the other end of his lead. My heart clenched. I wanted to run across the street and steal that lonely dog away and shower him with affection.

It occurred to me as I watched the guy sway a little on his feet that there were just some people who didn't know how to love. I had to wonder why, then, if they couldn't learn, they even bothered trying. Their attempts only harmed those foolish enough to try to love them in return.

CHAPTER 3

**I still don't forgive you. I just want to know
you're not dead.**

S taring down at the text message from my sister, I pondered what to
do. I'd been staring at the damn thing on and off for the last twenty-
four hours. And for the last twenty-four hours I hadn't been able to get
her voice out of my head.

*"When are you going to stop picking these losers to date? God, Shannon,
it doesn't say much about you, does it?"*

*"Another one bites the dust? What was it this time? Another woman?
Drugs? A pregnancy scare? All of the above?"*

*"You've done it now. You invite scum into your life and we're the ones
dealing with the consequences. You're so selfish, Shannon!"*

I suppose that meant it was selfish to leave her hanging.

I'm not dead.

I stuffed my phone into my big slouchy bag where I carried my sketch pad and pencils. It was Friday, my day off. Since the studio was busiest at the weekends, I got Thursday and Friday off instead. Yesterday I'd spent cleaning the flat and reading a book Rae let me borrow. Today I was going to the castle. I couldn't get the idea of trying my hand at landscape painting out of my head. I'd never painted before, but it wasn't the first time I'd fancied giving it a go . . .

"What the hell is that?"

I stared at the box of acrylic paint he was pointing to. "Paints."

"You don't fucking paint."

"I'm going to, though."

"No. You're not. You're going to return those expensive-as-fuck paints you can't bloody use."

Unsure now, I stared at the box.

Sensing my sadness, he wrapped his hand around my neck, forcing me to meet his eyes. They were soft, concerned. "Babe, I'm sorry. I just want you to get this art thing out of your head so we can get real. I don't mean to hurt you, but there's not much of a career in it for most people and you really need to be mega-talented to succeed. There's no point sinking your time and money into something you're not good at."

That conversation and the many that had come before it played in my head as I made my way to Edinburgh Castle. I paid the entry fee and hoofed it to the top, where I had a wonderful view of the city. Battling against the soft wind that fluttered the corners of my paper up every now and then, I began to sketch it, already imagining painting it in nighttime colors with streaks of electric tones for the lights.

I was going to use acrylic, I thought determinedly, anger burning in my gut.

I was going to use my first paycheck to buy myself those bloody acrylics I'd returned because of *him*.

Tears stung my eyes, and my mouth trembled as I glared out at the city. If it was the last thing I did, I would buy those acrylics and use them . . . and somehow, hopefully, along the way I was going to find the girl I'd lost because of him.

Pleased with the work I'd done at the castle, I returned back to the flat in a better mood than the one I'd left it in. Before going home I went food shopping, buying fresh fish, vegetables, and baby potatoes. I put it together with a sauce my gran had taught me to make and took pleasure in the fact that I'd rendered Rae speechless when she returned from work to a meal.

She took a bite of the fish in its homemade sauce and made a little moan of pleasure. I forcefully shoved the reminder of her sex noises out of my mind.

"You weren't kidding," Rae said with her mouth full. "Did you steam this?"

I nodded as I ate.

"It's lovely." She swallowed and took a swig of water. "You're full of surprises, wee fairy."

I rolled my eyes. "Don't."

"Stu told us how you reacted to him calling you that." She grunted. "I would have looked like I wanted to kick him in the balls too if he'd called me that."

My eyes grew round. "Did he say that's what I looked like?" At Rae's nod, I whispered, "Why did he hire me, then?"

"Said you had spunk. I didn't believe him, but now I do."

"I can die happy," I muttered.

Rae grinned. "So come on. Spill. Why did you leave Glasgow?"

Thankful I was already looking at my plate and could easily hide my instant dislike of the turn the conversation had taken, I shrugged casually. "No reason really. I'm not that close to my family. I got laid off at my last job. I decided it was time for a change of scenery. My gran used to live on Scotland Street, so I know Edinburgh pretty well and have always loved it here. It's different from Glasgow. I was looking for that."

"Aye, Cole mentioned he met you on Scotland Street years ago. Says you can't remember, though." She eyed me, smirking. "Somehow I doubt that." I shrugged again and Rae threw her head back in laughter. "Love. It."

Before my flatmate could plague me with any more questions I wasn't sure I was ready to answer, I said, "What about you?"

Rae put her fork down and gave it to me straight. And I mean *straight*. "Foster kid. Mum's a junkie. Dad's in jail—voluntary manslaughter. Lived in Edinburgh my whole life. Was engaged once when I was twenty. He died. I tried to commit suicide. Simon was my fiancé's best mate. He found me. He saved me, got me into the tattoo industry. Love him to bits. Five years later I met Mike at a gig. He works weird hours, but we manage. Hopefully you'll get to meet the man behind the grunts."

Bloody hell. That was a lot to process. The silence stretched between us as I tried to decide which part of that to acknowledge. I felt her gaze as she waited for my reaction and decided the best thing I could do was concentrate on the positive. Her life had been crap. She didn't need me to comment on the fact that it had been.

"How long have you and Mike been together?"

Her eyes twinkled at me and I was learning that this meant Rae was pleased. "Three years." She took another bite of dinner and asked through a mouthful, "No ex-fiancé in your past, then?"

I shook my head.

"But there was someone," she said.

Realizing it wasn't a question, I just kept eating. It was on the tip of my tongue to tell Rae everything. She'd laid it all out for me, so I knew she wouldn't think I was oversharing. But today had already been an emotional day and I just couldn't form the words.

Rae sighed. "Well, not everyone can be an open fucking book like me, I suppose. It's only with my life, though. I'm good at keeping my fat mouth shut when it comes to other people's shit."

I smiled and got up to clean my empty plate. "I'll tell you all about it one day."

Rae got up and joined me at the sink. She took my plate out of my hand to clean it. "Fancy getting pissed?"

The last two days had been quite relaxing for one very big reason. I hadn't seen Cole. Not once.

Until I decided that I did fancy having a drink with my new friend and flatmate and completely forgot that Cole was likely to be there too. And not just Cole. I discovered that his leggy friend Tamara was still in the city when we walked into the Voodoo Rooms and found her at a corner table with Cole, Simon, and Tony. I said a polite hello to them, thankful that Tony was a compelling character who required my entire focus when we met.

"Simon has been talking nonstop about you," Tony said in his musical accent, before kissing me on each cheek. "I can see why."

Whereas Simon was the epitome of casual earthiness, Tony was the opposite. Incredibly handsome in a very pretty way, Tony was dressed head to toe in a well-fitted three-piece suit. He was warm, cultured, and sophisticated.

"It's lovely to finally meet you," I said after he let me go.

"No, no." He shook his head. "The pleasure is all mine. You make Simon's life easier and he loves you already, so I am happy, yes."

Rae huffed. "I don't remember getting a reception like that when we first met."

Tony gave her an insouciant shrug. "I didn't like you at first. Such a bitch, darling."

"Takes one to know one," Rae countered.

Tony grinned. "Doesn't it, though?"

Rae laughed and threw her arm around him, planting a kiss against his cheek. He pretended to shoo her off him, but it was clear he was only kidding and that there was a lot of affection between them.

I suddenly felt very out of place.

But that feeling didn't last long. They wouldn't have it that way.

Simon bought us all a round of drinks and Rae and I stole a seat and shared it. Luckily we both had a tiny arse or one of us would have been on the floor. Across the table, Cole's attention was being commandeered by the lovely Tamara. I was fine with that. It meant avoiding his eyes was easy, and I could gab away with Simon and Tony, two opposites who somehow made a perfect right. I was falling in love with them and I imagined anyone who spent just a little time with them would feel the same way.

"So I have this woman come into my salon and she asks for my price list," Tony said. I'd already learned from Simon that Tony owned a hair salon in Old Town. He was so successful he was just about to finalize plans to open a second salon in Stockbridge. "She turns up her nose and says, 'Oh no, darling, I never get my hair cut in a salon that charges less than eighty pounds for a cut and blow-dry.'" He rolled his eyes. "So I say, 'But, darling, there are so many gorgeous woman who can't afford high-end prices. Here I offer high-end cuts at an affordable rate.' And the old witch has the nerve to say loudly in front of all my beautiful customers, 'And that's why you'll never have high-end clients.'"

"I hope you stuck it to the bitch," Rae said.

Tony harrumphed. "I look her over very deliberately and I say, 'In my salon, darling, you *can't* put a price on class.' I dunno what these women think . . . that I'm going to sniff after their gold-covered bottoms?" He leaned into me now. "I start with very little and it was the students and young working people that help me build my business. I'm not going to forget where I come from, you know." He chuckled. "Although my mother tells me all the time I forget I am Italian."

"She doesn't know what she's talking about." Simon shook his head. "Half the time I can't understand a fucking thing coming out of your mouth."

Tony grinned wickedly at him. "It has its uses, though, yes?"

While his boyfriend threw his head back in laughter, Rae yelled, "No! No, no! No sex talk tonight."

I raised an eyebrow. "Really?"

She frowned. "Really, what?"

"*You* have a problem with them discussing their sex life. *You*," I emphasized. "The squealer?"

Simon, Tony, and Cole burst out laughing. I hadn't even realized Cole was listening to our conversation. Rae fought a grin as she stared at me.

Tony raised his glass to me. "I knew we were going to get along."

Rae pretended to huff but then stood up. "My round." She pointed at me. "Use those fucking earplugs."

"They only *muffle* the squealing."

This set the boys off again.

She shook her head at me, eyes glittering with amusement. "I guess I can try to be quieter."

I smiled. "That would be appreciated."

"You're lucky you're fucking cute," she said, and strode off to get us more drinks.

"Told you you could handle her," Cole said.

I threw a tight smile in his direction, successfully avoiding his eyes.

The guys and Rae pulled me into hilarious conversation, each little tidbit from Tony proving that despite his intimidating sense of confidence and style, he was down-to-earth. But I was hyperaware of Cole. He was just that guy—he exuded charisma. There was this aura about him and I imagined I was not alone in being drawn in by it.

I did my best to fight it, though, winning the battle every time I looked over and saw him flirting with Tamara. *Player. Player. Player,* I reminded myself.

After a few drinks and lots of conversation, I excused myself to use the ladies'. The bar was near closing and many of its customers had cleared out. Glad there was no line into the ladies', I took my time, and as I washed my hands I stared into the mirror above the sink. I looked less tired, less stressed. The pinched, tight lines around the corners of my mouth had disappeared. My hair tumbled down my back in thick waves and ringlets, and my violet eyes were bright with alcohol. I wasn't drunk, but I was definitely tipsy. That mixed with the good company meant I was in the best mood I'd been in in forever.

That mood plummeted as soon as I stepped out of the ladies' and was confronted by Cole coming out of the men's.

Before I could say a word, he came at me, crowding me against the wall as he had crowded me against the reception desk the other day. He put his hands on the wall just above my head, his eyes searing down into me. "Tamara is just a friend."

I jerked my head back in surprise, whacking it on the wall. "And I would care why?"

This close I could see the frown lines between his eyebrows and the hint of darkness in his beautiful green eyes, a gloom that not even the mesmerizing flecks of gold striations around the edges of his irises could counter. "You've been quiet with me, Shortcake."

I tensed against the wall. "I've been talking to Simon and Tony. And Shortcake?"

"Mmm. I'm a fan of strawberry shortcake. You remind me of it."

"I remind you of strawberry shortcake?" I asked, completely befuddled.

"Sweet strawberries, whipped cream, and sugary biscuit. That's definitely you." He frowned now. "You're telling me you're not icing me out because of Tamara."

"Why would I?"

He leaned closer and I sucked in my breath as his citrusy cologne hit me in delightful waves. "Because of what's between us."

Trembling now, I whispered, "There's nothing between us."

The gloom disappeared from Cole's eyes and the gold seemed to flare as heat entered them. "Nothing but a shitload of chemistry I've wanted to explore since we first met. And you can stop pretending you don't remember that because I know you do."

Feeling the heat flood into me, I became desperate to get away from him. I reached up and pushed my hands against his chest, but he wouldn't budge. I was tiny as it was. Next to Cole I was an ineffectual . . . *wee fairy*. I glowered at him. "You should know I find arrogance a real turnoff."

Cole leaned forward and his lips whispered across my cheek before resting against my ear. "Bullshit."

A shiver rippled down my spine at his hot breath on my skin, and my nipples tightened. My chest rose and fell as I lost control of my breathing—the air between us felt much, much too thick.

Cole pulled away just enough to look into my eyes, and whatever he saw there made him turn liquid with triumph. I'd never felt an attraction so powerful before, and although there was a mini version of me screaming from the back of my brain to get the hell out of there, I ignored it. Later I would blame the alcohol for just standing there as Cole leaned down to meet my lips with his.

I waited, breathless with anticipation—

"There you are!"

I slammed back against the wall, the moment ruined. Cole squeezed his eyes shut, his jaw clenched with obvious annoyance. He took a few seconds to gather himself. When he opened his eyes the annoyance was gone, but something else was there. It felt like he was trying to send me a silent message.

Pretending indifference, I stared up at him blankly, only managing to breathe properly when he spun around to speak to Tamara.

I didn't like her.

But my God, I was grateful she'd interrupted us.

That was it. There would be no more overimbibing when Cole Walker was in the vicinity.

CHAPTER 4

W orking a weekend at INKarnate proved to be manic. The studio was abuzz with noise from the needles, music, and conversation. It was a constant flow of people, and the guys took a shorter lunch break to keep up with their appointments. I thought Sunday might be slightly quieter, but it was one of Simon's days off, so it worked out to be just as busy, if not more so.

It made avoiding Cole extremely easy, however, and he never got a chance to bring up the charged moment between us at the Voodoo Rooms.

For some reason Monday was busy too, so despite the fact that a busy studio meant a far-too-busy-to-flirt-with-me Cole, I was somewhat relieved when I walked into work on Tuesday morning to a quiet environment. I started up where I'd left off on the digitizing of the files.

Half an hour later the door opened and a young woman, perhaps a few years younger than me, walked slowly over to my desk. I tensed at the darkness behind her eyes and her pale face. "Larissa Jones," she said, her voice extremely quiet. "I have an appointment for a tattoo removal."

I checked the appointment book, confirmed it, and disappeared into the back to Rae's room where she was setting up to let her know her first appointment had arrived. When I returned to tell Larissa that Rae would be five minutes, I was surprised to find the girl sitting in the waiting area crying into her hands.

Alarmed, I hurried to retrieve the tissue box on my desk and made my way over to her. I sat down beside her. "Are you all right?"

She sobbed and lifted her tearstained face to mine. She shook her head. I understood the pain that was etched into her every feature and I felt my heart clench in compassion. Shuffling closer, I slid a comforting arm around her shoulders and held the tissues to her.

"Bad breakup?" I guessed as she took one.

Larissa sucked in a huge breath. "Yes." Her lips trembled. "It's his name I'm getting removed."

"Oh, sweetheart," I murmured softly, rubbing her back.

"He was a shit," she cried. "I know that. I do. But . . ." She wiped at her face.

"Hey." I tugged on her hand, and she leaned into my comfort. "I understand. You're allowed to be sad. You are. But just know . . . no regrets, yeah? You're doing the right thing. This is a fresh start. A new beginning for you."

Meeting my eyes, Larissa gave me a tremulous smile. "Thanks."

"Everything okay?"

I snapped my head up, surprised to see Cole there. I hadn't even heard him approach. His green eyes were on the girl and me. Concern wrinkled his brow.

"Yes." Larissa nodded, looking embarrassed. "Had a bit of a meltdown." She smiled sheepishly at me. "Sorry."

"Don't be," I reassured her. She should have had a friend come along and help her through this, I thought, sad for her.

"What's all this, then?" Rae strode toward us. As soon as she saw Larissa's tear-streaked face, she rounded the coffee table, gently took her hand, and guided her out of her seat. "I'm Rae. Come on, honey, let's get a start on removing that fucker's tattoo from your skin. You'll feel all better soon."

I watched my flatmate lead the girl into the back rooms and couldn't help my smile. I was coming to learn that beneath the bluster and bravado, Rae was a big perceptive softie.

Suddenly the air changed.

I sucked in a breath, feeling Cole's gaze burning into me.

Not wanting to but needing to nonetheless, I looked at him. I sucked in another breath.

He was staring at me with what appeared to be tenderness.

I didn't like it. Nope. I really didn't.

"What?" I said, my tone impatient.

His answer was to give me a small smile, walk casually over to me, place a kiss on my forehead, and then walk away.

My skin tingled where his lips had touched me.

"What the heck?" I muttered.

That night I had the pleasure of meeting Rae's boyfriend, Mike, for the first time. At first it wasn't a pleasure. At first I was a little mortified as Rae introduced him, because all I could think was that I knew the noises this guy made during sex.

Once I worked my way through the embarrassment, I was a little surprised by Mike. For some reason, I'd expected this superedgy, gruff guy with a personality to match or outmatch Rae's. Mike wasn't anything like that. He was tall, leanly built, had a nice face, kind dark eyes, and short blond hair. From the band on his T-shirt and from what Rae had told me, Mike liked the same music as his girlfriend. But that seemed to be where the similarities ended.

"We were feeling a bit frisky, shall we say?" Rae continued, telling me a story about the second gig she and Mike had attended together. From the moment we'd sat down in the sitting room to have a beer, Rae had done all the talking for Mike and he seemed okay with that. "So I suggested the ladies' toilets and lo and behold, the place was empty. I dragged Mike in there, locked the main door, and we started going at it against the tiled walls." She grinned at her boyfriend and he gave her a small smile, not at all put out that she was divulging details of their sex life. It occurred to me that perhaps this was because it wasn't the first time she had done so in company.

I waited, not sure what my reply was supposed to be. I'd never had sex in a public place. In all honesty I'd never wanted to. My ex had tried to coerce me into having sex with him once in an alley in Glasgow City Center and had been more than pissed off when I told him to take a run and jump off the nearest bridge.

"She *thought* she'd locked the door," Mike suddenly murmured, his lips twitching with amusement.

I gasped. "No."

Rae laughed. "Yup. There we were, my knickers off, skirt around the waist, Mike's jeans around his ankles as we did it against a cold wall, and all of a sudden we heard, 'I'm not sure that's very hygienic, sweetheart.' We turned and this old lady, with long, hippy-length gray hair—cool-as-fuck old biddy—is standing in the door holding out a cloth handkerchief. 'You might want to give those tiles a wee clean before you continue,' she says."

I laughed. "What did you do?"

Rae's eyes sparkled at the memory. "Mike took the hanky and I said, 'I want to be you when I'm older.' And she replied, 'Well, you're going the right way about it.'" Rae chuckled. "Seriously. My freaking heroine."

"She sounds like a character."

Rae nodded and then launched into her next story. Although Mike was rarely given a chance to speak, and it appeared Rae could be quite bossy with him, I deduced that from what I could see so far, their relationship was quite balanced. When Mike got up to get himself another beer, Rae shooed him back down in his seat. She stroked his cheek tenderly. "You've been working such long hours, baby. I'll get it for you."

Every day I discovered new facets to Rae's personality, and although she could be abrasive and she used the F-word way too much, I was nonetheless charmed by her. For the longest time I'd been surrounded by people who were either negative or fake. With Rae, what you saw you got—and although she teased people often, I knew that it never came from a mean place unless that person was not very nice.

In only a week of acquaintance I knew where I stood with Rae, and I was coming to learn that that was worth its weight in gold.

While Rae got the beers, Mike smiled at me. "How are you and Rae getting on?"

"Good."

"I know she can be a bit . . . well, everything, but she's a really good person."

I smiled reassuringly. "I'm getting that."

"Talking about me?" Rae sauntered back into the room. "Are you discussing my absolute fabulousness, darlings?" she asked, imitating Tony and doing it so well, I couldn't help giggling.

"Something like that." Mike smiled indulgently at her.

An hour later, Mike put down his empty beer bottle and stood. "I'm sorry, ladies. I'm going to have to hit the hay." He gave me a nod good night and leaned down to press a soft kiss to Rae's lips before heading toward her bedroom.

As soon as we heard the door shut behind him, Rae turned to me. "What do you think?"

I smirked. "Like you care."

"True." She grinned. "But I'm curious."

"He seems like a really good guy."

"The very best," she said, her gaze drifting past me to the dark sky outside.

Comfortable silence fell between us only to be broken a minute later by Rae. "I had a good foster parent when I was a kid."

The brittle quality in her voice made the hairs on the back of my neck stand up.

"Sally McIntyre. Her husband passed a year before she got me, but she kept on fostering." She took the last drag of her beer and looked me direct in the eye. "Sally's brother raped me when I was fourteen."

My whole body jerked back like I'd been shot, and my lips fell open, ready for the right words, the right response, but my brain couldn't think of one. The blood rushing in my ears drowned out any possible response.

"Sally found out and she got the police involved. She lost every-thing, though. I was put back into a girls' home and I was examined and questioned until I wanted to die. That kind of thing leaves a mark on you. My fiancé, Jason, worked his arse off to help me through all the ugliness I'd been left with from my teenage years. He was patient with me, made me feel safe, in every way. With sex too. He gave me back to me." She smiled but the gesture didn't reach her eyes. "I fought tooth and nail to enjoy sex and not to be afraid of it, so I kind of went the opposite way, you know—as sexually free as I can be. But that mark . . . it never really disappears, and it leaves something behind in the back of your eyes."

I couldn't believe someone as strong as Rae had gone through so much. "I'm sorry that happened to you."

She nodded her thanks and then continued to shake the ground beneath me. "Shannon, were you raped?"

I felt like all the air was sucked out of the room, and the blood rushing in my ears only worsened. Sweat prickled under my arms and along my palms. Trembling a little, I held her gaze. "Almost," I whispered, fighting the tears.

A fierce quality entered Rae's eyes. "You fought the bastard off?"

I nodded and suddenly I was telling her everything. "His name was Ollie . . ."

Everything but the very worst of it, I told her. I didn't want anyone to know the worst of it—my blame, my guilt, the devastation I'd caused my family. But everything else just poured out of me until I was sobbing in her arms.

Rae held me tight, rocking me, whispering words of comfort I'd had no idea I needed until somehow the pain lessened. Exhausted, I fell asleep in her arms.

The next morning I woke up in my own bed and I realized it was the best sleep I'd had since it all happened.

CHAPTER 5

Although Rae and I didn't mention her confession or my own at breakfast the next morning, there was definitely a shift in our new-found friendship. Not only did I know where I stood with Rae, but now she knew where she stood with me.

Feeling raw after having purged so much from the dark closet in the back of my mind where I kept the events of the last few years locked up tight, I was thankful that Rae continued to be her usual sarcastic, unfiltered self. Her pity would have killed me. It was her day off and for once it coincided with Mike's, so I was really quite glad to be leaving for work. From the look on her face, I was guessing Mike was in for a sexathon.

Despite Rae's support and willingness to act normal around me, as I walked into INKarnate I still felt really fragile from my breakdown the night before. Cole had an early appointment, so he was busy, but

Simon came out to greet me, took one look at me, and immediately asked me if I was okay. I managed to convince him I just hadn't slept well, and he left me to get on with the filing.

I blame the edginess I was feeling for what happened next.

A few hours later, I was standing in the back of the closet that held all the files when the light in the room dimmed a little. Sensing I wasn't alone, I spun around and found Cole leaning against the door-frame, his arms crossed over his chest, one ankle over the other. The pose said *casual*, but his gaze was assessing.

The attraction I felt toward him was suddenly overtaken by an overwhelming burning anger centered in my gut.

"You look very pretty today, Shortcake," he said softly.

The seriousness in his words, the lack of flirtation, the tenderness in the silly nickname he'd given me, only made my anger simmer over. At least when he was being blasé and sexy I could fight it, but now he was being underhanded—trying out that soulful "I really do like you" rubbish on me. "I'm busy," I bit out.

Sighing heavily, Cole stood from the door and took a few steps inside. "Look, I'm sorry if I came on a little strong before. I'm not usually like that." He gave me a cheeky smile, returning to his natural form. "You just bring it out in me."

"Oh, I'm sure."

Hearing the acidity in my response, Cole tensed. "Have I done something to upset you?"

Had he done something?

Mad as hell, I turned on him, feeling all the dislike and fear and loss that was running through me coalesce in his direction. Later I'd realize how unfair and irrational it had been, but right then Cole Walker represented everything wrong with my life and the choices I'd made thus far.

"I can't stand guys like you." My words were low, filled with venom that caused Cole's body to jerk back in surprise. "Good-looking guys who assume every woman will just fall at their feet, grateful for a crumb of their attention. Well, I'm not one of them. I don't respect players like you. I don't like you. I don't trust you. There's nothing behind that charming smile but empty promises. You have nothing real to offer me or anyone who finds herself a victim of your flirtation. The difference between me and them, however, is that I'm smart enough to see you for what you really are." Breathing ragged, I concluded, "Nothing."

As soon as the words were out of my mouth, I wanted to take them back. The look on his face . . . utter disbelief. I didn't say ugly things like that to people. That wasn't me.

But the fact that he'd reduced me to it just made me even angrier.

The muscle in Cole's jaw flexed and he took one menacing step toward me, causing me to stumble back. He stopped, noting my retreat with something like disgust. "You don't know the first fucking thing about me . . . but thank you. Thank you for showing me what a judgmental bitch you can be. I won't waste my time on someone who's not worth it."

To my astonishment his words cut me.

I hid it, though. Practice made perfect. "Am I out of a job?"

His upper lip curled. "You really do think I'm a prick, don't you?"

I made no response since the vitriol I'd just dealt him seemed evidence enough.

"No, Shannon," Cole snapped. "Your job is safe as long as you do it well. As for me, I'll be sure to stay out of your way as much as I possibly can."

. . .

Unfortunately for Cole and me we shared the same two days off, so it wasn't even as though we could avoid each other at work.

The hostility between us was bad.

I was sure Rae noticed it at work on Tuesday, but she didn't say anything. I didn't know if that was her being scarily perceptive or if she just didn't give a crap. Sometimes with Rae it was hard to tell. It was Simon's day off, so he didn't know anything was going on. He returned to work on Wednesday.

We made it obvious pretty quickly that something was amiss.

Cole had just finished up with a customer. He'd been all friendly and smiles, bringing the older woman to the reception to pay, but as soon as he turned to me his expression turned blank. "An hour for Marie here."

I didn't even look at him. Just as friendly as he had been with Marie, I took her cash with a smile and bade her a good day. As soon as she was out the door, Cole informed me, "I'll be out for lunch today, so I won't need you to get me anything."

"Fine."

He grunted and strode away.

Half an hour later his next appointment came in. Just the thought of having to go into Cole's room to tell him caused me butterflies and not the good kind. The moth-eaten-winged kind.

Bracing myself, I hurried to his room only to find he and Simon were in there joking together. Cole looked up and the laughter died in his eyes at the sight of me. "What?" he said impatiently.

I glanced at Simon and noted his eyebrows were halfway up his forehead, he was so taken aback by Cole's tone. Annoyed, I gritted my teeth and looked at my boss with invisible daggers shooting out of my eyes. "Your next appointment is here. Thought you'd like to know."

"Fine." He looked away quickly to resume conversation with Simon, but Simon's mouth was hanging open as he stared at me.

I made a face and whirled around on my heel and stomped out of there.

I heard Simon say gruffly, "What was that?" but was moving too fast to hear Cole's reply.

That was pretty much how Cole and I treated each other for the rest of the day. My favorite part was when he finished up with the pretty young blonde who'd gone in for a tattoo of her favorite lyrics on her lower hip (I knew this because she couldn't shut up about the Killers lyrics, what they meant to her, and what it meant that *the* Cole Walker would be inking them on her skin) and he ended up taking her out to lunch. Her name was Jessica and after she paid, she leaned over the desk to me with this massive grin on her face and whisper-shouted, "Cole's taking me out for lunch."

I couldn't help it. My eyes sought his with a will of their own.

Cole stared right through me. Without a good-bye, he held the door open for Jessica and followed her out into the cool spring day.

Ignoring the burn of something I refused (once again) to admit was jealousy, I fiddled with the files, trying to remember what I'd been in the middle of doing before Cole turned a client meeting into a date.

"Hmm."

My head jerked up at the noise.

Simon was standing in the middle of the studio staring at the door.

"Hmm, what?"

He shrugged before slowly turning his gaze on me. "Cole rarely does that."

Not that I cared . . . but, "Does what?"

"Asks clients out. Did it once a few years back, but she was a regular and they dated for about six months, I think."

I snorted. It was hard to believe Cole lasted *six* months with a girl.

"I'm saying"—Simon stepped toward me, sounding just as impatient as Cole had sounded earlier—"perhaps he just did it to piss *some-one* off."

Someone as in me?

I made a face, staring at the door where he'd left. "How very mature," I muttered.

"What happened between you two?"

"Nothing," I hurried to assure him. "Absolutely nothing."

Now it was Simon's turn to snort. "Funny how absolutely nothing can make the most laid-back guy I know act like a pissy little fucker."

"Funny, that," I murmured, looking down at my work and refusing to look back up again until I felt him leave.

It would be an understatement to say I was glad when Thursday rolled around. I jumped on a bus that took me to Portobello. I sat at an angle at one end of the beach promenade and began to sketch the houses along it where the land curved around the sand and water stretched out in front of me.

It was peaceful and for a little while I didn't think about my family or Cole or anything upsetting.

I thought Friday was going just as well until later that evening Rae invited me out for a drink. I wanted to say no because I knew Cole would be there, but I'd already declined the previous night and I knew Rae wouldn't take no for an answer again.

Weirdly, Rae's friendship had come to mean something to me. I was lonely in Edinburgh and she was the only thing keeping me from feeling not so lonely. I didn't want to inadvertently push her away in my bid to avoid Cole.

To my everlasting relief, however, I discovered Cole wasn't at the pub. Just Simon and Tony.

Rae and I sat down with a fresh round for the boys. "Where is His Gorgeousness tonight?" she asked.

Simon grinned. "Getting sexier. He, Cam, and Nate are at that judo tournament in London. They get back late tonight."

Curiosity got the best of me. "Judo?"

Rae nodded. "Our boss is a badass. Not only is he a kickboxer, but he has a black belt in judo with some number attached to it or something. I don't know. Suffice to say he's good at it. His brother-in-law, Cam, and Cam's best mate, Nate, are also black belts. I think Nate coaches."

Well, that explained Cole's fantastic body.

Clearly I wasn't the only one who thought he had an amazing body, because Simon started laughing at the glazed look that had come over Tony's eyes. "Snap out of it, man."

"Sorry." Tony smiled wickedly. "I just got lost in the picture of those three throwing one another around."

The others laughed, but Rae sensed my confusion. "Cole's brother-in-law is this rugged, sexy guy in his late thirties. Nate's the same age, I think, but he's—"

"Fuck me," Tony interrupted. "Nate is fuck-me gorgeous."

"And straight," Rae said, causing Tony to stare stonily at her. She turned to me. "Cam married Cole's sister years ago when Cole was fourteen or fifteen or something. Jo is a female version of Cole—so fucking beautiful you want to hate her. But she practically raised Cole on her own, so she's kind of awesome. She also gave birth to the most disgustingly cute little wretch ever. Her name is Belle, she's nearly four, and she could charm your last tenner off you." Rae pulled out her phone and started flicking through it. "Here." She put it up to my face, showing me a photograph of Cole laughing as he held a stunning little girl with a mass of strawberry blond curls in his arms. She had her arms wrapped tight around his neck while her head rested in the crook of it. She was facing the camera wearing this wide, delighted grin.

My eyebrows drew together. The image of Cole as an adoring uncle pricked at something inside me. "They look close."

"Oh, they are." Rae put her phone away. "I tease the shit out of him about it. Big fucking softie. He'd kill for that wee girl. For all of his family."

"Aye, they're close," Simon agreed.

"Fucking Brady Bunch." Rae grunted.

"Jealous, darling?" Tony raised an eyebrow at her.

"Abso-fucking-lutely."

As I listened to my new friends tease one another, I began to feel a little uneasy. The idea of Cole as a family man just didn't sit right with the person I'd drawn in my head. I began to worry my lip between my teeth.

"What about you, Shannon?" Simon's voice jerked me out of my grim thoughts. "Will we get to meet any friends and family from Glasgow?"

I tried not to visibly tense. "I'm not really close to my family."

He nodded as if he understood. "What about friends, then?"

Friends?

No. Unfortunately I'd lost most of those . . .

I sipped at the glass of wine I'd poured myself. I was almost ready for my first night out with the girls in ages, and I was giddy with excitement. I couldn't wait to catch up with them in Merchant City, have some good food and a few drinks, and party the night away. It felt like forever since I'd blown off some steam.

I slipped on the black stilettos that would take me from a small five foot three to a less small five foot six. As always I left my hair down in its natural waves, and I was glamming up the tight black miniskirt, black stockings, and black tank top I was wearing with a bunch of red and silver bangles and ear-

rings. I grabbed at my glittery red clutch and turned to face the mirror, only to come out of my skin at the sight of my boyfriend, Ollie, sharing my reflection. He stood in the doorway, his eyes roaming over me. I hadn't even heard him come in from work.

I tensed.

"You're not going out wearing that," he said quietly. "You look like a whore."

Without another word he walked out of the room.

Hot with embarrassment and hurt, I changed out of the skirt with shaking fingers and pulled on a pair of black skinny jeans.

I didn't say anything when I walked into our open-plan sitting room and kitchen to put my empty wineglass in the sink. I'd downed the remnants of it only moments ago. Fortification.

Transferring my purse, keys, and phone from my everyday bag to my clutch, I could feel Ollie's eyes burning into my back.

Seconds later I heard him approach and then his heat hit me as he wrapped his arms around me, pulling me into his chest. He started kissing my shoulder, his lips trailing up to my neck.

Still mad, I stiffened. "Stop it. I need to leave."

He gave me a squeeze. "Don't go, babe," he said, using his soft voice full of apology and placation. "I've had such a shit day at work. I could really use a quiet night in with my girl."

I sighed and turned in his arms. "I'm sorry but I've had this night out with the girls planned for ages. I haven't seen them in so long."

His hold on me tightened, his eyes pleading. "Please, babe. You have no idea how bad it's been."

I chewed my lip. "I'll leave early. I promise."

Ollie's arms instantly dropped, disappointment clear in his face. "It's cool. Don't bother. Your friends are important." But the way he said it might as well have been "Your friends are more important than me."

Feeling a mixture of guilt and annoyance, and knowing that if I didn't stay in he'd be pissed off at me for days, I sighed. "I'll text them to let them know I can't make it."

I was rewarded with a long, sweet kiss. "I'll order in," he said.

"Chinese," I muttered as I pulled out my phone.

"Nah, I'm in the mood for Indian."

Ugh, Indian. I sighed again and texted my friend Jennifer.

A few seconds later I received "You are fucking kidding me, right? Haven't seen you in ages and then you cancel at the last minute? This friendship is a one-way street right now, and I'm done with it."

Furious—at myself, at Ollie, and at Jennifer—I stomped back into our bedroom and ripped off my clothes, scrubbed off my makeup, and pulled on my pajamas in a huff.

Ollie had put on Top Gear *and had gotten us a beer out of the fridge. I joined him on the couch, where he instantly pulled me into his side, but I couldn't relax. I sat there worrying for the next few hours, scared I'd really, truly ruined my friendships.*

Ollie's phone rang and he answered it. I wasn't really paying attention to his conversation, so it was a surprise to me when he got off the phone and turned to me. "Come on, we're meeting Bill and the lads down the pub."

Disbelief and anger coursed through me. "Are you kidding?"

Confused, Ollie shook his head.

I stood up, my hands flying to hips. "I just gave up a night out with the girls because you said you needed a quiet night in with me."

"Oh, don't start," Ollie groaned. "I can't be bothered with your fucking drama tonight. Are you coming or not?"

"No! I'm not!" I yelled. "You selfish arsehole."

Ollie's face instantly darkened.

· · ·

I pulled myself quickly out of the memory, blinking it away as fast as I could. He'd been a prick for a long time. I couldn't believe how long it had taken me to see him for what he was, to see the damage he'd done to me and to my life.

"Shannon?"

I threw Simon a quick, tight smile. "We lost touch."

"I need another drink," Rae suddenly said, changing the subject, and I suspected (gratefully) that it was deliberate. "Anyone else?"

CHAPTER 6

Although the hostilities did not cease between Cole and me, time passed pretty quickly while I grew more accustomed to my job at INKarnate and living with Rae. Sometimes I couldn't believe it had only been a little over a month since I first came to work at Stu's studio. Not much had changed: I worked, avoided Cole when I could, snapped back at him in retaliation to his cold impatience, and watched him disappear out to lunch every now and then with Jessica, whom he'd been dating for the last few weeks.

Not that I cared.

I had Simon and Rae to use as buffers in the situation with Cole. They found the tension between Cole and me weirdly hilarious. They just went with it. Honestly it was almost becoming second nature to ignore him, or glare at him when I couldn't ignore him.

That was exactly what I was doing on Tuesday midafternoon. Rae had a client; it was Simon's day off; Cole was free but keeping himself busy (i.e., avoiding me) in Stu's office. I was sort of on my lunch break. I'd been late that morning, so I was making up for it by having my lunch break at my desk. That way I could still deal with customers if they came in or called. I was trying not to think about why I was late getting to work.

My nightmares had returned.

For ages after everything that had happened in Glasgow, I'd had bad dreams. When I moved to Edinburgh they were quickly taken over by stress dreams of the "my teeth falling out" variety. They were better than the nightmares, though, and they didn't wake me up in a sweaty mess at night, so I dealt with them. Then I got the job and a new roommate and the dreams had disappeared completely.

Now they were back and after waking up early that morning a complete trembling, clammy mess, I'd eventually fallen asleep but then slept right through my alarm.

I frowned and buried my nose deeper into J. B. Carmichael's latest book as I munched on a homemade sandwich. I was just getting into the story when I heard footsteps approaching from the back hallway. I didn't even have to look to know it was Cole—I'd grown that aware of him.

Concentrating with all my might, I attempted to ignore him as he walked into the main studio, his footsteps nearing me. I felt him hover around me, but I'd buried my nose so deep in the book that now all I could see was paper and black lines.

I heard an exasperated sigh seconds before I felt hands on my waist and then my whole body was lifted up out of my chair. I gasped and froze in shock as I was gently lowered to my feet near the filing cupboard door. I still held my book and sandwich in the exact same position, my eyes peering over the top of the book, as Cole steadied me and then pulled my chair out of the way of the desk. As he bent down to retrieve an empty folder from the drawer my shins had been pressed against, I finally found my voice.

"Couldn't you have just said 'excuse me'?" I was trying not to look at his arms. I knew I was small, but he'd just lifted me like I weighed less than air!

Cole turned his stony stare on me and suddenly started toward me. I refused to back up, but he got so close I had to smoosh my sandwich and book against my chest. I sucked in my breath as the heat radiating from his body hit me along with the tantalizing and mouthwatering smell of his cologne. I now knew that irresistible scent was the sport version of L'eau D'issey by Issey Miyake because I'd found Rae wrapping a gift set of it just the other day only to be told it was for Cole for his upcoming birthday. At the time I resisted the urge to grab the bottle off her, spritz my bedding, and roll around on it naked like a crazy lady.

Perhaps the tension between Cole and me was getting to me just a little.

Maybe.

Eyes wide, I watched as Cole's face came closer . . . and then completely bypassed mine as he reached behind me for a pen sitting on the top of the filing cabinet behind me.

Unfortunately my body responded to his proximity in a way I really wished it wouldn't. It was completely out of sync with my brain. Confused and upset, I held still as Cole pulled back with the pen in his hand. His expression was hard until he caught sight of mine. It made him pause.

Cole's eyes flickered over me before coming to a halt at the cover of my book.

"J. B. Carmichael fan?" he said.

I swallowed hard, trying to pull myself together. "Yeah."

He nodded and then lifted his eyes from the book to meet my gaze. "She's best mates with my sister. She lives in New Town."

What?

Wh—

My mouth fell open as I visibly fangirled. "Seriously?" I whispered, visions of meeting her and having my books signed dancing in my head. I'd known she was an American living in Scotland. Her series was set in Richmond, Virginia, and Edinburgh also featured, but I had had no idea I'd been this close to her for the last few weeks.

Something wicked glinted in Cole's eyes, but I was too busy freaking out to really notice what it meant. "Yup." He made a tsk noise. "Shame, that."

Viciously I was yanked out of my excitement at the tone. That wicked look registered and I knew exactly what it meant. Any hopes I had of meeting the author had been dashed from the moment I'd started a war with Cole.

He gave me a tight, triumphant smile and walked away.

My anger got the best of me. "You're an immature idiot!"

"I could give a fuck, Shortcake," he threw back at me. "And you started it."

Usually I enjoyed Rae's particular brand of conversation, but that night at dinner I wanted her gone already. Mike was taking her to a movie, but he was running late. Rae had decided to have dinner with me before heading out to meet him, thus stopping me from throwing a snack together and hiding out in my bedroom where I was going to pull out my acrylic paints for the first time.

I'd done as I promised myself and bought the paints with my first paycheck, and now I felt like a kid at Christmas, waiting for an empty flat so I could use them without fear of discovery. The first landscape I wanted to work on was the cityscape I'd drawn from the top of the castle.

However, Rae was taking her sweet time with dinner. She was also being strangely quiet.

Since my flatmate didn't like anyone asking if she was okay (she usually responded with something sarcastic that made me wish I'd never bothered to be concerned in the first place), I ate in silence.

Until Rae had the notion to speak again. "I haven't said anything, but I've got to tell you my curiosity is killing me." She dropped her fork and leaned across her plate, her eyes trapping mine. "Why the fuck are you and Cole acting like shitheads to each other? It's like working with psychos. You're all nicey-nicey to everyone else and then your attitude turns to ice the second he walks in the room and vice versa. Split personalities much?"

Honestly I was impressed that she'd managed to restrain herself for this long. I blew out air between my lips before answering her. "He kept coming on to me, so I put him in his place."

Rae laughed. "Why would you do a silly thing like that? It's *Cole*."

"It's Cole—so what? Just because he's hot and talented and confident I should fall at his feet? I know his type, believe me. I don't do bad-boy players anymore. They chew you up and spit you back out. As for Cole, he's like the Thor of the bad-boy world and . . ." I trailed off as Rae started laughing hysterically.

Glowering at her, I waited for her to stop.

My annoyance only made her laugh harder, so it took her a while to finally calm down. I'd finished my dinner, in fact.

"Oh." She wiped tears from her eyes. "Forget the hilariously random analogy that didn't even make a lot of sense but totally did anyway. What the hell are you talking about?"

I stared at her blankly. "Cole. Bad boy."

"Right." Rae snorted and started chuckling again.

"What?" I said, more than annoyed now.

"Nothing." She stood up and took our plates over to the sink. "I'll let you figure this one out on your own, you bloody numb nut."

Bewildered, I stared at her as she cleaned the plates. Finally I got up and left the kitchen but not before murmuring somewhat huffily, "*You're* the numb nut."

Her only response was to keep laughing, which she knew would bug the crap out of me.

The next day something different happened. Something unusual.

Like every day I let myself into the studio just before nine o'clock knowing that Cole and either Rae or Simon were already there setting up for the day. Sometimes, nearly almost always, if it was Simon's day to work he came out to greet me and retrieve the cappuccino I brought him. If it was Rae's day she came out to tease me about something and retrieve the black coffee I'd brought her.

Cole never came out to greet me in the morning. Not since we'd declared war.

So I was more than a little taken aback to see him striding toward me as I shrugged out of my jacket.

"Today we call a truce," his deep voice boomed into the room.

Ignoring the familiar butterflies that took up residence in my belly whenever Cole entered the room, I crossed my arms over my chest in defiance. I might have looked intimidating and impressive if it wasn't for the fact that I had to tilt my head back so much to look up at him. "I don't see the point."

The muscle in Cole's jaw flexed. I ignored the warning sign that I was pissing him off.

"Well?" I shrugged, flicking my hair over my shoulder.

His eyes followed the movement before he could stop it.

"Cole?"

Transferring his focus from my hair to my face, Cole sighed. "Can you just pretend to be a grown-up for two seconds? One: I don't like acting like this. I rarely acted like a teenage brat when I *was* a teenager, and it bloody galls me that a two-foot-nothing Glaswegian has reduced me to one."

Irritated at the suggestion I was the reason he couldn't maintain a level of professionalism (he was the one who started snapping at me when I shot him down), I opened my mouth to argue only for Cole to silence me by cutting the air in front of me with his hand.

"Don't." His tone and body language suggested it might be safer for me to listen. Cole waited a beat to see if I was going to obey his command. It hurt to do it, but I couldn't help remembering the way he lifted me out of my chair as if I were inconsequential. "Two," he continued once he realized I wasn't going to back talk him. "Stu is popping in today with an old friend who wants a new tattoo from him. If Stu senses even the tiniest bit of the bad atmosphere you and I have created this past month, he'll fire your arse so fast your knickers will turn to ash."

Oh, crap.

That never even occurred to me.

I was immediately consumed by anxiety.

What I was feeling must have shown on my face, because Cole's expression actually softened. "I can pretend to get on with you if you can."

The thought of losing my job caused me to nod quickly in agreement. As we stared at each other I wanted to ask why Cole would think to protect me, to protect my position here. I would have thought he'd be glad to see me fired.

Too scared to ask him in case it made him change his mind, I kept my lips sealed and Cole gave me a determined nod before heading into the back.

I stared after him for a while, beyond puzzled that he'd been considerate enough to do this for me. For some reason a surge of uneasiness began to slosh around in my tummy for a while.

No more than forty minutes later the front door of the studio opened and the mammoth that was Stu Motherwell strode inside. Although I was anxious I was also pleased to see him. He had a natural merriment about him that really did remind me of a biker version of Santa Claus.

As he walked in he was talking to the man behind him. The man was almost the same height, same build, same hair, with the same beard.

"There she is!" Stu bellowed cheerily. "Steely, meet Shannon. Shannon, Steely."

Steely and I exchanged hellos as Cole strolled into the main studio. He reached Stu and it was hard not to miss the affection in the older man's eyes. I'd known Cole meant something to Stu during our interview. He spoke about Cole with such respect. But now I could see it was more than that. As he clamped a hand on Cole's shoulder, giving him a manly shake and asking him how he was, it was in the gesture of a father asking a son.

He said something, but I wasn't quite paying attention to what; I was so focused on witnessing the dynamic between them. But then Cole laughed at whatever Stu had said and it was a deep, rumbling, full-on laugh that lit up his eyes and completely mesmerized me. I'd never seen Cole laugh like that before.

It occurred to me then that I didn't really know Cole Walker at all.

I'd made assumptions (which I still believed were true), but I didn't know a thing about Cole's past, his present, or what made him tick.

"Shannon?"

I blinked out of my musings. Stu grinned back and forth between Cole and me in a way I found disturbing. "How you getting on?" He looked at Cole. "How's wee fairy getting on?"

Cole immediately threw me a kind smile that caused this weird flippy feeling in my chest. "She's doing great. She's revolutionizing your filing, Stu."

Doing my very best to hide my shock, I grinned gratefully back at Cole.

He appeared almost dazzled by the smile, blinking rapidly at me.

"Good stuff," Stu said, apparently not noticing the strange interplay between his two employees. "Which room am I in today, then?"

"Mine," Cole said. "It's Rae's day off, so I'll take her room." He nodded past Stu to Steely. "How's things?"

"Aye, no bad." He frowned, though. "After fifteen years together, the wife finally noticed I've got a woman's name scribed on my shoulder." He looked at me in disbelief. "Fifteen years. Talk about a lack of interest, eh?"

"To be fair, it is a tiny script and the name is 'Cherry,'" Stu said.

"Aye, that was *her* argument. I asked her what the hell she thought 'Cherry' meant if it wasn't a woman. She said she thought it was a fucking song title." Steely sighed. "Anyway, she's annoyed about it, so I promised I'd get one done for her to prove some such nonsense or whatever. I don't know. So let's get it done." Cole chuckled and Steely pinned him to the wall with a serious glower. "Never get a woman's name inked on your skin. Never."

Stu grinned at Cole. "He'll ignore that, Steely. I know him too well." Cole barely responded with a mysterious smile and a half shrug. "And will it be the fair . . ." Stu frowned. "Fuck, what's her name? Jessica, is it?"

I immediately wanted to bury my head in my files. I really didn't want to know anything about the fair Jessica, but Cole stopped me from turning away by flicking an enigmatic look at me before answering.

"Nah." He glanced back at Stu. "Broke up."

I stopped breathing.

"Ah, and what happened this time?"

"You're a nosy bugger," Steely ribbed his friend.

Stu ignored him. "Well?"

"She started redecorating my flat in her head after only two weeks of dating."

Stu shuddered. "Cling-on."

"Oh God, yeah."

Cole's pained expression stayed painted across my mind's eye as I bent my head and started pulling out the files I'd last been working on. I still hadn't come anywhere near to finishing the digitization of them. As I began to work, all the warm and fuzzy feelings I'd been afraid to admit to developing since Cole called a truce for the day dissipated upon new evidence that Cole really and truly *was* the kind of bad boy I needed to avoid.

I felt sorry for Jessica.

She'd probably only suggested Cole get some cushions for his sofa or something, and he'd misinterpreted it as a threat to his bachelorhood.

Arse.

I lifted my head to wave Stu and Steely a temporary good-bye as they disappeared into the back to get to work on Steely's new tattoo, and then I looked back down at the files.

But I could feel Cole's gaze on me.

Steadying my nerves, I looked up at him and somehow I managed to unstick the words blocked in my throat. "Thank you."

Cole's lips twitched with amusement. "See? That wasn't so hard, was it?"

"I *still* don't like you."

The humor left his eyes. "The feeling is mutual." He shook his head, his expression unreadable now. "You really are the biggest disappointment, Shannon MacLeod."

Without another word he followed our boss into the back, leaving me reeling.

His words had almost sounded . . . sad.

At that point I'd really thought the worst was over for the day. Cole and I had put on a united front and Stu seemed happy enough. However, I was wrong.

I knew I was wrong when Stu showed Steely out after he'd finished the tattoo and then turned to me once the door shut behind his friend. He scrutinized me in a way that made me squirm as I scanned photographs of a guy's tattoo Stu had done fifteen years ago. It was of a muscled naked chick riding a motorbike toward the gates of hell. It was disturbing, but the artwork was awesome.

"Glad to hear you're getting on so well here, Shannon."

Was that a question? It sounded like a question.

I tensed.

"Yeah, it's going great." Cole suddenly appeared and walked toward me.

Weirdly, I'd never been happier to see him.

Stu looked at us both and then nodded. "Great. Glad to hear it. So I'll see you at Cole's birthday party, then?"

Birthday party?

Say what?

Panic. Yes, that was definitely panic causing my heart to do that horrible fluttery thing in my chest. "Uh—"

Cole reached me and slid his arm along my shoulders, pulling me into his side. I tried my best not to stiffen, in fact allowing myself to relax into him. I flushed, feeling his lean, hard body pressing into my soft one.

My head barely reached his shoulder.

I hate him, I hate him, I hate him, I hate him, I chanted in my head to remind myself as I quickly grew heated and turned on.

"Of course she'll be there." Cole gave me a squeeze and my left boob was crushed against his chest.

Oh boy.

I tried for a grin, but I was pretty sure it came out tremulous because Stu got this suspicious look on his face. However, the suspicion melted into a gleam of delight that quickly made me realize he'd gotten the wrong impression about what was going on between Cole and me.

"Oh." He nodded and tapped a finger against his nose. "I got you."

No, he did not get us! He did not get us at all.

"Have fun, kiddies." He laughed and threw open the entrance door. "See you soon!"

The minute Stu was out of sight of the front windows, I wrenched away from Cole's embrace, my hands flying to my hips. "Birthday party?"

Looking beleaguered, Cole nodded. "My friend Hannah is on maternity leave. She's bored. Extremely bored. I am not telling my bored, pregnant best friend that she can't throw me a birthday party no matter how much I don't need that shit right now."

There was a lot in that sentence I did not want to deal with. "I don't think I should go."

"That's entirely up to you, but Stu will be there and he'll wonder why you're not there since the two of us get on *so* well. *Everyone* I know will be there."

I growled in frustration.

Cole raised an eyebrow at my reaction. "Don't worry, sweetheart. It's not likely that we'll cross paths at this thing. I'll barely even know you're there."

And once more the irritant walked away with the last word!

CHAPTER 7

The room was naturally dark since it was a basement room, but warm lighting had been placed in alcoves all around and rugs covered the flagstone floors. To the left of the bar situated in the back of the room were two long tables with enough buffet food to feed a small family for a good couple of weeks. Booths were situated around the edges of the room, and people had already laid claim to most of them.

There were no balloons, no banners, nothing but a birthday cake to suggest this was indeed a birthday party, which told me that Hannah knew her best friend quite well.

"Why am I here again?" I said to Rae.

Somehow despite protesting against it for days, I was standing next to Rae and Mike in the entrance to the basement bar that was part of a split-level nightclub called Fire. The basement had been turned into a private function suite for Cole's party, organized by his friend Hannah, and hosted by the owner of the club, Braden Carmichael. And yup, Rae told me that Braden was J. B. Carmichael's husband.

"Because you look hot and it'll annoy the fuck out of Cole and greatly entertain me," Rae said, leaning into Mike's side.

I pulled a face at her, but secretly I was pleased by her compliment. It made no sense, but I wanted to look my best tonight.

As always my hair was down, but I'd taken special care to make sure it was soft and not wild. I was wearing a black figure-hugging short dress, black stockings, and black suede ankle boots with a thin silver heel. No accessories. My makeup was fresh and light—my lipstick, eye shadow, and nail polish peach because it was a color that worked nicely against my skin tone and hair.

Since the dress was short and the heels were high, my legs looked longer. Wearing no jewelry and no color meant that the dress and my hair were doing all the work tonight.

Tony waved from across the room, just this mere action drawing gazes my way. He strolled toward us in another beautifully fit suit, his hand clasped in Simon's. Simon wore dark jeans and a white T-shirt with a Banksy print on it. As soon as Tony reached me I received a kiss on either cheek. When he stepped back his eyes raked over me with a thoroughness you'd expect from a straight guy. "You look *bellissima*," he murmured throatily.

Seriously, the guy oozed sexual charisma.

The strangers beyond him were looking at us again, and as I scanned the group I halted on a familiar face. Cole. I flushed and turned my attention back to Tony, murmuring my thanks.

Tony turned to greet Rae and Mike, and Simon took his place beside me. "You do look sexy as hell, Shannon."

I smiled gratefully. I felt completely out of place and out of my depth, but looking good and being appreciated, especially by Tony and

Simon (whom I'd come to adore) made me feel a little better. "You look sexy too. But you always do." It was true. He could wear a bin bag and look hot.

"Simon," a low, pleasant voice said, and I turned to my left to see it belonged to a stunning and very pregnant blond woman. She held her arms out and Simon stepped into her, enfolding her in a gentle embrace.

"Hannah, you look great, sweetheart."

Oh. So this was Hannah. I studied her while she smiled at Simon. This was Cole's best friend.

Her gaze moved to me and I could see her brown eyes were brimming with curiosity. "Introduce me, Sy."

He did so and then promptly left me alone with her.

Hannah held her hand out to me with a friendly smile and I took it with my own. I nodded at her small baby bump. "Congratulations."

"Thanks." She patted her stomach and then gave a nod to the left. "It's our second."

I followed her gaze to an exceptionally tall, broad-shouldered too-good-looking-to-be-true guy with fantastic caramel skin. He was talking to a dark-haired man I didn't recognize, holding a little girl with dark curly hair in his right arm, while a little boy, the spitting image of him, gripped his left hand.

"My husband, Marco," Hannah said. "And our daughter, Sophia, and my stepson, Dylan."

"You have a beautiful family," I said with genuine feeling.

Wistfulness caused a light ache in my chest.

She smiled. "They keep me busy." Just like that, her gaze turned questioning. "So, you're the new receptionist at INKarnate?"

It occurred to me I had absolutely no idea what Cole had said to her about me. My answering "yes" was cautious.

"Hmm."

I waited, but that was all I was going to get out of her on the subject apparently, because the next words out of her mouth were "You have the best hair ever."

I laughed and some of the tension between us broke. "Thank you."

"How do you get it to do the ringlet thing? With straighteners or a curling iron?"

"The ringlets are natural," Rae butted in. "The bitch's hair looks like this naturally, all the fucking time."

Clearly used to Rae, Hannah didn't even blink at her calling me a bitch. She just laughed, told us to help ourselves to the free bar and buffet, and wandered off to mingle with other people.

I looked around at the gathering, at the faces I didn't recognize, at the small children laughing and running in among the adults. I wouldn't have expected there to be kids, but it suddenly made sense why the party had started so early on a Sunday evening. Stu had even closed the studio early for it. I saw our behemoth of a boss over by the dip, talking to a curly-haired blond girl who was staring up at him in awe.

This was a family party, completely at odds in my mind with the man it was being thrown for.

"Cole knows a lot of people."

"Yeah," Rae said, and grabbed my hand. "And I know which one you want to meet."

Without mercy Rae began to drag me through the room. Struggling against her would only draw more attention to us, so I just went with it, even though I was sure I was about to be mortified.

When I stumbled to a stop at Rae's abrupt halt in front of an attractive blonde I recognized from her author photo, I knew I was right.

I froze as I took her in. She leaned into a tall, rugged older guy. His dark hair had some gray in it at the sides, but this only made him more distinguished looking than he already was. His amazing pale blue eyes seared right through me.

Rae and I had interrupted the couple's conversation.

Floor, swallow me. Please.

"Joss, Braden," Rae said in an almost militant manner. "This is Shannon." She gently nudged me forward and I gave Joss a strained smile. "She's my new flatmate and our receptionist at INKarnate. She's a fan of your books, Joss."

Joss gave me a kind smile, as though she sensed my discomfort. Admittedly it wouldn't have taken a writing genius to sense that. I shook her hand, surprised by how nervous I was to meet her. That was probably why the next words that spilled out of my mouth were unfiltered and revealed way more than I'd meant to. "I just want you to know that your books are important. They've helped me through the worst months of my life this last year."

I tensed as soon as the words were out of my mouth, and my three companions noticed. *Rae* noticed. She put her arm around me and pulled me close so she could press a kiss to my hair. She gently released me and walked away, leaving me staring after her.

Sometimes that woman could surprise the heck out of me.

When I turned my attention back to Joss and Braden, I discovered they both now wore identical expressions of concern.

"That really means a lot," Joss said, and I noted that her American accent was interrupted quite a bit by Scottish inflections. According to Rae, Joss had lived in Scotland for seventeen years. "I hear you've moved from Glasgow. How are you settling in?"

"Good, thank you. I've always loved this city."

She smiled in response, but I could see that she was still assessing me. "Well . . . you know we're a tight group here . . . if you ever need anything . . ." She shrugged.

I was stunned.

Her offer of support, her acceptance of me as part of their group of friends when she'd only just met me blew me away. I thought about the fact that my own family hadn't contacted me at all since my sister's blunt text weeks ago, and I had to look away because this stranger's kindness had moved me to tears.

I blinked them back hurriedly, staring at the girl with the head of blond curls again. Now she was herding a group of younger children toward the buffet table. Looking more closely, I could see she had Joss's tip-tilted eyes and smile. "Is she yours?"

"How can you tell?" Joss said, following my gaze, a smirk playing on her full mouth. "That's our daughter, Beth, and the little dark-haired boy holding her hand is our son, Luke."

I glanced around the room, taking everyone in. "Big family," I muttered.

"We're kind of a tribe, really," Joss joked.

I smiled and took a step back. "Anyway, I'll let you get back to your evening. It was a pleasure to meet you."

"You too, Shannon."

"And remember," Braden spoke up, and I was instantly transfixed by him. The air around him crackled like it did with Cole. I hadn't noticed because I'd been so focused on Joss, but her husband was really kind of sexy. "If you ever need anything just ask."

Wow. That was nice. "That's very kind." I nodded my thanks and walked away, thinking Cole was one lucky son of a bitch to have people like them in his life.

An hour later I'd met almost everyone and also caught up with the twins and Karen. I hadn't spent much time with them since meeting them that first night weeks ago, but from their friendly demeanor it was clear they didn't know about my war with Cole.

I was trying desperately to remember everyone's name, but the only ones that stuck were the names of Cole's extended family—or tribe, as Joss called it. First Tony introduced me to a tall, slender woman who was quite possibly the most beautiful woman I'd ever met in real life. With her gorgeous light, clear green eyes, I wasn't surprised to learn she was Cole's sister, Jo. Her husband, Cameron, reminded me of Cole—not in looks but in manner. I could tell from the way he dressed and held himself that he'd been a huge influence in Cole's life. They had their daughter, Belle, with them and the minute she saw me she threw herself at me and asked if she could play with my hair. Of course she was even more adorable in real life, so I let her do just that as Jo introduced me to her boss and uncle, Mick, his wife, Dee, and Mick's daughter, Olivia.

Olivia was an attractive brunette, American, and bubbling with a humor and personality that dazzled me almost as much as her smile and her husband, Nate, did. Although Tony had warned me about Nate, there was really no way to prepare myself for the reality. He was just *that* good-looking. Everything about his looks, his smile, his confidence, screamed *player* . . . until he looked at his wife and their two daughters. Anyone could see they meant the world to him.

Finally I met Braden's sister, Ellie, and her husband, Adam, and their two boys. Ellie was one of those women you couldn't help liking immediately. She was down-to-earth, warm, and endearing and she just knew how to put a person at ease. After meeting her mum and stepfather, Elodie and Clark, I knew instantly where she'd inherited the qualities.

It was overwhelming meeting the tribe.

Even more overwhelming was that uneasiness I'd been feeling every now and then, an uneasiness that churned in my gut and came at me in waves as I met Cole's friends and family.

Trying to shrug it off, I wandered over to the bar to order a glass of wine, hoping to sneak in a few minutes to myself.

I knew the instant he neared me.

I felt him.

From my peripheral I saw Cole slide in next to me. I turned to watch as he leaned against the bar. Tonight he looked even more amazing than usual, in a crisp white dress shirt rolled up at the sleeves, a fitted black waistcoat, and black suit trousers. A quirky silver pocket watch was attached to the waistcoat. He was wearing a leather aviator watch along with the black leather bracelets he always wore. For some reason that watch and those bracelets were incredibly sexy on him. Perhaps it was because it drew attention to his wrists, which then drew attention to his strong forearms, which then drew attention to his tattoos, which then . . .

You get the picture.

My eyes drifted up to his face, and heat instantly suffused me. His greedy gaze was roaming over me in a way that was blatantly sexual and at the same time consternated. Our eyes met.

"So, all I've heard tonight from my family is how bloody lovely Shannon MacLeod is."

I flushed inwardly with pleasure, glad they'd liked me, but I didn't respond to him. I didn't really know what he wanted me to say.

No response was the wrong way to go, because it clearly exasperated him. "Want to tell me why I've not met this version of you? No . . . wait." He leaned in close, those green eyes hot with anger. "I have met her, but she was fifteen."

I looked away quickly, willing the bartender to appear.

Seconds later I heard a frustrated growl and then I felt Cole melt away from my side. I let go a huge sigh of relief only to choke on the remnants of it at the sight of Hannah hurrying toward me. She frowned as she came to a stop in front of me.

"What was that?" she asked, gesturing in the direction of where I assumed Cole had headed.

"Nothing."

Hannah narrowed her eyes. "Cole is my best friend and he tells me everything, so I know he came on to you and you shot him down. I also know you shot him down in a probably not very nice way because of his reaction. Cole spends most of his life horizontal he's so bloody laid-back, so it takes a lot to make him this frustrated and fucked off. It's not like him."

"I only said the truth." I defended myself because I didn't want these seemingly good people not to like me. "I told him I knew he was a player and that I wasn't interested."

Hannah looked taken aback. "You're kidding me, right?"

I shook my head.

"Cole? A player?" She guffawed. "Are you high?"

I grew very still, not liking her reaction at all. She smiled, but there was disbelief in the look. "Shannon, I've known Cole Walker since he was a shy fourteen-year-old that could barely say two words to me. Cole is definitely not a player."

I struggled to deal with what she was saying, and I doubted I kept that struggle out of my expression. "He's such a bad boy," I squeaked out.

She chuckled. "No way."

"But . . . but he's so cocky and flirty . . ." I trailed off, that uneasiness in my gut starting to make sense all of a sudden.

"Well, he's spent his formative years surrounded by men incapable of restraint when it comes to flirting outrageously with their wives. Each one of them"—she gestured around the room—"is a cocky, arrogant, overconfident bugger." She grinned. "But you won't find men who are more loyal or loving to their wives." Her expression turned serious. "We've all been through a lot. As has Cole. Like us, he knows what's important. And he's been deeply influenced by the men in his life. Cole's never been a fan of casual. With the exception of Jessica and probably some alcohol-induced one-night stands, Cole has only ever been in relationships. He's looking for the right woman to settle down with. He's a romantic." Her eyes glimmered with deep affection. "He's also one of the best men I've ever, ever, ever met. I love him dearly, and . . . I only want the very best for him," she concluded pointedly.

I felt awful as soon as she finished speaking. Absolutely, truly awful.

"I don't respect players like you. I don't like you. I don't trust you. There's nothing behind that charming smile but empty promises. You have nothing real to offer me or anyone who finds herself a victim of your flirtation. The difference between them and me, however, is that I'm smart enough to see you for what you really are . . . Nothing."

"Forget the hilariously random analogy that didn't even make a lot of sense but totally did anyway. What the hell are you talking about?"

"Cole. Bad boy."

"Right."

"What?"

"Nothing. I'll let you figure this one out on your own, you bloody numb nut."

I squeezed my eyes shut tight at the memories. "I am such a bitch."

Feeling Hannah's hand resting on my arm, I opened my eyes to find her staring at me with a surprising amount of kindness. "Somehow I don't believe that's true."

And on that enigmatic comment she walked away, leaving me to drown my guilt in a large glass of red wine.

CHAPTER 8

Once when I was ten I had helped my granddad throw out some old things because Gran was doing her yearly spring clean and somehow Granddad's belongings always ended up taking the brunt of the clear-out.

My granddad had books everywhere. I remembered grabbing books that were piled randomly in the corner of the sitting room and asking him if they were to be thrown out. His response was an immediate and very adamant no. I made a face and asked him why since no one else had probably even heard of the books with their very boring covers. Granddad had tutted at me and told me that inside the books were the best stories he'd ever read, and that I shouldn't judge them solely on their bad marketing.

I hadn't really understood at the time, but I guessed he was quite literally telling me not to judge a book by its cover.

An old cliché.

A cliché it might have been but one lesson I should never have forgotten. After Hannah's revelations about Cole's true character, I left his party quickly. I barely slept that night, consumed with guilt for judging Cole on what happened to be bad marketing from my perspective. Amid the guilt was regret and something bigger. Something a little like panic.

The next day at work I didn't know how I was supposed to act around Cole. It seemed it was back to business as usual for him, because he didn't come out to greet me when I pushed open the front door of the studio.

Simon did, looking a little worse for wear as he took his coffee from me. "Thank fuck," he muttered. "I started in on the whisky after five beers last night." He took a sip of his coffee and frowned at me. "Where did you run off to?"

I shrugged, already uncomfortable. "Home. Headache."

He gave me an incredulous look.

With a heavy sigh I told him the truth. "I think I may have made some not very nice assumptions about Cole."

"Has this got anything to do with the cold war between you two?"

I nodded. "And now I don't know how to fix it."

"Why not start with just being nice to him?"

"Nice?"

"Nice."

Not sure how to go about making that change after being such a bitch, I looked down at my coffee to avoid Simon's gaze. I felt ashamed of my behavior these last few weeks. How the heck did I go about trying to make amends?

I contemplated my coffee. "What does Cole drink?"

Simon chuckled. "A cortado. One sugar."

"The coffee shop is right around the corner," I mused.

"It is." Simon grinned. "I'll man the desk for you."

I returned his smile with a grateful one of my own before shrugging into my jacket and hurrying out to the coffee shop. Not even five minutes later I was back in the studio. As soon as I stepped inside with Cole's cortado, Simon winked at me and left the reception for his workroom.

I looked down at Cole's coffee and felt the butterflies in my belly go wild. Bolstering myself against nerves, I threw my shoulders back and headed toward the workrooms.

Stopping in the doorway of Cole's room, I almost completely lost my nerve. He was sitting with one ankle resting on the opposite knee, his sketch pad on his lap, and his head bent, as he concentrated on what he was drawing.

He was really handsome. I knew this. I'd known this from the moment I met him, but that feeling was back—that feeling I'd had when I was fifteen years old and I was staring up into his green eyes in absolute delight. That feeling you get when you realize something special about another person and he goes from being attractive to downright kick-you-in-the-gut good-looking.

I'd learned a lot about Cole in the last few days.

He was so damn kick-you-in-the-gut good-looking now.

Catching sight of me out of the corner of his eye, Cole lifted his head in surprise.

In response to his silent question I took two steps forward and thrust the coffee at him.

He raised an eyebrow. The gesture was too sexy for words.

My hand trembled.

Cole watched the coffee cup shake with the tremor and reached out to take it from me.

Once it was in his hand I backed out of the room and practically fled down the hall.

Standing at my desk, taking in a ragged breath, I inwardly berated myself for being quite possibly the most uncool person to have ever worked in a tattoo studio.

Not even ten minutes later I had to find the nerve to face Cole again because he had a customer. I informed him of this with a warmer politeness than usual, and I could feel his curious gaze on my back as he followed me out into the reception area.

I buried my head in my work, sighing a huge sigh of relief when he returned to his workroom.

An hour later, my mind still mostly on the recent turn of events, I was more than taken aback when the front doorbell rang, signaling a customer, only for me to look up and be faced with Cole's recent ex, Jessica.

She strode to the desk with her usual exuberance. "Hi, Shannon. Is Cole free?"

Confused, I shook my head. "He's got a client."

"I'll just wait."

"Um . . . okay . . ."

She smiled and planted her bottom on one of the leather couches and made the impression of someone who was settling in.

Cole *had* broken up with her . . . right?

For the next forty minutes I attempted to put my head into my work, but every now and then my eyes would lift to check on whether the young blonde was still there.

She was.

As I studied her I decided she was definitely all wrong for Cole. Too young, too bubbly and in your face, and much, much too blond.

Not that I was biased or anything.

Hearing Cole's voice approaching, I waited curiously to see how this scene would unfold. Appearing in the main studio, Cole was too busy discussing aftercare with his customer to notice Jessica in the waiting area. He brought the guy over to me and while I smiled, I subtly nodded in Jessica's direction.

Cole flicked his eyes over and was about to return them to me before he did a double take. His eyebrows immediately drew together.

Handing Cole's customer his card back, I bade him good-bye, as did Cole, and waited for the gentleman to leave.

"She's been waiting for you for the past forty minutes," I told him under my breath.

Cole appeared frustrated. Exhaling, he wandered over to her, not even halfway to reaching her before she jumped up off the couch and dashed toward him. She threw her arms around him like a little girl and Cole staggered back, immediately gripping her elbows to gently push her away. "Jessica, what are you doing here?" he asked.

"We need to talk," she said, batting her pretty eyes at him.

She was good. I'd give her that.

Apparently not good enough. "Jessica, we said all we had to say."

"But I miss you." She went into instant begging mode that raised my hackles. "I can do better, I promise."

It took everything within me not to scream, "Have some self-respect!"

I was beginning to think that maybe, perhaps, more than possibly, Jessica was indeed every bit the cling-on Cole had accused her of being.

"Jessica, you don't have to do anything." Cole continued being nice, which I thought was decent of him considering most guys would have bounced her arse out of the door by now. "We're just not right for each other, sweetheart."

Her eyes filled with tears. "We are. I love you."

My mouth fell open.

Yup. Total cling-on.

A red warning sign began blinking in my mind's eye.

Cole seemed as stunned as I felt. "Jessica . . ."

The urge to rescue him overtook me. "Cole," I called out. "Simon needs you in the back."

His startled gaze flew to mine, relief in them. "Right, of course." He turned to Jessica. "Look, this is a really bad time. I'm sorry if you got the wrong impression, but we're just not . . . going to happen."

When she continued to stare at him incredulously, I found myself slinking out from behind the desk and hurrying over to the front entrance. The bells tinkled as I yanked it open, drawing Jessica's attention.

She caught my look, and her jaw hardened at the silent point I was making. With an overdone sniffle she hurried out of the studio, clutching her bag to her chest as though we'd just killed her puppy and refused to apologize.

I shut the door behind her and mouthed, *Wow,* at Cole before heading back behind my desk.

Cole cautiously approached me, his expression filled with suspicion. I returned his stare with an innocent one of my own.

"Thank you," he said with not a tiny amount of wariness.

"You're welcome," I said, my tone kind.

He blinked rapidly and it was clear his suspicion had only increased.

Cole stared at me for a few seconds longer, but I managed to maintain perfect politeness.

Backing away slowly, Cole held my stare, silently questioning me with every step he took. He turned around, but then just before he stepped into the hallway he looked back at me, confused.

I gave him nothing and he disappeared into the hall. I broke out into a massive, amused grin, a grin I quickly hid when Cole's head popped back around the door. The hilarious sight of his seemingly floating head was made only more entertaining by the distrust in his narrowed eyes. Schooling my features into innocent politeness, I endured a short staring match with Cole's head before he gave up.

His head disappeared and I began to shake with silent laughter.

"You're freaking me out a little bit," Cole said the next morning as he took the coffee I offered him.

Although I quite enjoyed the fact that I had him feeling off balance, I gave him the speech I'd prepared for the moment he called me out on my unusual behavior. "I've decided you're right. I'm sick of acting like a brat. I'm sorry for what I said. I don't know you. It was uncalled for and unprofessional of me."

Cole didn't even try to hide his surprise, and I liked that about him. I was beginning to realize that Cole was pretty transparent. He didn't play games like most people. He wore his mood on his sleeve for everyone to see, and most of the time his thoughts were out there too. "Wow. Did not see that coming."

I grimaced, feeling unsure all of a sudden. I'd been holding on to Hannah's assessment of Cole's character, using it to assure myself that we'd move on like nothing had ever happened. "Does that mean you accept my apology?"

He stared at me a second and I think he did it to make me squirm. It worked. He finished off, however, with a nod. "Of course. Thanks for the coffee."

His response was mature; it was what I thought I wanted, but I walked out of his room weighed down with disappointment. He'd accepted my apology with all the warmth of a wet bath towel.

Muttering under my breath, I berated myself. I did have only myself to blame if Cole wasn't really feeling all that friendly toward the woman who completely annihilated his character without an ounce of proof to back up said annihilation.

"Making nice with the boss?"

I let out a startled squeak and spun around to find Rae mere inches from me. "Jesus!"

Rae laughed and pushed me gently down the hallway and into the main studio away from Cole's ears.

"I take it you were listening?" I glowered at her as I headed toward my desk.

"Of course."

"You are a nosy pain in the arse."

"Yeah, yeah, I'm a horrible flatmate. Now fucking spill."

I lowered my voice. "Hannah informed me that I had the wrong impression about Cole. She told me he isn't a player or a bad boy after all."

"Took you long enough."

"*You* could have told me."

"And where is the fun in that, pray tell?"

I was not amused. "You know, there are times when you're a bitch and then other times when you are a *bitch*."

Rae sighed in exasperation. "Look, you need to learn how not to bring your past into your present. It's a lesson I had to learn on my own, and having someone baby you through that isn't going to teach you what you really need to discover for yourself. If you fuck this up— whatever this is with Cole—you'll learn never to do it again. But I'm hoping there is a better lesson here."

"And what's that?"

"Someone tried to take something from you. You didn't let them. Why start now? Especially when it comes to the things you want, and the things you need." She smacked her hand down on the counter with an abruptness that startled me. "Enough of this Miyagi crap. Point is, fight for what you want, and while you're doing that I'd like an egg mayo sandwich without that fucking cress shit on it this time."

I tried to keep up with the change in subject. "It's three hours until your lunch break."

"I'm hungry now and I've got a client in fifteen."

"I get lunch for everyone at the same time. I'm not a gofer. I'm a receptionist."

She eyed me carefully. "Sometimes your tiny height is deceiving." And on that weird comment, Rae strode outside. I assumed in search of a sandwich.

CHAPTER 9

In high school I took art class every year, and a lot of still-life drawing is involved in the Scottish curriculum. Luckily for me I liked those classes, yet there were moments when I'd be sketching a flower or flowers stuck inside a skull, or a stuffed animal, or even a person in life drawing class, when I'd step back from my work and to my disappointment I'd see that it wasn't quite right. There was something lacking, something that was stopping it from being brought to life.

If it was a sketch of a person, my problem was usually in the hands. Hands were so difficult to draw and it took me forever to get them right. There were times I just couldn't manage it, and every time I stepped back from the sketch it fell short because of the bloody hands.

That was a little how I felt about my interaction with Cole.

Things were definitely better between us, but it was just sort of friendly on his part. For some reason his attitude completely threw me off balance. I couldn't stop thinking about him, which I knew was ridiculous because it wasn't as though I wanted to be in a relationship with him. I didn't want to be in a relationship with anyone. My life here had just started and I didn't need another man screwing up this new start.

That didn't mean I could switch off whatever I was feeling about Cole. I went for drinks with him, Rae, the twins, Karen, Simon, and Tony and it was a really good laugh. Part of me sat there grateful that in just a few short weeks Rae had helped me build a life, with good friends and good times that helped me ignore the bloody awfulness of what I'd left behind in Glasgow. However, there was this other part of me that would glimpse Cole out of the corner of my eye, stealing glances whenever I could, and I'd feel this disappointment in my gut that all the joking and closeness he shared with the others he didn't try to share with me.

The only thing that could take my mind off my complicated feelings was my newfound love for painting. Somehow I'd managed to keep my artwork a secret from Rae by either working outside the flat or waiting until she was occupied elsewhere. I was already working on my second landscape after having completed the one of Edinburgh at night. I knew it was probably far from the quality of professional artists, but I actually loved it. After experimenting I found I was most comfortable with broad brushstrokes and a minimal approach. I loved how this gave the cityscape energy and movement. I was hooked. I couldn't wait for my holidays off work. I was planning on booking a last-minute budget break somewhere like Italy or Budapest or Prague—somewhere exciting where I could set myself up on a riverbank, or a café, anywhere I could just relax and draw and forget about every single thing that worried me, including Cole Walker.

. . .

A week had passed since I started being nice to Cole. It felt longer. Much, much longer. I frowned over at him while we worked. He was standing in the gallery area, showing tattoo concepts to a prospective customer, as well as going over his video portfolio for the guy. Cole was completely lost in conversation about his art and I was becoming increasingly transfixed by the animation in his face and the way his eyes were lit up. His passion for his work took Cole from a ten to an eleven, and eleven had, heretofore, never seen the light of day in my hot-guy ranking system.

As if he felt my stare, Cole suddenly looked over at me while he continued to talk and I casually smiled at him and looked in the opposite direction like I hadn't just been caught ogling my boss.

Looking out the window, the blood beneath my cheeks hot, I wondered if he was still staring at me. I fidgeted, trying to maintain my cool.

I was just about to lower my gaze to my work in the hopes of making out like I'd just needed a break from staring at paper, when the sight of a familiar blonde out on the pavement caused me to freeze.

Jessica.

She was staring up at our signage, chewing her lip.

Oh, heck no.

I knew from Rae that Jessica hadn't let up on Cole. She'd turned up at his flat last Thursday, and while I was with him on Friday night at the bar she had texted him a dozen or so times. Even if Rae hadn't told me, I could see for myself that Jessica's behavior was really starting to stress Cole out.

I'd heard of girls like her, girls who just couldn't take no for an answer, but I'd never met one in real life. She was beginning to piss me off. Cole had had to deal with my craziness when I first arrived here only for Jessica to jump on the crazy train when I jumped off.

Well, I thought determinedly, *I can make up for my craziness by getting rid of Jessica once and for all.*

Utilizing my often-underused, rapid-fire typing skills, I logged on to the Internet and looked up the info I thought might be useful in taking her down. Once I had it I glanced up to see the crazy girl had decided she was coming into the studio.

I immediately hopped off my chair and hurried across the studio to Cole, hearing the bells over the door jingle just as I reached him. I practically elbowed his customer out of the way and hissed, "Everything I do next, just go with it."

His eyebrows had just begun to rise in surprise when I lunged at him, causing his whole face to slacken with shock. On tiptoes, and having to crush my chest against him to reach him, I wrapped my arms around his neck and yanked his head down. My mouth hit his and for a few seconds he tensed in my grasp.

I pressed my lips harder against his, my legs trembling as I had to stay on tiptoe to reach his mouth.

Just like that, Cole relaxed into me, his hands coming to a gentle rest on my hips, his mouth now moving against mine.

Oh boy.

He had good lips.

Good, good lips.

And he smelled wonderful.

I had no idea a kiss without tongue could still curl your toes.

Um . . . Shannon . . .

Forcing myself to remember why I was doing this, I pulled back from him and stumbled a little as I dropped my arms and returned my feet flat to the floor.

Cole's fingers pressed into my hips as he steadied me. "What—"

"Jessica," I whispered. "Smile, like we're together."

"Excuse me," the bewildered customer said in annoyance behind me, but he was cut off by a screeched "What the hell is going on?"

I turned around and Cole's hands dropped from my hips. Jessica was standing by the reception desk, eyes round with horror.

"Jessica," Cole began impatiently, but I cut him off.

"Stop stalking my boyfriend," I said with as much menace as I could muster. I didn't really *do* menacing, but I think I pulled off angry redhead well enough.

Cole grew still at my back.

Jessica, however, gasped, her hurt gaze flying to him. "Boyfriend? But . . ."

I'd so lost my patience with her crap. "How many times do you have to be told that it's over?" I took a few steps toward her, but she didn't back away from me like I'd hoped. "Or is this your game? You think you can bug the crap out of a guy until he gives in just to get you to stop? Well, not *my* guy."

She made a huff of disbelief. "I don't—"

"I'm not finished," I snapped.

Her mouth clamped shut and that hurt puppy dog look was back.

My expression turned mean with calculation. "I take it you're counting on graduating from Edinburgh College of Art?"

Confused, she nodded.

"I happen to be Professor Kris Lowery's goddaughter. You'll have heard of Kris, right, seeing as she's the principal of the college?"

Jessica's whole demeanor changed. *Now* she took a wary step backward.

"See, I don't know if you're stupid, selfish, or crazy, but I do know that harassment is beyond stressful, horrible, and downright criminal. I also know for a fact that Kris will not be happy to hear that one of her students has a report filed against her with the police for harassment. In fact, I'm thinking Kris will not like that *at all*."

Jessica's anxious gaze drifted over my head to Cole and then back to me.

I sighed, pouring every ounce of pissed-off impatience into the effect. "That look in your eyes tells me at least you're not stupid. Just selfish, then."

"I really like him." She shrugged pathetically.

"Well, he's a little preoccupied liking me, so from now on don't call, don't write, don't turn up at his home, his work, or try to contact him in any way, because I'm a jealous girlfriend with a very doting godmother who will do just about anything for me. Understood?"

Flushing, Jessica nodded quickly.

"That's your cue to leave."

It was almost tragically comical how fast she flew out of the studio, slipping on the marble floor tiles. She had to grab on to the door to right herself, before yanking it open and fleeing the building. If she hadn't put Cole through the ringer these last few weeks, I would almost have felt sorry for her.

I turned to face my boss and laughed at the twin looks of shock on his and his customer's faces. "You're welcome."

"Is it always like this in here?" the customer said to Cole.

Eyes still on me Cole nodded. "Lately it feels like it."

The customer left fifteen minutes later (after having booked an appointment, so we couldn't have scared him too badly), and Cole waited until the door closed behind him before turning the full force of his inquisitive green gaze on me. "Thank you, Shannon."

There was a question in there somewhere, but there was also warmth that pleased me beyond measure. "You're very welcome."

"Professor Kris Lowery? You knew that how?"

"I looked her up. Good bluff, though, eh?"

"Fantastic," he agreed. "But why?"

"Her constant harassment was stressing you out. I felt bad for you."

Cole leaned on the counter, creating a deeper intimacy in our proximity and thus our conversation. "About that kiss . . ."

Not wanting him to think I was expecting anything, I hurried to reassure him. "I was just trying to help you out. I don't have a lot of friends here, Cole, and apparently you're a good one to have. I was trying to help out a potential friend."

His smile was kind, but there was something troubled in his eyes. "I can be your friend, Shannon. I know when you first came here I was too forward with you, with the flirting and what have you, but that was then. It won't happen again."

"It won't?" I blurted out before I could control myself.

"I find you attractive," he said carefully. "I think we both know that, but you and me . . . we're different. We're better as friends."

I knew I should accept his words and move on, but I was feeling a little put out. "Different?"

"We didn't get off to the best start because of that difference . . ."

It dawned on me what he was talking about. "Me being overly judgmental." I deflated when I saw on his face that I'd grasped what he was trying to say.

Cole grimaced. "I don't operate like that, and being in a relationship with someone who does would drive me nuts, and as gorgeous as you are, I don't do casual. So friends it is."

To my horror and surprise I felt more than a little winded by his declaration. I wanted to tell him that he'd gotten me wrong, that I had a reason for the way I treated him and that I wasn't usually like that. However, the words got stuck in my throat when my pride kicked in.

I was not going to beg for his attention like Jessica had done.

Instead I gave him a nod of agreement. "Sure. Friends."

"Great." He gave me that boyish grin again, and it made my stomach twist with lust and regret. "In fact, we have the same days off, so we should do something sometime."

"Sure," I repeated, not *actually* sure I meant it at all. Did I really want to spend time with Cole outside of work when he didn't know who I really was?

"You know I've wanted to go to the new prizewinner exhibit at the modern art gallery. They've put the winner and runners-up from the college of art graduates for the John Watson prize on display. Do you fancy coming along to it on Friday?"

I knew if I said no, if I shut him down once more, that would probably be the last time he'd make a friendly overture. So, attempting to hide my reluctance, I smiled. "Sounds good."

CHAPTER 10

By sheer force of will I got through the rest of the day and the next by pretending that everything was all right and just as it should be. The truth was I wasn't sure everything was okay.

I didn't want a relationship with Cole. As much as I'd grown to like him, I still didn't trust him. Plus, I worried about what my family would think of him if they ever found out. At the same time it was really rubbish to have to go on with him thinking the way he did of me. That wasn't who I was.

And now . . .

Now he was acting like there was no attraction between us at all.

Exhibit A: He took a sip of my latte without even asking and he did it without batting an eyelash. He walked away like it was no big deal, leaving me to stare at the place where his lips touched my coffee cup. Weeks ago our lips touching the same cup would have caused loads of meaningful staring and flirty eyes!

Exhibit B: I was working innocently at my desk when I felt Cole press in behind me and take the mouse from my hand. Cheek nearly touching mine, he leaned into my space to look through the computerized appointment book. I held my breath the entire time, my whole body zinging with awareness of him.

It didn't affect him at all!

Thankfully for the first half of Thursday I got a break from Cole. I hoofed it to Old Town in the morning with my sketch pad and set myself up in the back room of the Elephant House Café. With the great view of the castle outside the window, my music playing through my headphones, and my sketch pad and pencil in hand, I drowned out the world for a while.

Until my phone vibrated in my pocket.

Meet me outside the Gallery of Modern Art at 10:30. Cole.

From that point on I was a jittery mess.

And it wasn't even a *date*.

Dressing for the nondate with Cole turned out to be a heck of a lot harder than I thought it would be. Over the last few weeks I'd managed to pick up some bargain buys, so my wardrobe wasn't nearly as pathetic as it used to be, but still . . . how did a girl dress when said girl wanted to look her best without seeming to have tried to look her best?

I finally decided on dark blue skinny jeans tucked into brown suede ankle boots that had a little heel just to give me some height. I wore an oversized yellow sweater because I'd once been told that yellow was one of my best colors. I was hoping that hadn't been a crock of crap from a well-meaning friend.

The gallery was in Stockbridge, so I jumped on a bus. When I approached the gallery my gaze immediately zeroed in on Cole. He stood near the entrance, laughing into his phone. Watching as he talked with a mystery person, I felt this wild fluttering starting in my chest and a lump forming in the back of my throat. He was wearing a dark blue knit sweater with a shawl collar, faded dark jeans, and worn black engineer boots.

He was seriously tall, which I already knew, but as I looked at him it dawned on me that he was *seriously* tall and very broad-shouldered. He struck quite an imposing figure.

I was going to look small and silly next to him. I wasn't going to look like I fit at his side at all.

I stumbled at that thought, feeling my blood heat.

That wasn't my voice in my head. That was someone else's and *he* did not get to win like that.

So, throwing my shoulders back, I strode toward Cole with more confidence than I was feeling, a confidence that grew when his eyes lit up at the sight of me.

He smiled. "I've got Hannah on the phone. She wants to know if you fancy coming over for dinner tonight."

Somewhat stunned at the kind but abrupt offer, I gave a jerky nod. As Cole relayed my "yes" back to his best friend, my mind whirled. Dinner with his best friend and her family? Wasn't that something you took your girlfriend rather than your friend to?

This whole "thing" was perplexing.

Cole got off the phone. "After you." He held out an arm, gesturing for me to lead the way inside. Admission was free, so there was none of that awkward nondate fighting over which one of us paid.

Despite my nervousness, I realized as we walked into the exhibit together that there wasn't an uncomfortable awkwardness. There was awareness (on my part anyway), but that was entirely different.

We stopped in front of the first piece of art.

After a few seconds of looking at it, Cole stared down at me. "Do you like it?"

"No," I said honestly.

"Why?"

Surprised that he seemed genuinely interested in my opinion, I turned my attention back to the photograph. It was taken from somewhere on Loch Fyne (as detailed in the title) and the artist had used recyclable material to build a cityscape over the loch. "It doesn't say anything that hasn't been said before. Many times. And in far more creative and meaningful ways. It's . . ."

"Amateur," Cole finished. "Agreed." He shook his head in consternation. "I'll grant you the construction of the cityscape is well-done, but art in this landscape"—he gestured around the gallery—"should always say something new or at least say something old in an original way."

We moved on and I was quickly caught up in our shared passion. A lot of the times we agreed, but even when we didn't Cole listened to why I thought differently and accepted it as though it was my right. Thoughts of Ollie's bullying opinions intruded, but I forcefully pushed him out of my head.

An hour later we wandered out into the cool day and Cole smiled thoughtfully at me. "I didn't realize you were so into art. Do you draw, paint, sculpt?"

Still not ready to share that part of me with anyone just yet, I successfully avoided the question by pointing out a café across the street. "I've always wanted to eat there. Fancy brunch?"

Cole apparently didn't think anything of my change of subject and soon we were seated in the café, having coffee and scones brought to us.

"Have you always been into art?" I said.

Cole chewed and swallowed his bite of scone and brushed off his crumb-covered fingers. "Yeah. It used to be mostly comics and cartoons as a kid, but as I got older I got more and more into my art classes. I was influenced a lot by my brother-in-law, Cameron. He's a graphic designer and he spent a lot of time encouraging me and my art."

"What about your sister? Your parents?"

Cole smirked, but there was a sadness in the look. "Jo, definitely. She's supported me since the moment I came screaming into the world. As for my parents, I don't remember my dad and he's been out of my life since I was a baby. I wasn't close to my mum." He looked down at his scone. "She passed away when I was nineteen."

Feeling awful for bringing it up, I whispered, "I'm sorry."

The muscle in his jaw ticked. "Don't be."

At the cryptic and quiet, emotion-fueled response, I decided it might be better to change the subject. "Do your tattoos mean anything?"

Cole's whole body relaxed and when he looked at me it was with a grateful smile. His fingers brushed the tattoo on his neck. "J and C. Jo and me. Jo and Cam. The three of us. Cam has the same tattoo."

"You guys must be really close."

"Jo's the best sister anyone could ever ask for. I'm really proud of her. And Cam . . . I owe him a lot."

I was pleased for him that he had that in his life. Smiling, I gestured to his wrist. "And the tattoo there? I've been trying to read the script for weeks now."

He laughed and turned his hand over, pulling the sleeve up so I could see the tattoo on the underside of his wrist. He held it up and I leaned across the table to read it, just stopping myself from touching him. As I took in the words, I felt a little dizzy with the rush of familiarity and rightness that rushed over me.

"Arm your fears like soldiers and slay them."

"TATE lyrics," I murmured, referring to the band The Airborne Toxic Event. The lyrics were from the song "All I Ever Wanted" off their second album, *All at Once*. That album was the anthem of my young adulthood, and those were my favorite lyrics of all time.

And Cole Walker had them tattooed on his body.

I didn't know if I was turned on or in love.

Or both.

"My favorite TATE lyrics," I added.

Cole gave me a slow, hot grin that edged me more toward the whole turned-on thing. "Mine too."

For the first time in weeks we shared one of those long, meaningful looks.

I broke it before I could no longer breathe under the intensity of my attraction. "Left arm?"

In answer, Cole took his sweater off and thankfully (or not so thankfully depending on how you looked at it) he was wearing a T-shirt underneath it. He pulled the short sleeve up his shoulder so I could see the woman and the wolf tattoo more clearly on his muscular arm. Her hair billowed against a full moon I hadn't seen before because it was usually covered by the sleeve of his T-shirts.

"What does it mean?"

That boyish grin of his made another appearance, but this time it was edged with something akin to shyness. "It's sort of a tribute to the women in my life, and mostly it's a reminder that there are women like them out there." He shook his head, the spark in his eyes dimming. "Let's just say I had a shit mum, Shortcake." He tapped his fingers against the sleeve tattoo. "I wanted this reminder that not all women are like her. There are women who know the importance of family, and will do anything to protect that. I wanted the symbolism of it on here, but I also like paranormal stuff and thought as art this particular idea worked better with that element involved." He chuckled now. "Stu did it and he thought the woman howling at the moon would be more sexual, and I quote, 'Will dilute all the sentimental shit so you don't look like a fucking pussy.'"

I laughed. "Men and their macho-man bull crap."

Cole joined in my laughter and nodded. "He meant well."

"He did a good job. But then again, he's Stu Motherwell. Did he do the eagle and the pocket watch?" I pointed to his right sleeve tattoo.

"Yeah." Cole pulled up the fabric of his T-shirt, attempting to show me that the tattoo actually started on his right shoulder before curving around his upper biceps and down.

"And it means?"

He sighed. "This one is a little morbid. Well, it used to be."

I eyed the pocket watch. "I get what the tattoo's general meaning is. Time is prey. It's short-lived, right? Live it while you can."

He nodded.

"But does the time you've got on the pocket watch have meaning?"

"That was the morbid part." He eyed me, almost challenging me to judge him. "The time is when the paramedics called time of death on my mum."

Uneasiness moved through me as I began to realize that Cole's mum had really done a number on him.

"Now, thankfully, it means life as well as death. It's also the same time my niece, Belle, was born."

"That's actually very cool."

"Yeah." We smiled into each other's eyes as we took a sip of our coffees. Cole lowered his cup. "What about you? Any tattoos?"

"Nope."

"Have you never wanted to get one?"

The question forced me to remember when I did want to get one and I lowered my gaze to the table to avoid Cole's eyes. "Once. But my ex-boyfriend talked me out of it. He had tattoos, but he didn't think they were attractive on women."

He hesitated and I waited, my heart beating fast for him to dig at that. To my everlasting gratefulness he sidestepped my sudden change in demeanor. "What would you get if you decided to go for it?"

I smiled up at him from under my lashes. "A small dragon on my lower back."

"Why a dragon?"

"I've always had a fascination for them." I used to draw them all the time and collect all things dragons when I was a preteen. "They were the epitome of cool to me." I didn't even realize my tone had grown flat, hard. "I was so fascinated I forgot the pertinent fact that they would fry my arse without even blinking if they got the opportunity."

Cole was quiet. He studied me and I knew he understood so much more about my dragon than I'd let on. Instead of commenting he said, "Let me do it. Your tattoo."

"Seriously?" The thought of Cole putting ink on me, touching me . . .

"I'll draw it up, and if you like it we'll get you into the studio next Thursday when we're both off."

I bit my lip, unsure I could handle it.

"You get the employee discount," he urged. "One hundred percent off."

Seeing as it would be incredibly silly to turn down a free tattoo from one of the best tattooists in Scotland, I found myself agreeing to it.

The tattoo wasn't a bad idea.

The tattooist on the other hand?

He just might have been a *very* bad idea.

Upon discovering that I hadn't visited the National Gallery on Princes Street in years, Cole ushered me onto a bus and we returned to New Town, where we wandered around the gallery, discussing our thoughts on fine art. I discovered that Cole's knowledge of art history was tremendous.

I had no idea knowledge could be so sexy.

From there we walked around the city center—through the gardens, along Princes Street, onto North Bridge, along the Royal Mile, into Old Town, around the university, and back. I barely even felt the walk we were so lost in conversation. Art, music, film, books—we talked about it all.

It was one of the best days I'd ever experienced. Cole had a way of making me feel special, like I was the only person in the world he wanted to be around. He made me feel smart and interesting and important, and I'd never had that before except from the one person I couldn't bear to think about.

By the time we arrived at Hannah and Marco's house in Morningside, I was pretty sure I was harboring a beyond-serious crush on my boss.

Soon I wavered from crushing on Cole to insta-crushing on Marco when I got to know him better. Hannah introduced him as she closed the door to their gorgeous Victorian terrace, and as I shook his hand, staring up at this mammoth man who somehow managed to tower over Cole, I found myself a little dazzled by his good looks. "Nice to meet you," he said in this rumbling voice, surprising me with an American accent.

"You too." I found myself staring (hopefully not openmouthed) into his stunning green-blue eyes, astonished to find someone with eyes as gorgeous as Cole's.

Okay, maybe not as gorgeous, but they were close.

I was quickly distracted from Hannah's husband when Dylan walked into the hall, carrying his little sister, Sophia. Adorable didn't even cover it.

Things just got worse from there.

Cole strode to Dylan and took Sophia into his arms, saying hello to her before bestowing his attention on Dylan, who clearly idolized his uncle Cole.

The evidence that Cole was freaking awesome with kids just kept mounting. My crush deepened.

As we sat down to dinner, Hannah began to ask me about my family, and my awkward attempts to avoid the conversation caused some tension. Finally I smiled through the discomfort. "You know, I spent a lot of time in Edinburgh growing up. My grandparents lived in a beautiful Georgian house on Scotland Street."

"Next to Ellie and Adam's house," Cole added.

Of course. "It's where I first met Cole."

"So you do remember?" He grinned, and it was a cocky look.

I gave him an apologetic smile. "I said you had a hero's name."

Taking in Cole's absurdly pleased expression, I found myself turning to mush on the inside, only just managing to keep the longing out of my eyes when I caught Hannah watching me.

It occurred to me that to be a friend to Cole I was going to have to pass the best friend test. Enigmatic answers and puppy-love eyes probably weren't going to work in my favor.

The rest of dinner was easier because I just asked Hannah and Marco a lot of questions, discovering they'd known each other since they were kids and that they lost touch for a few years only to almost immediately become an item when they finally found each other. They didn't go into a whole lot of details, but it sounded romantic, and seeing the hot, adoring look in Marco's eyes whenever he turned them on his wife made me think I was probably right.

Once we finished eating, Cole offered to help Hannah with the dishes and they left the living room. I'd been busy listening to Dylan tell me about his swimming certificate, so I'd missed the chance to offer to help. Despite Marco's protestations, I thought it would be unforgivably rude not to help Hannah out, and I didn't want to lose best friend points by not doing so.

I gathered the rest of the plates and wandered out of the room, turning in what I assumed was the direction of the kitchen.

As I neared it, however, I stilled at the sound of Hannah saying, "I don't know what the problem is. It's obvious you're into each other."

Heart pounding, I waited in tense expectation for Cole's reply.

"Hannah, drop it. Shannon is just a friend."

I sagged against the wall, feeling an unexpected rush of disappointment. I thought we'd had a wonderful day together, and although I wasn't sure I could trust him, I couldn't deny the way Cole made me feel.

Apparently it really was all one-sided.

"She's . . ." Cole hesitated. "It's a shame but she's just not the girl I'm looking for."

Crushed.

Absolutely crushed.

"What she presumed to know about me when she first started working at the studio—"

"Cole, she apologized for that."

"Look, it's not what she thought. It was what she said and what she's capable of saying when the mood strikes her. I grew up with that shit, Hannah. I'm never going back there."

"Cole," Hannah whispered sympathetically.

"It's fine." His voice was gruff.

"If it makes you feel better, I don't believe for a second that that girl out there is anything like your mother."

I tiptoed back up the hall, coming to a rest against the staircase. I was reeling.

"There's nothing behind that charming smile but empty promises. You have nothing real to offer me or anyone that finds herself a victim of your flirtation. The difference between them and me, however, is that I'm smart enough to see you for what you really are . . . Nothing."

Nothing, nothing, nothing!

I felt tears prick my eyes as I wondered how many times his mother had called him that.

Ashamed, I sucked in a huge breath, blinked back the tears, and drew up the strength to approach the kitchen, this time noisily. Acting like everything was fine, I handed off the dirty dishes and returned to the sitting room to engage in small talk with Marco about his job as a construction site manager.

I didn't care if Cole ever saw me in a romantic light again. That ship had clearly sailed for him, and I couldn't see how we'd have a future anyway given my track record with failed romances. But I *was* coming to care for this man and I couldn't bear the thought that I had genuinely hurt him.

I had to make him see that all the crap I'd dealt to him that awful day came from a place that had absolutely nothing to do with him. I knew I needed to fix any damage I'd caused him, even if it meant revealing all the damage someone else had caused me.

CHAPTER 11

Not long after overhearing Cole and Hannah in the kitchen, Cole made our excuses and we bade the couple and their young family good night. I walked in silence beside Cole in the darkening night toward the main Morningside Road.

"Is something wrong?" he said, bringing me out of my musings.

Looking up at him, I was confused to find concern in his eyes. It amazed me that he could spend this whole day with me when he thought so little of me.

I stopped on the quiet street and Cole halted too. "Why did you spend today with me?"

Now it was his turn to appear bewildered. "What are you talking about?"

"If I've discovered anything real about you, it's that you're pretty straightforward, so why do this today? Why spend time with me . . . ?"

After a moment's contemplation he said, "Because you're friends with my friends. We work in a close-knit environment. I thought we should try to put our differences behind us."

"Does that mean that this whole day has been torture for you?"

"What?" He grimaced. "No. Today has been . . ." He looked almost frustrated. "You're like two different people. It confuses the fuck out of me."

"I'm not two different people, Cole. If you can stand to spend a little more time with me tonight, I'd like to talk to you about something."

He studied me carefully, and I could see lots going on in those gorgeous eyes of his. "Okay," he eventually said. "My place is five minutes away. We can talk there."

I was so nervous on the walk to Cole's I couldn't speak at all. Thankfully he seemed to understand. He led us to a Victorian apartment building just off Bruntsfield Road. Once inside his flat on the second floor, I was distracted by its beautiful high ceilings and polished hardwood floors. Cole had furnished the flat in masculine dark woods, strong textures, and artwork that had obviously been carefully chosen. The living room had a gorgeous bay window dressed in heavy chocolate brown suede drapes to match the suede L-shaped sofa. There was an old Victorian fireplace in the center of the room. It was minimal and there were splashes of color in the cushions and rug, but none of it was deliberately coordinated. Everything had been chosen for comfort and function and yet somehow still worked stylishly in its period setting.

The place also smelled like Cole.

"Coffee?" he offered as I stood awkwardly in the middle of the room.

"Please. Milk, two sugars."

He left to make it and I lowered myself to the edge of the sofa, my knee bouncing up and down with my jitters. I was about to lay myself bare to him.

I felt sick.

When Cole returned, the concern was back on his face as he took me in, shivering. He handed me a mug of hot coffee. "If you like I can start the fire."

"Not if you're warm."

His answer was to start the fire for me.

I smiled gratefully at him as he took a seat in the armchair under the bay window.

"So, what do you need to talk about?"

Attempting to control my nerves, I took a deep breath and exhaled shakily. "That day I told you you were nothing . . ."

Annoyance flashed in his eyes. "Look, Shannon, we've been over that. It's done. Let's move on."

"It's not done," I insisted. I was so scared at the thought of telling him about what I'd fled from in Glasgow, but at the same time I needed to open myself up to him if we were going to have any chance at real friendship. "For once I'm not going to be selfish with you. You deserve the truth even if I don't want to tell it."

Cole scooted forward on his seat, eyebrows drawn together. "Shannon, what's this all about?"

"I'm not here to dump my problems on you. But I need to explain something about why I came to Edinburgh so you can understand why I said what I said to you and why, in the end, it really had nothing to do with you."

When he waited patiently, I continued. "I'm not a judgmental person, Cole. Not really. In fact, I've been known to forgive people even when their actions are beyond the point of forgiveness. I've always accepted people for who they are, always believing there was something special in everyone, something that others couldn't see. And every time I've done that with the men in my life I've been proven wrong and everyone else right."

"Shortcake, I'm not following."

"I'm a bad-boy magnet," I said with no humor, because as silly as it sounded out loud it was true. "A player magnet. To start there was a lead singer in a rock band who cheated on me, the biker who cheated on me, the secret drug dealer who stole from me, and my last boyfriend—the pièce de résistance. We were together for two years and his name was Ollie. He worked in a restaurant by day and was a drummer in a band at night. Tattooed, good-looking, cocky, charming, confident . . ."

An understanding was beginning to dawn in Cole's eyes.

"Before Ollie, I'd already pissed off most of my family with the choices I'd made when it came to men. I'd been hurt so many times they believed it was my own fault, and I don't think they're necessarily wrong. They predicted Ollie would be a disaster, but I was so sure he was different from all the rest. He was romantic and into me, and to begin with he made me feel really special. Until slowly that started to change.

"It was so subtle it took me a really long time to even realize what he was doing to me. How he had started to chip away at pieces of me. He belittled me, made me feel talentless and stupid. He made me feel like it was a miracle I'd managed to land him."

"He was a dick," Cole snapped.

"Like I said, I didn't even know it was happening or how much he emotionally manipulated me into constantly choosing him over my friends and family. Almost two years—that's how long it took me to wake the heck up.

"It was so stupid," I whispered, feeling the pain in my gut and in my chest. In fact, I ached all over with the memories. "It was a stupid thing that made me wake up. I was supposed to be going out that night with the girls. I hadn't seen them in a while and I was always blowing them off for Ollie. So I was excited and all dressed up.

"Ollie came into the bedroom. He told me I looked like a whore, which was his favorite word weapon. It hurt, like always."

Lifting my gaze to Cole, I sucked in my breath at the blaze of anger in his eyes. He gave me a taut nod of his head in a gesture to carry on.

"I changed my clothes and gave him the silent treatment. He tried to placate me. And then somehow like always he manipulated me, attempting to make it out as though I was choosing my friends over him when he needed me. He'd had a bad day at work or something and he just wanted a quiet night in with me. So I blew the girls off. They were beyond annoyed. Like, no-longer-speaking-to-me annoyed. And then a while later he said he was going out with the band.

"I was so angry. I never argued with him, but I was so, so mad at him that night that I let him have it." My eyes held Cole's as I silently tried to prepare him. "Ollie didn't say anything. He just swung his arm out and backhanded me across the face. He's six foot and a drummer. I went flying across the room and caught my hip on the coffee table as I went down."

"Shannon . . ." Cole's teeth were gritted and he was rising from his chair, but I halted him with tears in my eyes.

"He was so apologetic. He cried. He promised it wouldn't happen again. I believed him." The tears fell. "I'm so stupid."

"I don't know if I can hear much more without breaking something," Cole said, his voice shaking.

"I need you to. I need you to try to understand."

Muscle flexing in his jaw, he nodded.

"I didn't tell anyone. And although I stayed with him, what he'd done to me festered inside me. I couldn't bear his touch, in bed or out, and he grew frustrated." I exhaled heavily, my fingers trembling. Sometimes it felt just like yesterday. "He punched me one night when I shoved him off me.

"The next morning he went to work and I called in sick. I packed all my clothes, only taking what I'd need—the rest could burn in hell along with Ollie for all I cared. However, it was like he had a sixth sense or something, because I was just about to leave when he walked through the door. He'd cut out of work early. I should have called Logan before it even got to that point."

"Logan?" Cole frowned.

"My big brother." The ache inside me intensified. "It's just me, Logan, and my sister, Amanda, and our parents. But I've never been close to any of them, just Logan. My mum and Amanda had always resented how close Logan and me were. He was one of my best friends."

"I'm almost afraid to ask what happened next."

"Ollie took one look at my suitcase and he flipped out. He started yelling that I wasn't going anywhere, that I was his, only his." The stinging in my nose began again, the tears welling up fast as I heard his voice replaying in my head. "And then he was shouting . . . just nonsense and he . . . he started beating the living daylights out of me. I tried to fight." I wanted Cole to know that. "I tried, but he was so much bigger than me—"

"Shannon—"

"He stopped hitting me." I sucked in a shuddering breath. "And he started touching me, tearing at my clothes, repeating over and over that I was his. And I—I knew. I knew he was going to rape me."

Cole stood up suddenly, fists clenched at his side.

I shook my head at his pleading eyes. "No. It was the last straw for me. He'd taken so much. I couldn't let him take that. The adrenaline kicked in, numbing the pain, and I was clawing and scratching and biting at him. Eventually I kneed him between the legs and he lost his grip on me. I got out from under him, the adrenaline kept me going, and I got away." That was when I started to cry in earnest and apparently Cole couldn't deal with being across the room anymore.

Suddenly he was on the sofa beside me, his arm around me, holding me close.

"I should have gone to the hospital," I sobbed. "Or the police. I didn't think. I didn't realize what a mess I was in. I went to Logan." I stared up into Cole's soulful gaze, brushing angrily at my tears as I pleaded silently with him to understand. "I didn't think. I didn't mean to be so selfish."

"Shh." His grip on me tightened. "You went to the one person who made you feel safe. There's nothing to feel guilty about."

"You're wrong. There's everything. I made the choice to be with a bastard like Ollie. And when things went horribly wrong I turned up at my overprotective big brother's work covered in my own blood." *My shoulder hanging out of its socket, my right eye swollen shut, my clothes torn . . .* "How did I think he would react?"

Cole brushed his thumb over my cheek to catch a tear. "The way any man would react when someone he loves has been violated. He went to teach that fucker a lesson."

"Logan put Ollie in a three-day coma."

"Shit."

I nodded, lips trembling. "My brother got two years in prison." And there it was. The worst thing I'd ever done.

"Shannon," Cole murmured in sympathy, tucking my head under his chin and tightening his arms around me.

Rae knew about the attack, but she didn't know about my brother. It was the first I'd spoken of it since leaving Glasgow.

"I had to leave. My parents, my sister . . . they hate me for ruining Logan's life."

"Your brother's actions are his own," Cole said, and I heard the tremor of anger in his words. "Don't take that on. Your family is wrong."

"It would never have happened if I hadn't made the choice to be with Ollie and men like him." I pulled out of the comfort of Cole's strong embrace and met his worried gaze. "The whole point of me telling you this is so you understand where my head is at. I came to Edinburgh to start over and to keep my distance from my old life, my old choices. From bad boys." I laughed hollowly. "And the only interview I got was at a tattoo studio where the good-looking tattooed manager began flirting with me immediately like I was a sure thing."

Cole winced. "That wasn't why, but I can see after everything you've been through——"

"Why I thought that." I smiled weakly. "But I presumed to know you because of that and I assumed you were like all the men who'd buggered up my life. All the men who had hurt and disappointed me. In doing so I said some unforgiveable things."

"Shannon——"

"I need you to know that you are *not* nothing and when I said that, that was *my* issue. Not yours. You shouldn't have to carry that."

In answer Cole bent his head toward mine, bringing our faces close as he cupped his hand around the back of my neck. He wanted all my focus and I gave it to him, somewhat transfixed, in fact. "It's now completely forgotten, Shortcake. Think no more on it."

Relief, an overwhelming amount of relief I had not been expecting to feel, rushed over me, and the tears were back in my eyes but for a totally different reason now. "You forgive me?"

"Sweet girl," he murmured, his voice thick with an emotion I didn't get. "How can you even worry about me after everything you've been through?"

"Because you're a good person," I said.

He gave my neck a squeeze in answer, but his eyes had turned hard. "What happened to Ollie?"

"He recovered. He got a prison sentence—thirty months."

Cole curled his lip in disgust. "Is that it?"

"The lawyer reckoned he would have gotten more, but Logan's attack was detrimental to my defense."

He did not look happy, but he nodded.

It was then I realized how close we were sitting, and how intimate we were as we gazed into each other's eyes. It was suddenly very important to me that Cole didn't misunderstand the reason why I'd told him my story. I didn't want him to think this was some ploy to turn him around and . . .

Feeling naked and vulnerable all of a sudden, I shifted back and his hand fell away. "I should go home."

"I don't want you to leave when you're upset. Stay," he suggested like it was no big deal. "You can sleep in my guest room."

Just the idea of staying with Cole was too much for me to handle. I smiled kindly. "I'd like my own bed tonight."

He nodded and leaned down to press a kiss to my forehead. I

stared at him, my blood hot, as he stood up. "Then let me see you home."

"You don't have—"

Cole cut off my protestations with just a look. A very stubborn, concerned, warm look.

A look that knocked on my heart.

A look I kept in my mind's eye as I closed my eyes to sleep that night.

CHAPTER 12

I didn't know how Cole would act around me the next day at work. I did know it was Saturday, so there was a possibility he'd use how busy he was to avoid having to interact at all. On the weekend I'd taken to coming into work at the same time as the tattooists—half an hour before opening.

Although nervous, I also felt relieved that he knew the truth, so I was in a fairly good mood as I came in bearing coffee for everyone.

I took Cole his coffee first.

When I knocked on his door and stepped inside, he looked up from a document he was reading and his expression brightened at the sight of me.

It winded me.

He stood up, grinning when I held his coffee out to him. Instead of taking it, he wrapped his hand around mine and we held them there. "How are you feeling?"

Noting the dark circles under his eyes, I had to wonder if my troubles had caused Cole to have a sleepless night. That was sweet; it really was. But now I felt terrible because for the first time in a while I'd slept like a baby.

I gave him a reassuring smile. "I'm fine. Honest."

He let go of me, taking the coffee with him. The look he gave me . . . it was as if he wanted to protect me in Bubble Wrap.

"Cole." I smiled again, more than a little enchanted by him. "I know I had a meltdown last night, but honestly I'm okay. I have a good life here—a good job, good friends. I've found more than I ever hoped to find when I moved here, so please don't worry about me."

"That's a tall order." He shook his head, his smile wry. "You're made of stern stuff, Shannon MacLeod."

"It's the hair. It's magic hair."

Cole laughed. "It is definitely magical."

"Am I getting my coffee any fucking time soon?" Rae yelled from next door.

I giggled at her irate tone and I swear Cole's eyes lit up at the sound of my laughter.

I felt all warm and gooey inside. "I'd better . . ." I gave him a little wave and walked out, sure I could sense his eyes on me until I disappeared out of sight.

I stepped into Rae's room and walked over to where she was lying on her tattoo chair with her eyes closed. She opened them at my approach and glared at me as I handed her a latte. "Thank God," she growled. "You don't know how excruciating it is having to listen to you two lovebirds when I haven't had my caffeine fix."

She said it so loud I knew Cole had heard.

I wrinkled my nose. "Don't be mean."

"Why?" she huffed, and then snorted, "Are you going to kill me with your magical hair?"

I rubbed a strand of hair between my finger and thumb. "It is thick. It *would* make good rope."

"Dark. I like it, wee fairy."

I rolled my eyes at the irritating nickname she'd adopted from Stu and wandered out of her room and down the hall to Simon. He was sleeping in his chair, his arms crossed on the counter and sink space in the back of the room, his head resting on his arms. I quietly walked over to him and nudged him awake, wafting the coffee below his nostrils.

"Argh," he groaned, blinking sleepily. He saw the coffee first and wiped drool from his mouth as he sat up to take it from me. He sipped at it before throwing me a grateful smile. "Tony kept me up late last night."

"No fucking sex talk!" Rae yelled.

"Since when?" I whispered at Simon, smirking.

"I heard that!"

My eyes bugged out. "She has radar ears."

"So what? You have magical fucking hair!"

I laughed and heard Cole's laughter join mine.

Sighing, I sipped my coffee as Simon chuckled into his. I felt almost content for the first time in as long as I could remember.

I felt part of something here.

I felt part of a family.

There really wasn't much of an opportunity to talk with Cole at work that weekend, but as we closed up for the early evening on Sunday, Rae announced Cole was having dinner with us. I was surprised because if Cole could cut out early on a Sunday to catch up with his friends and family who got together for lunch at Ellie's mum's house, he would. I wasn't complaining, though. There was something new between us now. Although we didn't get a chance to talk much, when we did Cole was warm toward me, and there was a glitter in his eyes when he looked at me.

Mike was at the flat when we returned on Sunday, and the four of us had a good laugh together. Cole and I had formed a bond and we were a team against Rae's sarcasm. She said it pissed her off that we were defending each other, but secretly I think she liked the challenge of finding a way to outwit us both.

From Monday through Wednesday Cole was in my space as much as he could be. He took me out to lunch twice, and when he didn't have a client he hung out in the waiting area distracting me from my work with silly stories and jokes. When he wasn't distracting me he was drawing, and what he was drawing were different ideas for my dragon tattoo.

I finally decided on a predatory black-and-petrol-blue dragon in profile.

The truth was I was nervous about the tattoo—not so much about the pain, because as Cole had told me many times since deciding to get the darn thing, everyone had different experiences and pain levels with tattoos. No, I was nervous about the fact that Cole was going to be the one giving me my tattoo. As in . . . touching me. Since Friday evening this new tension had grown between us. As much as I had always been aware of Cole, it seemed as if he was very much aware of me again. Not like he had been in the beginning—he was more careful now, like he didn't want to scare me away or upset me.

But I caught him looking at me.

There was a huge part of me that loved that he was looking again. Yet there was this other huge part of me that loved the small taste I'd gotten of being Cole's friend, and I didn't want to ruin that.

"Ready?" Cole greeted as I walked into his room on Thursday afternoon.

I exhaled nervously and shut his door behind me. "I'm not going to lie. I've got butterflies."

He smiled. "You're in safe hands."

Oh God, did he have to say that? I flushed inwardly, desperately looking anywhere but at his hands.

He was still grinning as he lowered himself to his stool and nodded to the chair. "You can straddle the chair and lean on the armrests."

I swallowed hard and moved to do just that, painfully aware that he was probably getting a good look at my butt as I did so.

"I'm just going to increase the height on the chair," he said a second before I felt the chair rise.

Suddenly his hands were in my hair and I tensed.

"There's a lot of it. I'm just shifting it out of the way." He gathered my hair and draped it over my shoulders. His fingers brushed my skin. "You can either take your top off or lift the hem and hold it out of my way."

The thought of taking my shirt off in front of Cole almost fried my brain. "I'll . . . uh . . ." In answer I lifted the hem and clutched it tight in my grip. "Is that high enough?"

"Yeah. But if you get uncomfortable let me know."

I nodded and tried to relax.

That was really hard to do when his fingers brushed across my lower back. "Everyone feels different levels of pain," he said, his voice soft as his fingertips lightly stroked my skin. "I will say you'll probably find the outlines the most uncomfortable, because as I sketch it I'm dragging more definitively on the skin."

"Okay." My hands turned into fists as I prepared myself for pain.

Cole chuckled. "Now you've tensed up. Just relax. It won't be as bad as you think."

I nodded again and a few seconds later the buzz of the needle filled the room. I braced myself and attempted not to flinch as Cole brought the needle to my back.

At first it stung, like a constant scratching over my skin. Soon enough it stung like a mother. However, as time wore on I got used to the pain. It wasn't nearly as wretched as some people made it out to be.

The needle stopped buzzing. "Are you okay?"

"I'm fine," I said. "You?"

I could hear the amusement in his voice. "I'm good, Shortcake."

I attempted and failed to ignore the thrill that went through me at the endearment. "How does it look?"

"Like I just started it three minutes ago."

I giggled, trying not to shake, and he laughed. "It's going to be pretty cute when it's done." I stopped giggling. Sensing why, he hurried to assure me, "Cute but fierce." His free hand squeezed my hip. "Perfect for you."

I laughed now, liking that. "Cute. That's my lot in life."

"How do you mean?"

"That's how people describe me. 'Oh, Shannon, you look so cute in that picture,' et cetera. I suppose it's better than 'You look like you've been pulled through the bushes backwards,' so I'm not complaining."

"There's more to you than cute. People call you cute because you're petite . . . but you're sexy too . . . Mostly you're beautiful in a way that stops a man in his tracks."

Did he just say that?

Flabbergasted, bowled over, blown away . . . I didn't know how to respond to the best compliment in the history of compliments. In the end I went with a lame, choked "Thank you."

Cole gave my hip another squeeze and the tattoo needle started up again, as did the pain. Thankfully he didn't stop, because getting used to the pain all over again wasn't fun.

About an hour from when Cole started, the needle stopped. "Done."

"Really?" I was surprised. I'd been lost in a daydream about different things (not Cole . . . uh-uh . . . no, siree), and time had flown.

He chuckled. "Really. I'll put some film wrap over it to protect it." I could feel him doing that.

"I know you've probably heard the aftercare speech a million times, but I have to give it to you anyway."

"Hit me with it." I glanced at him over my shoulder with a smile.

There was something intense in his green eyes as he proceeded to "hit me with it." "Take the film off in four to six hours. Clean the tattoo with a mild soap—Rae will definitely have some—and warm water. Massage, don't scrub. If you're showering tonight or in the morning, don't let the spray hit the tattoo at full force and keep the water lukewarm. It also helps to run the shower at ice-cold on just your tattoo before you get out—this closes any pores the warm water might have opened, allowing the tattoo to heal better and keep the ink vivid. You don't need to rebandage, but moisturize it lightly twice a day—again, Rae has the best product to use. Do this for the next few days. Wear loose tops, low jeans, so your clothing doesn't rub against it." I felt him stand up from his stool seconds before his hands came to rest on my hips. Realizing he was helping me down from the chair, I stood up and stumbled a little as I tried to back off it. "I

should have lowered the height on the chair," he murmured apologetically in my ear.

I shivered at his nearness, and his fingers tensed on my hips.

"It might be better to sleep on your side tonight, and for the next
few days try not to rub your tattoo against anything and . . . eh . . .
missionary is probably out for the next few days as well."

I swallowed my gasp but jerked out of his hold, turning to face
him with a million questions in my eyes. His gaze was burning hot
and I could barely breathe under the stifling tension. "That won't be a
problem," I whispered.

Cole took a step toward me just as his door flew wide-open.

"Can I see it?" Rae strode in and I quickly lowered my gaze so she
couldn't see the excitement Cole's tactility and overall sexy behavior
was causing me. I turned and lifted up my shirt.

"Cool," Rae pronounced upon inspection. "I'll be able to see it
better when the cling film comes off." When I turned back around she
grinned. "So, what did you think?" she said. "Did it hurt?"

"Not as bad as I thought it would."

"Are you going to get another one?"

I snorted. "I think I'm good for now."

Rae abruptly clapped her hands together so loudly I blinked. "Tomorrow night! Drinks to celebrate Shannon's tat."

"Sounds good." Cole smiled, busying himself with his tattoo
equipment.

I felt shy and uncertain now that I could no longer sense his eyes
on me. "Okay. But I'm buying for Cole since he won't let me pay for the
tattoo."

Rae's lips parted. "Free?" She whirled around and Cole raised an
eyebrow at her bristling aggression. "You only gave me fifty percent off!"

His lips twitched as his eyes flicked from her to me and then he just shrugged and turned back to switching out the tattoo needles. Unwilling to make himself a target for her annoyance, Cole unwittingly set Rae on me.

"Fucking magical hair, all right!"

And with that she stormed out of the room.

Cole glanced over his shoulder at me and winked.

I burst out in peals of laughter, already contemplating whether a coffee or a donut or both would pacify Rae.

CHAPTER 13

I spent the rest of that day attempting to concentrate, but I was too aware of my tattoo to manage it. I was trying not to rub or lean against anything . . . and, admittedly, I was trying not to think about the fact that Cole had very definitely been flirting with me.

And the flirting wasn't like before either. This time it was like he couldn't help himself. I had to admit that made me feel more than a little bit giddy. Cole was the hottest guy I'd ever met and he also happened to be one of the nicest.

Nice.

It seemed like such a blah little word, but it was a quality that was too often completely underappreciated.

Not by me.

I appreciated the hot, *nice* tattooist I worked with.

I appreciated him a whole lot, so much so I was thrilled to have caught his attention.

Yet, at the same time, I was also apprehensive.

I knew Cole wasn't Ollie or Nick or Bear the biker, or Rory the thief. I knew that. I believed Hannah. I believed what I could see with my own eyes, but that didn't mean my fears were just going to disappear overnight. No matter how great he was, Cole could still end up hurting me, and I had this feeling in my gut that getting hurt by Cole Walker might just break me.

"Smells good," Rae said as she got in from work that night. She kicked off her shoes and sank into a kitchen chair just as I laid her plate down in front of her. "Tattoo okay?"

"Yeah." I sat down in the seat beside her. "Bit itchy, though."

"That'll get worse as it heals. Whatever you do, don't scratch it. You'll ruin the fucking thing."

"Yeah, Cole already cautioned me."

Rae nodded while chewing. As soon as she swallowed she said, "Speaking of Boss Man, what did I walk in on today?"

In all honesty . . . "I have no idea."

"Do you like him?"

I looked up to meet Rae's direct gaze and I nodded.

Rae smirked. "Well, every idiot with a pair of eyes in their head can see Cole likes you back. So, what's the problem, kiddies?"

I knew if anyone might understand, it would be Rae. "I know he's a good guy. Honestly I do, but I've been burned too many times not to be scared about starting something with him."

"You would feel that way about any guy."

"True." I eyed my plate, no longer hungry now that turmoil had filled my belly.

"You want my advice?"

I gave her a small, wry smile.

"Go for it. Cole is the real fucking deal."

"I told him," I said, the words hushed. "About Ollie."

Rae's eyebrows rose. "You told him that? So he knows you come with a shitload of baggage and he's still eye-fucking you across the room?" She grinned. "I knew I loved that guy."

"I don't want to ruin my friendship with him."

"Since when were you two friends? The sexual tension between you since the moment you arrived . . . Well, it's like living in an episode of the latest teenage drama series."

I frowned. "I think there's an insult in there somewhere."

"There was also some advice I think you should take. If you blow off Cole again, he's going to move on, and Cole does not do casual, so the next girl he moves on to is going to be around for a while, if not forever. Do you really want to have to make friends with Cole Walker's girlfriend or do you want to *be* Cole Walker's girlfriend?"

Tamara's gorgeous face flashed in my mind.

I grimaced.

Rae nodded. "Mmm-hmm. That's what I'm saying."

When I strolled into the Walk the next evening, Rae at my side, I found myself filled with anticipation. I didn't know why . . . I just had this feeling in my gut that something was about to happen.

Cole, Simon, and Tony had grabbed a table in the corner of the room and had started drinking without us. As soon as Tony spotted us across the room, Cole turned his head and held my gaze as we approached.

I couldn't look away.

He smiled and stood up when we reached the table, pulling the chair out next to him for me to take a seat. "How's the tat?" he asked once I'd settled.

"Itchy."

He chuckled. "It will be. Let me see it."

My hyperawareness of him meant that every interaction with him made me think of sex. When I shifted around in my seat, I couldn't look at Rae because my blood was hot and my mind was in the gutter and I knew she'd take one look at me and see that. Cole lifted the hem of my cardigan and the silk camisole underneath it so he could appraise his work. I braced myself for it, hoping I could control my reaction, but as soon as his fingertips brushed the skin around the tattoo I shivered.

"Have you seen it?" he said.

"Rae took a picture on my phone." I cleared my throat of its sudden huskiness. "It looks amazing. Thank you."

He traced the skin along the waistband of my jeans. "You're welcome."

The need to turn around and jump him was overwhelming. So overwhelming I jerked away from his touch and shrugged my hem back down. Everything felt too tight—my clothes, my lungs in my chest, even my skin. Never had I felt this explosive level of frustration before.

"It looks wonderful." Tony nodded his approval. "Very sexy."

"Agreed." Simon smiled.

"Thanks." I smiled weakly. Already needing some distance from Cole, whose ludicrously delicious aftershave was driving me nuts, I asked if anyone wanted a drink. Rae, however, stole my getaway by insisting on buying the round.

"So, I'm meeting Tony's mother for the first time," Simon announced. "Please tell me one of you is getting married, having life-threatening surgery, a baby, or some big-ass event on June twentieth?"

Tony scowled. "You are not getting out of this, Sy. Mama is very traditional and she needs to know that her darling child is being taken care of by a *man*." He frowned. "I've spent two years telling her you're all man and now you're acting like a little girl. Where are your bloody balls?"

Simon shrugged. "They jumped up inside me at the mention of in-laws."

Cole and I burst out laughing, sitting quietly, entertained by Simon and Tony as they argued. When Rae returned she regaled Tony with less than helpful stories of her encounters with Mike's straitlaced mother. The whole time I sat there in silence, aware every time Cole reached for his pint or shifted infinitesimally closer to me.

I kept glancing out of the corner of my eye, my gaze roaming his tattooed forearm, before fixating on the chunky Indian silver ring on his big hand.

Not only was I hyperaware of Cole's body; I was painfully aware of my own. My lips, my tongue, my breasts, the insistent throb between my legs . . .

It was ridiculous. And it had never happened to me before, so I didn't know how to deal with it. Finally I got an excuse to move away from Cole when it was my turn to buy a round of drinks. Walking over to the bar, I took a deep breath and attempted to mentally coax myself out of the desirous stupor I was in.

I'd only been standing at the bar a few seconds when a bartender freed up and took my drinks order. I was in the middle of trying to think of ways to resist the attraction to Cole when I felt eyes on me. I turned my head to the right and found two guys around my age, maybe a little older, smiling at me. Although I glanced away quickly, my noticing them seemed to invite their attention.

They slid their drinks down the bar and came to a stop at my side. I very deliberately ignored them. It didn't deter them.

"Having a nice night?" the one closest to me said.

"Yeah, thanks."

"I'm Gordon. This is my mate Barry. What's your name?"

I didn't answer because I didn't want to encourage them. As it was I could feel their eyes crawling all over me. I was wearing jeans and my olive green cami and matching cardy. My makeup was subtle, and I was wearing flat-heeled boots. There was nothing about my appearance that screamed I was out on the town. I had no idea why I'd attracted their attention, and frankly I didn't care. There was nothing that turned me off more than guys who sat at bars and constantly hit on anything that moved. There was a desperation about it, a soullessness, that the romantic in me revolted against.

"Oh, come on, we're harmless, sweetheart," the other one said.

I frowned. "I'm not interested."

The one farther away shrugged and began to retreat, but his friend actually moved closer to me. "Sounds like you're having a bad day. I'm a really good listener."

Eh . . . apparently not.

I snorted. "All evidence to the contrary."

"What does that mean?"

"It means I'm not interested."

He laughed, like I'd said something funny. My eyebrows drew together in confusion.

"You look like that actress," he said, shifting even closer. "That Australian actress. You look like her when she was younger. I had the biggest hard-on for her."

Really?

Before I could follow up my look of disgust with a verbal "get lost," a sudden heat engulfed me and a shadow fell over me. Two strong, tattooed arms caged me in as they came to rest on the bar at either side of mine, and a hard chest pressed against my back

I relaxed immediately and glanced up over my shoulder at Cole's handsome face. Currently it was turned away from me as he glowered at the persistent barfly.

Although the friend instantly backed up even farther than he already had done, the "good listener" just stared dumbly at Cole.

Cole raised an eyebrow at him. "Which part of this doesn't say 'fuck off' to you?"

The idiot studied Cole for a moment as if he was considering ignoring him, and then his brain finally seemed to compute what his eyes were telling him. Cole was bigger and much, much scarier than he was. He lowered his gaze. "Sorry, mate. Didn't know she was taken."

He shuffled off down the bar, already searching the pub for a new target.

Cole bent his head, his lips brushing my ear. "You okay?"

Unable to form a coherent sentence with him pressed up against me, I nodded.

Seeming to sense that, Cole hesitated a second. "Am I making you uncomfortable?"

My pulse raced with that feeling of anticipation I'd had earlier. "Yes. But not like you think."

I heard his sharp intake of breath and braced myself.

His lips were at my ear again. "Do you want me, Shannon?"

My legs began to tremble. "Yes."

Cole exhaled, as though he was relieved, and to my surprise he buried his nose in the crook of my neck, relaxing into me. The scratch of the bristle on his cheeks against my skin caused tingling in all my feminine places. He breathed me in and lifted his head just as the bartender served up the drinks.

It broke the moment between us.

Cole stepped away from me and I shivered at the loss of his heat.

To my confusion Cole didn't say another word as I paid for the drinks and we returned to the table.

He sat next to me, drinking his pint like nothing had happened. I stewed in uncertainty, ignoring our friends' questioning looks (they'd obviously seen our interaction at the bar) and sipping my drink. Tony didn't take long to dispel the awkwardness by launching into a story about a biker bar he once went to in Glasgow.

I tried to pay attention, laughing at all the right bits, but it was difficult.

After I finished the last sip of my rum and Coke, I put my empty glass on the table and wondered how rude it would be to leave early.

Apparently Cole didn't care if it was rude.

As soon as my glass hit the table, he pushed his chair back, grabbed my hand, and stood up, pulling me gently up with him. Our friends went instantly quiet. Cole gave them a nod and began leading me away. I had just enough time to snatch up my purse and throw Rae a wide-eyed look that was part "holy heck" and part giddy, before Cole had us outside the bar.

I looked at him for direction, but he was focused on finding us a taxi. His hand curled tight around mine, he strode quickly down the street, and his arm stretched up as soon as a cab with a light on appeared.

He opened the car door for me and I climbed in, my stomach just a flurry of butterflies. Cole settled in next to me, his right side pressed against my left, and he entwined the fingers of his right hand in my left before placing our clasped hands on his thigh. He gave the taxi driver his address and I immediately felt a quiver between my legs.

This was going to happen.

I was going to have sex with Cole Walker.

Hot, exciting, sexy images filled my head, so by the time the car pulled up outside Cole's building I was already ready for him.

It was easy to sense Cole's impatience as he practically threw money at the taxi driver and hurried us out of the cab and up the stairs to his flat. At no point did he let go of my hand as he opened his door and led me down his hallway to a room at the end of it.

The master bedroom.

Like the rest of his flat, it had high ceilings, deep coving, and a gorgeous bay window. Blinds were drawn down over them, giving us privacy. In the center of the room was a king-sized bed with a chunky, masculine walnut frame. In the corner of the room near the door to the en suite was a contemporary black leather reading chair. The walls were painted a warm mocha and buttercream, and the plush carpet beneath my feet was dark chocolate. Above the headboard was a huge black-and-white photograph taken from the backseat of a classic American convertible. The driver was turned in profile. He wore dark aviators and smoke billowed from his lips as he seemed to stare out at the world in boredom.

Beyond the car was a deep canyon, giving the impression that the car was mere inches from the edge.

The whole room was cool and sexy and completely Cole.

My eyes flew to him as he let go of my hand and walked over to the end of the bed. He turned and looked at me, almost taunting me with the heat in his eyes.

We both knew we were about to cross the line I'd drawn between us a long time ago.

Before we crossed that line, before there was no turning back, I had to be sure we were on the same page. "I like you, Cole. I do. And clearly I'm attracted to you . . . but you have to know there's a possibility that I won't ever learn to trust you. And you said you don't do casual . . ."

Cole's answer was to shrug out of his jacket and throw it on a nearby chair. His fierce gaze delved deep inside me. "Shannon, there is nothing casual about how I feel about you. There hasn't been since the day I stepped out of Ellie and Adam's house and found you on the stoop. I get you don't trust me and I get why, but I want you to give me the chance to change that. I think there's something here that's worth all the effort."

"Cole," I said as my lips trembled, my eyes misting. I felt too much, just too, too much . . . "I wish I'd never left you that day."

I knew he understood instantly all the many reasons I wished I'd never walked away from that strangely magical connection I'd felt with Cole when we were fifteen. If I'd never walked away, life would never have taught me not to trust this man—a man who just might deserve my trust much more than the others who had come before him.

I saw the pain and regret mingle with the heat in Cole's eyes and I understood without him having to say that he was feeling it too.

Suddenly I was in his arms.

His lips crashed down on mine as I stood up on tiptoe, my hands fisted in the back of Cole's T-shirt as I tasted him for the first time. Two seconds later he gripped my bottom in his hands and lifted me. I wrapped my legs around his waist and melted into him as the kiss turned wild. He had one arm around my back while his other hand threaded through my hair to hold my head, to hold me to his lips.

I wanted that kiss to go on forever—it was hungry and wet and hard. It was so crazy beautiful I didn't even realize Cole had moved us to the bed until he lowered himself on it and my knees hit the duvet on either side of his hips.

He pulled back from the kiss and we panted against each other's mouths. Cole brushed my hair back from my face and it took everything within me to tear my gaze from his gorgeous mouth. As soon as I looked into his green eyes, however, I swore I'd never look away. The gold flecks in them seemed brighter than ever as he said, his voice hoarse, "I want to see you. Just you and all that fucking hair."

I bit my lip on a shy smile. Although excited, I couldn't help wondering how I'd measure up to the tall goddesses who seemed to decorate Cole's past. I'd heard the stories and even seen some pictures, courtesy of Rae. However, I discovered a while ago that men generally didn't get as hard as Cole was right now unless you turned them on, and acting insecure would definitely take the sexy out of our very sexy—oh my God, too sexy to breathe—situation. "I'm starting to think you like my hair."

He touched a strand that fell down over my breast, his hands gently caressing it in a way I felt between my legs. I shifted a little impatiently against his erection. "I love your hair," he murmured, more than a little distracted. "You have no idea how many fantasies I've had about you and your hair."

Flushing hotter than I would have thought possible, I squirmed and whispered, "Tell me one."

"The most recent?" he said, dragging his gaze from my hair and breasts to my eyes. "You're naked on your hands and knees, and your hair is spilling down your shoulders, the ends touching my ink on your lower back. Some of your hair is wrapped lightly around my hand as I fuck you from behind." His eyes flashed. "Hard."

I was panting now at the visual, the hot puffs touching Cole's mouth. "I want that."

A possessiveness entered Cole's eyes, a possessiveness that given my history caused me momentary panic . . . but then he was kissing me again, his hand fisted in my hair. The feel of his tongue stroking mine, the taste of him, the smell of him . . . nothing else mattered.

The kiss broke but only because Cole was reaching for the hem of my camisole. "We need to be careful with your tattoo," he panted as he lifted my top up. I raised my arms to assist him, the cool air prickling over my skin and turning my already tight nipples harder. Cole threw my top somewhere over my shoulder and spanned my waist with his hands. "My thumbs almost touch," he said quietly, almost as if to himself. "You're tiny."

"Or you just have big hands," I murmured saucily.

"I do but you're still tiny." His eyes lifted to my breasts and I was suddenly glad I'd had the forethought before leaving the flat to put on my best bra—a satin and lace balconette in a pretty peach color. "These . . . not so much." He gave me a hungry smile and somehow I managed to melt even more. He met my hot gaze. "You really are perfect." His tongue wet his lower lip before he said gruffly, "The fantasy doesn't live up to reality, Shortcake."

Then I jumped him. His signature version of sweet and hot was pushing me to the combustion point. Cole met my aggressive kiss with his own fever, his hands carefully dodging my tattoo as they slid up my back, under my hair, to my bra clasp. I felt it loosen within seconds and Cole gently pushed me back so he could look at me as he removed it.

He sucked in a breath as the straps fell down my arms, his eyes fixated on my naked breasts even as he threw the bra aside. I swelled at the need in his eyes, my nipples puckering up under his focus, begging for his mouth.

Cole's fingers went to the button on my jeans. "Get these off," he commanded, and I felt the demand in my core. Trembling, I slid off the bed and began to undo my jeans.

"Undress," I demanded right back.

I stopped to watch as he removed his sweater and the T-shirt underneath it, my eyes drinking in his beautiful tan body. Sculpted and tawny and inked. The deep cut in his obliques made my throat suddenly dry. I wanted to lick the sexy definition in his muscles before moving on to his six-pack.

I'd known he was muscular, but I'd had no idea just how tightly roped he was. He was honed and toned and fighting fit and I almost climaxed just looking at him.

"Shannon," he urged as he stood up to unbutton his jeans.

I nodded and pushed my jeans down, stepping out of them and my underwear. "I get to lick your tattoos at some point."

His soft laughter filled the room. "Deal." He reached one of those tattooed arms out, grabbed my hand, and hauled me up against him. I'd gotten a glimpse of the rather huge erection that was standing to attention before I felt it hot against my naked stomach.

"Cole," I said, breathless.

He lowered himself back to the bed and pulled me onto his lap so I was straddling him again. I dropped my gaze to his cock as it pushed insistently against my belly. If anything it seemed to swell under my attention. Nick had been big, the biggest I'd seen, and Cole was definitely giving him a run for his money. I was at once turned on and a little apprehensive.

I felt his fingers graze the curves of my breasts and I turned my focus to his face.

"You're sure about this?" he said.

"You're asking me now?"

"If you wanted to stop ten minutes ago, we would have stopped. If you want to stop now, we'll stop. If you suddenly want to stop when I'm inside you, we'll stop." He cupped my cheek, casting his tender eyes on me. "I will never do anything you don't want to do. You're safe with me, Shannon."

"Fuck," I said, choking on the word and all the emotion that had formed a lump in my throat.

Cole blinked. "That's the first time I've heard you swear."

"Gran always said ladies don't swear, so I rarely do. But this seemed like a 'fuck' moment."

Humor glittered in his eyes. "Why? Aside from the obvious, of course."

I laughed as I slid my hands behind his ears, stroking his jawline with my thumbs. "Because I'm scared of you, Cole Walker. I'm scared you'll hurt me or I'll hurt you . . . yet I have no intention of turning back. I'm throwing myself off this cliff, consequences be damned."

His arms tightened around me and I pressed my lips to his, our kiss quickly turning from sweet and sensual to charged and erotic. My fingers tightened in his hair as I pushed against his hard cock. Cole's fingertips glided down the curve of my waist, across my belly, and down between my legs. I moaned into his mouth as he pushed two fingers inside me, the moan turning to whimpers as he pumped them in and out. He left my mouth, his lips trailing down my chin, my throat, my chest before they danced across my left breast and closed around my nipple. I threw my head back on a startled cry of pleasure as the pull of his mouth shot streaks of heat from my breasts to my sex.

I clasped his head to my chest as he sucked and licked my nipples. While he paid my breasts such glorious attention, my hips flexed against the thrust of his fingers between my legs.

I was panting loudly now, his name falling in pleading whimpers from my lips as the tension inside me increased. It tightened and tightened and tightened until I froze, breathless. Cole scraped his teeth against my nipple and quickened his fingers, and the tension snapped.

My eyes fluttered as bliss came to me. "Cole!" I cried out, the word ending abruptly in a gasp as my climax rolled through me, my inner muscles squeezing around his fingers as I jerked against them.

The orgasm was long and beautiful and I could barely catch my breath as it finally drew to a stop. I sagged against Cole, my limbs all warm and jellylike.

Cole lifted my head off his shoulder, taking my chin in his hand to bring my lips to his. He pressed a sweet kiss on them. "Are you on the pill?"

I nodded.

"I'm clean." He kissed me again before he pulled back to growl, "Take me inside you."

Uncertainty caused me to press my hand firmly against his chest. "Condom, Cole," I insisted.

He stared into my eyes, something working behind his as he realized that when I said I didn't fully trust him I had meant it. No matter how much I wanted him, or how much I needed him to be as great as he seemed to be, I couldn't let go of my past. I would not be fucked over by another man, and that included catching an STD.

Tense, I waited as Cole came to a decision. He kissed me again and then held me tight so I wouldn't fall off his lap as he leaned down to his bedside table drawer. I relaxed as he pulled out a condom packet.

To make up for my lack of trust, I assisted him, stroking him and squeezing him until he was groaning against my mouth. "Now take me inside you."

I felt a resurgence of energy at the blaze in his expression. I lifted myself up onto my knees and guided him inside me. I slowly lowered myself back down.

"Oh God," I panted, feeling overwhelmingly full.

I clutched Cole's shoulders, watching the way his teeth gritted and his eyes darkened as his dick slid snugly inside me. His fingers bit into my hip as I lowered as far as I could and lifted myself back up. He pushed me back down and then back up, taking control of the rhythm. I wrapped my arms around his neck, bringing us flush so my hard, swollen nipples rubbed against his chest as I rode him.

We gasped against each other's lips, our grip on each other tightening as we soared toward climax.

"Come for me, Shannon," Cole grunted. "Come."

I nodded on a whimper as I neared the heights. Cole slid his hand between my legs, and his thumb pressed circles around my clit. The sensation blew the top off my head and I screamed.

"Fuck, fuck, fuck!" Cole yelled hoarsely, his fingers digging into my hips as he jerked up in one last hard thrust. I felt him swell even thicker inside me before he throbbed and his hot, wet release filled me. "Oh, fuck." His chest heaved against mine as I collapsed on him, my head burrowing against the crook of his neck. He held me tightly.

His penis continued to pulse inside me as my inner muscles quivered around it.

When our breathing finally calmed, Cole said, "We're not even close to done."

"I don't know if I can take much more," I replied. And I meant it. I was sated and languorous and all I wanted was to fall asleep while still wrapped around him.

Cole eased me back from him and I pouted playfully. He smiled and kissed the pout right off my lips. With ease, he lifted me off his cock and gently lowered me onto the bed. I watched his delicious, firm arse walk across the room and into the en suite. He returned, after obviously disposing of the condom, and when he reached me he pulled me up onto my feet. "Now you can sit on my face so I can taste you like I've been fantasizing about tasting you since you stepped foot into the studio."

I'd thought I was done.

But my sex clenched at his hot visual and unbelievably I knew I wasn't done.

A few seconds later Cole was lying sprawled out on the bed, the sexiest offering known to womankind, and I was crawling up his body. I'd never done this before. Of course I'd had boyfriends put their mouths on me, but I'd never done it this way.

My legs shaking—from this or my last two climaxes, I had no idea—I faltered above him.

Cole sensed my uncertainty and took control, guiding me over him.

I felt his tongue thrust into me, and that was all it took. I was lost again, shyness evaporating.

When I came again, this time was sharper and shorter but no less sweet, and by the time I was done, Cole was hard again. He wrapped me around him and lifted me up off the bed. I noted he grabbed another condom out of his drawer before carrying me as he walked out of the bedroom. "You weigh absolutely nothing." He squeezed my bottom, smiling as he entered the kitchen.

I felt the cold wooden table on my cheeks as he lowered me onto it. I stroked his sleek back as he spread my legs. My arms fell as he stepped back and I gripped the table edge, focused on my own thoughts as Cole's burning gaze roamed over my entire body. "Rae said your first big crush was on Nate's wife, Olivia."

Confused at the random turn in conversation, Cole frowned at me. "What?"

"Olivia," I repeated. "And I've seen pictures of past girlfriends and I've heard all about them. You have a type. And it's tall and leggy and curvy and often brunette. You have an attraction to tall."

Getting my point, Cole grinned and stepped back into my space, guiding my legs around his waist. "I have a new appreciation for tiny." His eyes smoldered as his hands glided along my outer thighs. "Delicate, beautiful, fragile. I want to protect you while at the same time I want to shatter you," he murmured against my lips, "but only in the best way possible." The glint in his eyes reassured me. "Tiny but curvy." His hands moved up along my waist to cup my breasts, his thumbs stroking my pebbled nipples. "Sexiest woman I've ever been with." His right hand disappeared between my legs as he held my gaze and slid two fingers into my slick heat. "Beautiful here too." His breathing started to escalate. "You feel fucking amazing." He groaned the last word and his fingers disappeared for a few seconds as he put on protection. A few more seconds after that he thrust inside me.

I cried out, my hands sliding back on the tabletop as Cole pumped into me. Our gasps and groans and the wet drive of his cock in and out of me echoed off the kitchen tiles, the sounds of sex turning me on just as much as the feel of Cole inside me.

I came for the fourth time that night, taking Cole right along with me.

Suddenly I was being lifted in the air again and sleepily I clung to Cole as he carried me back to his bedroom, too tired to ask him why he'd relocated us in the first place. There he laid me in his bed, my front to his front, and he pulled my leg over his hip so our bodies were as close as they could be.

I snuggled deeper into him, my nose pressed to his throat, and Cole's arms tightened around me.

CHAPTER 14

The chill seeped into me, raising goose bumps on my skin and pulling me out of sleep. I lingered on the edges of unconsciousness, too tired to come fully out of it.

"Shortcake, it's time to get up," a low voice said.

I groaned and buried my head deeper into the softness of the pillow.

I heard laughter. "Shannon, we have to get up for work."

"Mmm, no," I muttered, and followed up with a shiver. It occurred to me that the covers and warm body that had been keeping me nice and cozy all night had abandoned me. I patted down the length of my body, searching for the duvet, but before I could find it Cole grabbed my hand.

I supposed that would do instead.

I tugged on his hand with all my strength until his chest was against my back and his arm was over my waist. Warmer already, I tucked his hand beneath mine against my cleavage.

The vibrations of his chuckle from his chest to my back made me smile sleepily. A smile that left me quite abruptly when Cole lifted me right out of the bed.

I yelped in surprise, my eyes flying open. I clung to him as he climbed off the bed and started toward the en suite bathroom. Too tired to speak coherently, I made a few noises of complaint.

My brain started to wake up just as his gorgeous face came into focus. "I have a five-hour session today that I can't be late for." He stepped into the large shower and lowered me to my feet.

Thankfully he still kept a grip on me, because my eyes instantly closed and I swayed. We'd fallen asleep late and I'd definitely not had my eight hours of sleep. I needed my eight hours, or as close to it as possible, in order to function normally.

Cole snorted. "You really aren't a morning person, are you?"

I mumbled something about needing eight hours, but I'd have been surprised if it was intelligible.

"I'm going to put the shower on now. I really need you to wake up."

I nodded. "Mmm-hmm."

Apparently he understood I was giving him the go-ahead to turn on the shower, because the water poured down on me, too cold, and I gasped, my eyes flying open. Cole was smirking while he fiddled with the temperature dial.

"That was deliberate," I huffed, shoving him.

He grinned and grabbed my arm, pulling me into him. "It got your eyes open, didn't it?"

I frowned. "Meanie."

"You are really quite adorable when you're tired." He gently turned me around. "I'll wash you. You wash me."

I turned back to him. "You first. I'll just fall asleep again if we start with me."

Cole handed me the body wash, shampoo, and conditioner. The washing him part of the morning was fun and soon I was fully conscious. I had unfettered access to Cole's hard body, but unfortunately there was a time constraint, so it was a quick but wonderfully pleasant exploration. We ran into a bit of a problem when it came to washing his hair.

I wrapped my hands around him and pressed my cheek to his back. "I'm too short to reach your hair."

I felt, more than heard, him chuckling before he took the shampoo and conditioner and did it himself. I stood back from the spray and drank him in for a moment. He really was the most fantastic-looking man I'd ever had the good fortune to bed.

"Your turn."

Just as I'd thought I might, I almost drifted off again as Cole washed my hair. It was only when he started soaping the rest of me that my eyes flew open. I sucked in air as he slipped two fingers over my clit. I felt his erection dig into me. His warm breath puffed against my right ear as he bent down to whisper, "If you trusted me I could be inside you right about now."

Reluctantly I pulled away from Cole's tormenting touch so I could face him. Uncertainty made me want to run screaming from the shower, and yet at the same time I felt panic flare to life as I forced out, "I told you I don't want anyone to get hurt here, and as much as I want to trust you it's probably not going to happen . . . Maybe we should just stop before this goes too far."

To my surprise this amused Cole. He shook his head with a smile. "We're doing this. You *will* learn to trust me."

I wasn't convinced and I didn't hide my reaction from him.

To my consternation Cole laughed and held me in a naked, wet cuddle.

Unfortunately he gave good naked, wet cuddles and I found myself relaxing against him despite myself. "Has anyone ever told you you're exceptionally arrogant?"

He stroked my spine and murmured, "You say arrogant. I say optimistic."

I laughed.

"I love that sound." He caressed my bottom. "Now let's get out of here before we make each other late for work."

Holding my hand, Cole led me into INKarnate. The bell above the door chimed and Simon and Rae, who were chatting by the reception desk, turned to look at us. Their eyes immediately zoomed in on the handholding.

Rae had just opened her mouth to speak when Cole beat her to it. "Before you say anything, I'd like to remind you I'm your boss."

She replied with a long, drawn-out snort. "I don't think we're the ones who need that reminder since we're not the ones who just fucked an employee or our boss."

I glanced up at Cole. He looked comically affronted. "I did no such thing." Something wicked glinted in his eyes. "If anyone did the fuc—"

"Finish that sentence and die." I let go of his hand and crossed my arms over my chest.

He grinned and strolled over to Rae and Simon to give them the coffee we'd brought them.

To my relief, the ribbing seemed to be over. Rae sighed. "Big day today. Cole, you've got a five-hour piece, I've got two second sessions for removals, and that means, Simon, you've got a fuck load of smaller appointments to contend with. Try to keep up."

Simon gave her a wry smile. "No pressure, then."

I grabbed a pad of paper off the desk. "Give me your lunch orders now and I'll run out and grab some sandwiches. It'll be too busy later on today for me to be able to nip out for them."

They gave me their orders and Rae and Simon went to their rooms to set up. Cole, however, stayed.

I put the lunch money in my purse. "What is it?"

"Nothing." He shrugged. "Just trying to work out how I'm going to get through today—all I can think about is how good it feels to be inside you."

My blood instantly heated at the sudden turn of conversation. I pressed a hand to my hot cheek. "I'm so glad I'm not a typical redhead. I'd be wearing a constant beamer around you."

"Personally I think the blushing would be fun."

I rolled my eyes and gently nudged him aside. "Yeah, for you."

Cole's hand wrapped around my wrist and he pulled me back to him. He swallowed my gasp as he lifted me clean off my feet and crushed his mouth down on mine. Arms around his neck, I kissed him back for a few seconds before he gently lowered me to the floor, kissed my nose, and strode off into the back of the shop.

Feeling more than a little foggy, I had to physically shake myself out of the sexual stupor he'd put me in.

I was beginning to feel less and less in control of this whole situation.

It was an understatement to say we were busy. The odd few times I did see Cole he was completely professional around the customers and I didn't have to worry about him making any more heated comments that flustered me. I did, however, have to contend with an increasingly itchy tattoo.

"I want to rub myself up against a scratching post," I complained to Cole as we entered his flat later that evening with Chinese takeout in hand.

He smirked as I followed him into the kitchen. "Please don't. You'll ruin all my hard work."

"I won't. I just want to."

"It's healing. The itchiness will go away. You just need to persevere." He lifted up his kettle. "Coffee?"

"Please."

As he walked over to the sink I noticed he was a little stiff. He grimaced and pulled his shoulders back on a groan.

"Are you okay?"

He glanced over his shoulder at me. "Hunching over for a five-hour tattoo always pisses my back off."

It occurred to me I hadn't even thought about how physically uncomfortable Cole's job could be. Feeling like a shitty nongirlfriend that I hadn't considered this, I immediately thought of a way I could help. "I could give you a massage if you want. Years ago I had this friend Caro and when she was training to be a masseuse I was her guinea pig. I picked up a few things."

"You don't have to do that." He threw me a tired smile as he walked back to put the kettle on.

"I want to." I put the unopened takeout on the table. "Dinner can wait." I left the kitchen, glad to hear his footsteps following behind me. Once in his bedroom, I pulled down the duvet and pointed to the mattress. "Shirt off. Lie on your stomach." As Cole did as I said I went looking for moisturizer in the bathroom.

Finding it among other girlie stuff in the back of his bathroom cabinet, I felt a burn inside me that I could have likened to jealousy if I wasn't so sure Cole and I weren't ever going to be serious.

In the bedroom, Cole lay on his stomach, head on his arms. The sight of his broad shoulders and muscular back caused a little flip in my lower belly. Kicking off my shoes, I climbed onto the bed and straddled him.

"I like this already," Cole murmured.

I tapped some moisturizer onto my palms and rubbed them together. "Did you live here with a woman?"

I felt him tense beneath me. "Yes. Why?"

"There's still some girlie toiletries in your bathroom cabinet."

"There is? I'll get rid of them if it bothers you."

"No. I was just curious." I began to work gently at the muscles in his neck and shoulders first. The low groan he emitted shot straight between my legs and I squeezed my eyes closed. This was not a sexy massage. Cole was in real discomfort. I was helping him. *Dirty thoughts back into the gutter, please.*

"Her name was Elena." He sighed, his whole body relaxing under my touch. "We split up eight months ago."

Ignoring the sharp object that seemed to have lodged itself in my chest, I went for a casual tone. "What happened?" *Shannon, you are clearly a glutton for punishment.*

"We dated for nine months, lived together for three of those. First time I've ever lived with a girlfriend. It was a disaster."

"Why?" I held my breath, hoping despite higher reasoning that Cole had no lingering feelings for this Elena person. Rae had not told me about an Elena person, and that, in itself, caused me concern. Had she broken Cole's heart so badly no one talked about it? *Crap.*

"We weren't really compatible. You really get to know someone—" He groaned again as I found the knot that was bothering him. I began to gently work it out. "Feels good, Shortcake." His eyelashes fluttered closed and I almost growled in frustration.

"You were saying," I prompted, trying to sound casual.

"Mmm? Oh yeah, Elena. Yeah, you get to know someone when you live with her. She discovered that she couldn't deal with someone as laid-back as I am—apparently it means I don't care enough—and I discovered she was a bitch. She talked about her friends behind their backs and was always making negative remarks about people, even strangers on the street. It was when she started in on Hannah that I'd had enough."

I couldn't imagine anyone being mean to Hannah. She was so lovely. "Why would she start on Hannah?"

Cole grinned. "You like Hannah, don't you?"

"Eh, *yeah*. She's a pregnant superwoman. She's a teacher, she's a mum, she's a stepmum, she's a wife, and she's smart and organized and caring and somehow manages to be all those things while looking absolutely amazing. I kind of want to *be* Hannah."

He chuckled. "As nice as that it is, I like you just the way you are."

I grew quiet at the compliment and stopped to put more moisturizer on my hands.

"Anyway," Cole continued, "all of my girlfriends have had an issue with my friendship with Hannah. Elena never seemed bothered by it until one day . . . she just was. She started making underhand comments about Hannah, and then accusing me of being in love with her, until I couldn't take it anymore. We broke up."

I started massaging him again. I was relieved, but I really wished I didn't feel that way. Relief suggested real feelings were involved here. I shrugged the relief off. "It might have seemed out of the blue to you, but these things rarely are. Someone probably made a comment and she twisted it into something irrational. I'd take a guess it was one of her friends."

"You think?"

"Yeah." I curled my lip in annoyance. "Girls are idiots. Especially when it comes to attractive women. One of her friends probably got a look at Hannah and how gorgeous she is and then said something about you two until it made Elena paranoid about your friendship."

"Fuck. You're probably right," he grumbled. "Why do women do that?"

"Pfft, don't ask me. They confuse the heck out of me most of the time too."

"Makes them interesting, though."

I laughed. "If you say so."

"*You* confuse the hell out of me," he said. "But I'm enjoying it so far."

"Cole Walker, the patience of a saint."

"Is that what they'll put on my gravestone?"

"That and 'tattooist by day and time-traveling immortal high-lander by night,'" I teased.

His body shook with amusement beneath mine. "You never did dye your hair pink."

"Ach, it has sentimental value. It's the only thing I have in common with my mum." I quirked an eyebrow. "On second thought, maybe I should dye it."

He tensed under my hands. "No taking your family problems out on your hair."

I smiled. "I'll make a deal with you . . . I won't cut or dye my hair for the next six months."

"No deal."

"Why?"

"You'll not touch your hair for the next millennium."

I grinned again and started working his upper back. I would never *actually* change my hair, so it didn't hurt to concede. "Okay, since you like it so much . . ."

Cole relaxed again and we fell into a comfortable silence as I continued to massage him.

A little while later I heard a snore.

He'd fallen asleep.

My first instinct was to curl up next to him.

However, my brain told me not to get too attached. Cuddling up for a nap with Cole was definitely something I'd do if we were in a relationship. But we weren't in a relationship. You couldn't be in a relationship unless you trusted the person you were in said relationship with.

Ugh, I was giving myself a headache.

I slipped off the bed as stealthily as possible and gently eased the duvet over Cole. I ventured back into the kitchen for the takeout, my cheeks flooding with heat as I remembered what had happened on the table the night before. I still hadn't asked Cole why he'd taken me into the kitchen for sex.

Hmm.

With a plateful of heated-up chicken-fried rice and curry sauce, I made myself at home in the sitting room. Saturday night television wasn't brilliant, but it would do. I turned the volume low on a talent show so I wouldn't disturb Cole.

Half an hour later I heard the sounds of his waking. Eyes on the door, I waited for him to appear, his footsteps coming fast down the hall toward me. Cole drew to an abrupt stop at the sight of me. He was still shirtless and his cheek was sleep creased. His hair was rumpled too. I hadn't realized until that moment that it was possible for a man to be adorable and sexy at the same time.

His tense shoulders dropped when he took me in, curled up on the end of his sofa. "I worried you'd left."

I shook my head and he gave me a nod before heading back to the bedroom. A few minutes later he passed the sitting room with a shirt on and headed to the kitchen. When he returned and sat on the other end of the sofa with his plate of food, he said, "Sorry I fell asleep on you."

"Don't be."

"My back feels better. Thanks."

"You're welcome." Why was this suddenly awkward? I frowned at him. He wouldn't look at me and his tone was . . . weird.

He frowned at the television. "Next time wake me."

I frowned in return. "Not if you're exhausted."

He ate instead of answering, that little furrow on his brow deepening.

Was he . . . "Are you annoyed I didn't wake you or annoyed I didn't stay in bed with you?"

He shot me a dirty look and I had to bite my lip from smiling at his endearing disgruntlement. "No."

I burst out laughing because he was definitely put out. That was sweet.

Now he was glowering. "What?"

I shook my head, still chuckling. "You're the only guy I've ever met who's gotten pissed at me for not staying to cuddle." I tried to swallow more giggles, but it was impossible.

To my surprise and delight Cole's glower melted into a slow, wicked grin. "If you're trying to make me feel emasculated, you're wasting your time."

"Oh?"

He put his plate on the coffee table. "I'm perfectly secure in my own masculinity." His hand wrapped around my ankle and he pulled, sliding my body down the sofa toward him.

"You are?" I whispered as he moved over me, gently easing my legs apart.

He nodded, his green eyes hot. "And I'm about to show you why."

"A demonstration," I gasped as his hands slipped up my skirt. "How lovely."

Laughter glittered in his eyes, a laughter that quickly turned to a smolder as he got down to the business of proving there was more than a little alpha male in him.

Afterward as I lay in his arms watching the television, I remembered to ask him about last night and sex on the kitchen table. His answer: "Missionary was out . . . It was the next best thing. And the kitchen table is sturdy." He kissed me. "We broke it in."

"The table was a virgin?" I said, eyes round with mock horror.

"Yes, but I'm sure it was painless for it."

"Still, I wish I'd known. I would have been more of a gentleman."

Cole burst out laughing—a deep, full belly laugh that I hadn't heard from him until then. Knowing I'd made him laugh . . . well . . . it affected me. I spent the rest of the night fighting to ignore the warmth growing in my chest. I didn't succeed.

Later, as he spooned me in bed, I was thinking of ways to protect myself from becoming addicted to him. The best option, of course, was to go cold turkey and end it before it really started, but I knew I couldn't do it . . .

I cursed my willpower or lack thereof.

"You're tense," he said.

So I tried to relax.

I did not succeed.

Cole tightened his arm around me. "Everything's going to be okay, Shannon."

For some reason those simple words choked me up. Tears burned in my eyes and in my throat, and try as I might, I couldn't stop them from falling down my cheeks. I tried to swallow past the lump in my throat, but I ended up making this dreadful almost, but not quite, sob.

It was Cole's turn to tense and I suddenly found myself on my back as he leaned over me. Light from outside seeped through the blinds on his window to illuminate the concern in his eyes. "Shortcake," he whispered, his fingers brushing my wet cheeks.

"I don't know why I'm crying," I whispered back, brushing at them. "So stupid."

"It's not." He shook his head and pressed a soft kiss to my lips. "It's not." He rested his forehead against mine, hot air puffing over my mouth as he sighed. "If I was less of a selfish bastard I'd let you go."

I reached for him, my fingers digging into his waist. I didn't even realize I'd done it until Cole drew back to give me a small smile.

"I am a selfish bastard, though."

My body relaxed under his, and his smile widened. To my everlasting appreciation he didn't comment on the fact that my body clearly was at war with my brain.

"I can cheer you up."

"I'm not sad . . . It's just . . ." I shook my head and shrugged because I honestly didn't know what I was feeling.

"Well, I can get rid of those tears . . . Joss invited you to her book launch on Thursday night."

I drew in a breath, feeling a mixture of surprise, gratitude, and excitement. "Really?"

Cole's whole face warmed with affection. "What do you say? Fancy being my date to it?"

"Do you even need to ask?"

He laughed and lay back down, easing me against him. "Apparently not."

Smiling now, I wrapped my arms around him, snuggled my face

into the crook of his neck, and tried to envision a real, honest-to-goodness book launch. Would it be swish and sophisticated? Wine and cocktails and fun literary chats?

Ooh, I'd have to dress up for something like that.

Ooh, and I'd also get my books signed by Joss.

Giddy now, I let the happy thoughts pull me into a deep, contented sleep.

CHAPTER 15

The atmosphere at the bookstore on George Street was welcoming and relaxed. Although there were glasses of wine and champagne, there were also glasses of orange juice and water. The dress code was casual-smart, which kind of shot a hole in my plans to buy something a little fancier to wear, but it didn't detract from the excitement of being at a book launch for one of my favorite authors.

Everyone was there except for the kids, Nate, Mick, his wife, and Hannah's brother, Declan. Among the familiar faces were twenty or so strangers—all J. B. Carmichael fans. Joss's readership was growing since her last book hit the e-book top one hundred. Cole had told me that there were only a handful of people at her last book launch, and it read on her face that she was a little taken aback by the fact that her popularity had quadrupled since last time.

Her husband stood at her side while readers came up to chat to her, and anytime he tried to give her space, she'd grip his arm and not so subtly jerk him back to her.

I snorted and Cole followed my gaze. "She never crossed me as the shy type."

"She's not. But she also hates being center of attention, so this sort of thing is her least favorite part of being an author."

I grimaced. "I have to admit I'd probably feel the same way. I'm not a shy person, but *that* would make me shy."

"Me too."

"Really?" I said, eyeing him in surprise. "You? Shy?"

Cole grinned. "There is so much you don't know about me."

Before I could question him further, my curiosity was put on hold when Joss's publicist cleared her throat and introduced Joss. Braden squeezed her hand and gently nudged her toward the center of the room where everyone was now gathering in a semicircle around her.

"Hey, folks." She smiled at everyone, the natural coolness in her tip-tilted eyes warming anytime she made eye contact with one of her friends and family. "I want to thank you all for being here for the launch of my fifth book." She appeared to relax somewhat as she continued on less formally. "You know, I'm extremely blessed to be surrounded by family and friends who all inspire me. Believe me when I tell you there is never a dull year in the Carmichael-Clark-Sutherland-MacCabe-Sawyer-Walker tribe."

At that, said tribe all tittered, acknowledging the truth in her words. I knew there was truth in them because I had spent the last week asking Cole about these colorful, gorgeous people he was lucky enough to have in his life. Each one of them had a story to tell, and although he'd only given me the bare bones of them, I read between the lines and deduced their stories involved a lot of drama and plenty of heartache.

"That's why the plot for this book came to me so easily—it's inspired by one of my best friends. She knows who she is and I just wanted to say thank you for being you. You're a true heroine . . . and your tale makes one hell of a story." She grinned teasingly at the crowd and they laughed.

I looked around at all the women in Joss's life, wondering who she was talking about.

"I'm not going to say much, because my husband will tell you I'm not much for speeches, but I want to thank my publisher, my editor, Audrey, who flew all the way from London to be here, my publicist, Bill, my friends, and most important, my husband, Braden, who after a long day at work will find ways to keep the kids entertained while I hole up in my writing cave. I like you." She smiled at him. "A whole lot."

Braden laughed and I knew instantly what Joss saw in him.

Yum-ee.

While Joss walked over to him and the crowds began mingling, Cole squeezed my waist. Gazing up at him, I found he had his eyebrows raised. "Braden's forty-two," he whispered.

Damn. He'd caught me ogling.

I shrugged, going for nonchalant. "A *hot* forty-two."

He groaned as if in pain. "He's like a big brother, as is Cam. Don't call them hot."

"I won't." I shook my head. "Besides, Cam is more sexy than hot."

Cole made a gagging sound.

"And let's not leave out Adam, and my gosh, definitely not Nate and Marco. Those two are smok—"

His large hand clamped over my mouth and I looked up at him from under my eyelashes, my gaze mischievous.

"Don't say it."

I promised him with my eyes that I wouldn't.

180

Cautiously Cole removed his hand from over my mouth. I grinned. "I don't see the problem with me admitting they're all attractive. It's not like you didn't have a huge crush on Olivia."

"That reminds me. I need to speak to Rae."

"She's been very forthcoming."

"Stay here while I go find her and kill her."

"She's here?" I said, looking around the store for her.

"She came in while Joss was talking." He stilled and I followed his gaze to see Rae in the corner laughing with Ellie and her mum. "I'll be right back."

"Cole," I protested, but he was already striding off.

"Uh-oh, someone's in trouble."

I turned at Hannah's teasing voice. "Rae. Rae's in trouble."

Hannah smirked. "Why does that not surprise me?"

"She told me about Cole's crush on Olivia."

Delighted, Hannah burst out laughing. "Oh man, I almost forgot about that." Her eyes were bright with mirth. "She was his first big crush. It was so adorable."

"Yup." I giggled. "Which is why Cole's going to kill Rae."

"What are we laughing at?" Liv hurried over to us with Jo, her eyes filled with curiosity as she bestowed her freaking amazing smile on us.

My own gaze took in all her voluptuous gorgeousness. She wasn't beautiful like Jo, or glamorous like Joss, or stunning like Hannah. She *was* striking and sexy with unusual golden hazel eyes and killer curves. No wonder Cole had had a crush on her. She was a teenage boy's wet dream.

"Rae told Shannon about Cole's old crush on you. He's now killing her with words."

We all stared across the room where Cole was laughing with Rae.

I snorted. "Well . . . he was . . ."

"I hope it doesn't bother you . . ." Liv seemed unsure. "It was years ago. He was just a teenager."

"Of course not." I waved her concerns away.

"I'm just glad to see you getting along with Hannah." Jo took a sip of her champagne while Hannah tensed beside me.

I reassured her with a grin. "Oh, you mean because all his ex-girlfriends were crazy people?"

Cole's sister looked surprised. "Cole told you?"

"Yup. Don't worry. I'm not blind." I looked at Hannah now. "I can see you two are like brother and sister."

Relief glittered in her pretty brown eyes and it occurred to me this was obviously something she had to worry about every time Cole started seeing someone new.

"Anyway," I continued, "it's not like Cole and I are anything serious."

Just like that the mood in our circle changed. And not for the better.

Jo looked visibly confused and upset. "But . . . Cole doesn't do *casual*."

I opened my mouth to explain but found I really didn't know how. "Issues."

I spun around to find Joss standing behind us, apparently listening in.

She waved her wineglass at me. "I can spot someone with issues a mile off."

"Issues?" Jo and Liv stepped closer, crowding me in. I was starting to feel a little trapped. "What issues?"

"Yes, what issues?" I snapped, forgetting this woman was my current idol.

Joss shrugged. "If it were my guess, I'd say the whole 'not serious thing' was your suggestion and it was your suggestion because of a bad breakup."

Hannah, Jo, and Liv looked from Joss to me, expressions all the same. I was battered by three silent questions, each one the same. *Well, is she right?*

Yes, I definitely felt trapped.

"Jesus, women." Cole suddenly appeared, pushing past his sister and Hannah to get to me. "The four of you look like a pack of hyenas crowding baby Simba."

I wrapped my arm around his waist, thankful for the intrusion despite being likened to a lion cub. As much as I liked Cole's friends and family, I wasn't really up for sharing my past with them.

"We're sorry." Hannah looked like she really meant it.

Jo, however, wasn't ready to let it go that easily . . . "What does she mean you're not serious?"

"Jo." Cole sighed. "Don—"

"Since when do you do casual?" She crossed her arms over her slim chest, annoyance in her eyes. Eyes that were the exact shape and shade as Cole's.

I relaxed against her brother, remembering how Rae had told me Jo raised him. She was just being protective.

"Jo—"

"I don't think—"

"Jo, sheathe the mother-bear claws."

He said it in such an authoritative tone I wasn't surprised when she snapped her mouth shut.

Cole's fingers tightened their hold on my waist. "Shannon is my business, not yours."

"And you're my business," she argued, glowering at me.

"Awkward."

Everyone stopped talking and looked at me.

I blanched. "Did I say that out loud?"

Cole nodded, shaking with amusement.

Joss, Hannah, and Liv burst into laughter and even Jo's scowl cleared as her lips twitched. I was embarrassed, but I could take the embarrassment if it meant Jo would stop prying into my situation with Cole.

To my relief, over the next few weeks, Cole never brought up "our situation." I refused to call it a relationship even though very quickly I got lost in a blissful bubble with him. His attentiveness, his consideration, his cockiness and sweetness . . . it never wavered. It appeared that that was just who he was, and I had to admit it was nice.

Okay, so it was more than nice.

Cole didn't hide his affection for me, although he still maintained a distant professionalism in front of customers, and he didn't hide that he thought we were definitely going somewhere serious and that I'd eventually come to trust him. His optimism was kind of charming.

As was his good humor and his patience and . . . and, *and, and!*

I really wished I could find some kind of fault with him. But as we spent those weeks on dates at the movies, out to dinner, drinks with friends, quiet drinks alone, hanging out at his flat, and having the hottest sex of my life, I couldn't find anything more annoying about him other than the fact that he constantly flicked the channel on the television. And sure, that *was* really annoying, but it was just that one thing.

A thing I could deal with because . . .

I was happy.

And with the happiness came the guilt.

Logan was in prison while I shacked up with a gorgeous tattoo artist.

No wonder my family still hadn't bothered to get in touch with me. I was happily living my life while my brother suffered for having tried to protect me. My sister hadn't texted me since that last text weeks ago when she asked me to confirm I was alive.

And so for the last few days the worry over what my family would think if they found out about Cole had overtaken my contentment. It didn't matter if Cole wasn't really a bad boy at all. He looked like one, and that was all that would matter to my family.

I knew Cole could sense I was in a weird place, but thankfully he put it down to the fact that he was staying at my flat for the first time. I hadn't invited him to stay with me, because secretly I liked the idea that I could leave Cole's whenever I wanted. Not that I ever did, but the control was there. If Cole stayed with me . . . well, it was just much harder to kick someone out than it was to leave. But a few days ago Cole had insisted on staying the night. We'd argued. He'd won. Now he thought I was pissed off when in actuality I was neck deep in self-recrimination.

While I cooked dinner in the kitchen, Cole was in the sitting room watching a comedy show. He was perfectly at ease here, whereas I felt like it was our first night together all over again.

"Shortcake, have you seen my phone?" he called out.

"Try the bedroom."

A few minutes later I caught sight of him out of the corner of my eye. I glanced over my shoulder to find him standing in the doorway of the kitchen, holding a piece of canvas, eyes on me. He looked confused.

My gaze flew back to the canvas.

My . . . art.

The pulse in my neck began to throb. "What are you doing?" I croaked.

Cole held up the cityscape of Edinburgh. "Is this yours? Did you do this?"

I felt sick.

Concern emanated from him as he walked toward me. "Shannon?"

I nodded, my eyes glued to the painting.

"Shannon, this is amazing." His voice was soft, low, *amazed*. "Why didn't you tell me?"

Amazing? My eyes flew up to his face. "You like it?"

Cole gave a huff of laughter. "Are you kidding me? It's brilliant."

He liked it? He liked my painting. "Are you sure?" I squeaked.

"Yes," he insisted. "As are the three others you have hidden under your bed." He placed the painting carefully on the kitchen table and then wrapped his arms around my waist, drawing me into him. "Why didn't you tell me you paint? Why is it a secret?"

I was still in shock that he liked my work.

"Shannon?"

Trembling, I released myself from his hold to return to stirring my sauce. "It's . . ."

I didn't even know how to begin to explain to him.

Cole's chest pressed against my back as he leaned past me to turn the hob off. "Dinner can wait." He gently took my hand in his and led me to the bedroom. While I stood in the doorway he got down on his knees and pulled out all of my hidden artwork. He put the pile of sketch pads on the bed. "May I?"

Heart racing again, I nodded.

Cole began to flick through my work. After a few minutes he sat back on the bed and stared up at me. I didn't know what his expression meant. "I feel like I don't know you," he said softly, touching a sketch of my brother, Logan. "This is clearly a big part of you . . ."

It was only then I realized how stiff I was holding myself, my muscles coiled tight with tension. I released my hands from the fists I had them clenched in and tentatively made my way over to the bed. I brushed my fingers over the sketch of Logan. "He was the only one that ever encouraged my artwork. After Granddad passed and then Gran . . . I only had Logan."

"This is your brother?"

I nodded. "I used to love sketching people. I'm more into semiabstract landscapes now." I looked over at the acrylic paintings Cole had leaned against my wall. "I'd never painted until I moved here."

I flushed with pleasure at the surprise on his face. "You wouldn't know it."

"You really think I'm good?"

"Good?" Cole shook his head, bewildered. "Shannon, you're a beautiful artist. Why . . . why have you never pursued it?"

With his praise ringing in my ears I had to duck my head to avoid his gaze. I didn't want him to know how much that meant to me, or how it made me want to dive on him and kiss him all over. "After high school I decided not to go to uni like all my friends. I wanted to have some life experience, work experience. The plan was to defer for two years and then apply for art school." I sighed, a million regrets weighing on my chest. "Somehow I let it slip away from me. It was easier to have a job and some money and a relationship than it was to think about studying and getting into debt. But then I got a little bit older and I realized I wasn't happy. Being creative made me happy and I wanted it to be a real part of my life." I looked up at Cole and he flinched at the anger in my eyes. My words sounded brittle to my own ears. "When I decided I wanted to apply for art school I was with Ollie. He'd find my sketches lying around and he would mock and belittle them. He told me over and over and over again that I wasn't good enough, that I wasn't talented . . . and I let myself believe the son of a bitch."

"I hope I never find him, Shannon." Cole's voice was rough, his own anger scraping against the words. "Because I'll fucking finish what Logan started."

"Don't say that." I reached for his hand and he curled his fingers around mine. "He's not worth it."

"He's not worth this either," Cole snapped. "Hiding your talent under your bed like it's something to be ashamed of." His eyes blazed into mine. "He knew you were too good for him and that one day you would wake up and realize it too. So he did his best to make you feel small and worthless—to make you feel lucky to be with him, when the truth was the exact opposite."

"Cole . . ."

"This." He grabbed up a sketch pad. "Is out in the open from now on, and if you want to go to art school we'll find a way for that to happen. I'm still in contact with some of my professors from Edinburgh— I do special workshops every year there about tattoo art. We'll find a way," he promised. "If that's what you want."

So many feelings filled my chest that I was breathless. I stared at Cole in wonder. "Are you real, Cole Walker?"

He gave me this small half smile. "It's funny. Every day I look at you and ask myself if *you're* real."

"Don't." I squeezed his hand. "You'll make me cry."

"I want to know everything."

"Everything?"

The muscle in his jaw flexed. "About the others. Your exes."

Alarmed, I pulled out of his grasp. "Why?"

The determination in his eyes only grew more intense at my withdrawal. "Because I need to know what I'm dealing with. I need to know what they've done to you."

"No." I shook my head, ready for retreat. "You *want* to know, and I'm not sure I'm up for that discussion."

Cole removed my sketch pads, laying them gently on the floor like they were precious works of art, and then he moved closer to me on the bed. His fingers wrapped around my wrist and he tugged me toward him until my hip rested against his. "I *need* to know." He brushed his knuckles across my cheekbone as he stared deep into my eyes. "I need to know so I can try to reverse all the damage they've done."

My eyes and nose burned as his words prodded too closely at my raw emotions. "If you knew . . ." I shook my head, trying to pull away, but he wouldn't let me. "Cole." I tried to firm up my voice, but he held on tighter. "If you knew you'd know what an idiot I've been. You'll look at me differently."

"I won't."

"You will."

"Shannon." He gripped my chin tightly and I knew he was losing patience with my admittedly low assessment of not only myself but him. "I won't."

I tugged my chin from his grasp to look away, but I didn't retreat. I gave in. At some point he was going to find out. It had always only been a matter of time. "My first boyfriend was Ewan. The guy that picked me up that day on Scotland Street. His was a typical desertion and it didn't leave much of a scar. But Nick was next and his definitely did." I drew in a bolstering breath. "He was the first guy I had sex with. I thought I loved him." I rolled my eyes at my naïveté. "He was in a rock band. He was good-looking and too charming for his own good. He told me he loved me the night before I caught him screwing a blonde in a closet at one of his gigs."

I felt Cole's fingers dig into my waist and when I looked at him I saw turmoil in his gaze.

He hurt for me.

Something . . . something *big* lurched in my chest.

I wanted to wrap my arms around him and never let go, and yet at the same time I wanted to run in the opposite direction from this man who seemed too good to be true.

"I didn't learn my lesson," I continued, my voice now hoarse—affected by the events of the past and present. "A year or so later I started dating Bruce. He was a biker—everyone called him Bear because he was huge. He was really taken with me. At first." I smiled unhappily. "My size made him feel protective and powerful at the same time. He was always telling me how cute and sexy I was, how funny, how smart, how lovable. He was full of compliments. So it didn't matter to me that he was a fun-loving biker ten years my senior. I fell for him. He got me a job working in his best friend's tattoo studio and we dated for eighteen months.

"The last four of those he spent screwing a real honest-to-goodness biker babe behind my back. He decided she was more his speed, so he dumped me and he also made his best friend fire me."

Cole looked ready to kill someone.

"Are you sure you want me to continue?"

He nodded, his mood rapidly growing darker before my eyes.

For me . . . well, I'd thought it would be harder revealing all this to Cole. I'd gotten over my past grievances until Ollie, and these last few months the memories of what I'd allowed to happen to me had burned in my gut like acid. Yet sitting there with Cole, I realized that somehow over the past few weeks that bitterness had begun to fade.

I tensed at the realization.

I was allowing myself to forget because of Cole.

Don't be stupid again—you need to remember, to keep your guard up. It's when you feel safe that they hurt you. Every. Time.

Instinctually I attempted to pull away from Cole, but his hold on my waist tightened.

I exhaled, so confused, so unbelievably mixed up by all of the emotions churning through me. I should be terrified of Cole and yet . . .

"Fine," I continued. "Then there was Rory. We were only together a few months before I started to notice that money kept going missing from my purse. Eventually I discovered Rory was stealing from me even though he had a lucrative side business as a drug dealer. I then found out he was an ex-con. I got the hell out of there and went running right into the arms of dear Ollie. And you know all about him."

After a few seconds of loaded silence Cole said, "That's just a series of bad luck, Shannon."

This time I did pull away, jumping off the bed with an exasperated grunt. "Bad luck? No, Cole, that's having terrible taste in men."

"Present company excluded," he grumbled, getting up off the bed.

"Don't," I snapped, turning on my heel and heading back to the kitchen to finish making dinner.

"Don't what?" He followed.

"Be boyish and charming."

"That's kind of hard. I *am* boyish and charming."

I huffed and was just about to turn on the hob when his strong arms encircled me and I found myself up in the air. I landed on Cole's shoulder with a gasp. "What are you doing?"

"Taking you to bed. Dinner can wait." He patted my bottom and started striding back toward the bedroom.

"Let me down," I growled.

"Nope. First: Looking at your gorgeous artwork gave me a serious hard-on. I do love a talented woman." He stroked my bottom before dropping me on the bed. I stared up at him, wondering how we went from heartfelt confessions, messy confusion, and irate irritation to this.

My eyes dropped to his hands as he began unzipping his jeans. "Second, I'm going to fuck every bad memory of those unworthy gits out of you, even if it takes me a lifetime. Starting tonight."

My mouth dropped open at the lifetime comment. "Cole—"

"Be quiet, Shortcake," he murmured, crawling up the bed until he was straddling me. "Anything you say will only make me more determined."

I shot awake, my heart pounding so hard it was all I could hear. Sweat slickened my skin and I panted for air.

As my eyes adjusted to the dark, I saw I was in my bedroom. Cole was sleeping beside me. He was exhausted after spending the entire evening screwing my brains out. I'd been exhausted too. That was why I'd fallen asleep as soon as my head hit the pillow.

But the nightmare had returned.

I hadn't had it for weeks. Since I'd started seeing Cole.

I swallowed hard, running a trembling hand through my damp hair. It must have been all that talk about my exes that had spurred its return.

I had no idea what to do.

Things seemed and felt good with Cole, but hadn't they with all the others before it went bad? I should leave him. I should . . .

Taking my time, breathing in and out, I felt my heart starting to slow, and that was when I heard a familiar grunt followed by a low wheeze. Slowly the grunts got louder and the wheeze grew higher until it was more of a squeal.

Cole shifted beside me and groaned. His eyes opened reluctantly and he squinted up at me. "What the fuck is that?" he said, his voice hoarse from sleep.

I snorted and lay back down. "That's Rae and Mike."

The look of horror on his sleepy face was so comical I burst out laughing.

The grunting and squealing immediately stopped. Something pounded against the wall between Rae's and my room. "Shut the fuck up!" her muffled shout echoed through.

That set us both off. I snuggled into Cole, burying my giggles in his throat as he shook with his own choked laughter.

And just like that, my nightmare and worries were temporarily forgotten.

CHAPTER 16

At the press of a gentle touch on my lower back, I found myself inhaling the scent of Cole's cologne.

"I thought you could come over to my place tonight once I finish up at judo," he murmured in my ear.

I moved away from him, bending my head closer to the file I was working on. I'd almost completed the digitization of Stu's filing system. If I didn't have to endure too many distractions, I would be finished in a week or so. Cole didn't take my "I'm busy. I don't want you touching me" hint. The studio was quiet, and there was no one around to witness him crowding me against the reception desk.

"Shannon," he said, his voice a warning as his fingers gripped my hips.

I ignored the flush of arousal I felt at his touch. In fact, I was trying to ignore everything about him these days.

True to his word, Cole contacted a tutor at the College of Art inquiring about my chances of being accepted into a BA degree course for painting. She was kind enough to send me information on the kind of portfolio I'd need to put together for submission into the program as well as information on the student loan system. I was going to miss the deadline for that year, but after discussing it with Cole and being infected by his enthusiasm, I decided I was going to work on a portfolio over the next nine months that I would use, along with my high school qualifications, to apply for admission into next year's program.

Cole also outed me to Rae and Simon, and Rae insisted I use the sitting room to work in since there was more space and we had the view from the balcony. I was blown away by all their support, but mostly by Cole, who seemed more than determined to erase all the negativity Ollie had left me with.

His seeming dedication to making me happy scared the utter crap out of me. That was why when most girlfriends—*not* that I was his girlfriend—would be lavishing gratitude and affection on him, I grew distant. It wasn't even intentional. The need to protect myself was instinctual. At first I didn't even realize I was doing it.

It started with little things . . . like not meeting his eyes when we were talking at work and finding ways to let go of his hand whenever he reached for mine. Then I began to make excuses not to go home with him, and for him not to come home with me. Two nights a week he went to judo, and another two he went to kickboxing. In the past I'd meet him at his place after he'd finished up, but now I was using the classes as an excuse for us to spend the nights apart.

Cole had been patient.

I didn't know how long that was going to last. There was a possibility that his patience had just snapped.

"I'm working on the Royal Mile piece right now." I hurried to excuse myself from his company that evening. "Another time."

"Rae says you've finished it."

Dammit, Rae.

"Well . . . I'm tired because of it. I think I'll just have a quiet night in tonight." I tensed, waiting for his reaction.

His reaction was to hug me and kiss my temple. "Okay. But you've got the day off on Sunday. Simon's covering for me so I can take you to lunch at Elodie and Clark's."

Like he sensed my imminent refusal, he continued. "I've already told Elodie you're coming, so she's planned accordingly. She's also told everyone else. Hannah is really looking forward to seeing you, and Joss was hoping you would beta-read a few chapters in her new book while we're there."

I turned around in his arms and found him trying to quell a smirk. He'd completely outplayed me and he knew it. Cole grinned at my scowl and edged closer to me. My breathing stuttered at the feel of his hand on my thigh. He slid it up under my skirt, his fingertips caressing the soft skin of my inner thigh as his hand traveled higher.

"Cole," I gasped, and reached for his hand only for him to grab it with his other and press my palm against his chest.

He bent his head, bringing our bodies closer and his hand even higher up my skirt as he kissed my neck. I shivered as those kisses were scattered upward until his teeth were nibbling at my ear. "About tonight . . . ," he whispered, and his fingers dipped beneath my underwear. "Are you sure you're too tired?"

My hips jerked in surprise at the touch of his cool thumb on my clit. Heat and shock held me against him as he played with me in broad daylight in the studio. "Cole," I panted, my fingers curling around his shirt. My whole body was flushed and my thighs were trembling as I pressed my hips into his touch.

His lips brushed against mine, teasing me. "I'll take that as a 'no, I'm not too tired.'"

Senseless with want, I wrapped my hands behind his head and tugged him back down for a real kiss as my climax grew nearer.

I came with a breathless moan against his lips, my lower body jerking against him.

Cole groaned, slipping his hand out from beneath my skirt to smooth it back down. He kissed me again, his hands soothing and comforting as they glided down my waist and around my back.

Finally I came back to myself. I stiffened. I'd just let him bring me to orgasm in a public place and I hadn't done anything to stop him. Honestly I'd been mindless to have him.

So much for distancing myself from him. Or making up my mind about what I wanted.

I was such a mess.

Settling the last page on the small pile of chapters, I looked up at Joss, who was sitting at a dressing table in the corner. We were in the nursery at Elodie and Clark Nichols's house and Joss had been waiting impatiently as I read through the first three chapters of her latest manuscript.

"I know it's different from anything I've ever done before."

"Yes." I nodded seriously. Then I grinned. "But I love it."

Joss stood up, her gray eyes hard to read. "Really?"

"Definitely." I handed her the chapters. "It's still got your signature style—the dark humor, the earthiness, the somehow unsentimental sentiment. But you've added action and mystery and grit and intrigue. I love it. I can't wait to read the rest."

A slow, pleased smile lit up Joss's face. "Well, I have to write it first. I just wanted a reader's opinion before I continue any further—someone I can trust. Cole said I could definitely trust you."

I flushed inwardly at Cole's praise. Sometimes he made me feel guilty as sin for not trusting him in return. *Huh, sometimes? Try all the time.*

"Thanks for trusting me."

And as if she read my mind, Joss smirked. "Maybe you could try trusting Cole."

"Did he say something?" I could feel myself bristling inwardly. My business was my business. It wasn't for Cole to be telling people.

"Not much. But he finds himself surrounded by a lot of women who have adored him since he was a kid, so we tend to get a bit nosy and all up in his business." She grinned, like it was funny or something. I didn't really agree. "We managed to find out what I already suspected: You don't trust him because of a bad breakup."

Slowly the tension eased out of me. "But that's all he said?"

"Yeah, no details from Cole. He wouldn't do that to you. I'm not dumb, however, Shannon. I know bad in your case means *bad*." She gave my shoulder a comforting squeeze. "But you can trust Cole. He cares about you."

I didn't respond, because I didn't know what to say. My chest began to ache as we walked downstairs and the sounds of laughter and conversation hit our ears. Cole deserved to be with someone who could not only trust him but give herself to him the way that he was willing to give himself in return.

Oh God.

Was it time already? Did I need to walk away?

Feeling sick at the thought, I found it took everything within me to smile at Cole as Joss led me into the dining room. The place was a crush with one large dining table and a smaller one at the end of the room where the kids were sitting. Apparently I was visiting on one of the rare days that everyone was free for Sunday lunch.

Cole tucked me in beside him and I had Hannah and Sophia on my other side. Somehow Elodie miraculously managed to get food in front of everyone.

"Nate, tell them the what-if story." Liv chuckled at her husband.

Nate smiled across the room and I followed his gaze. His and Liv's daughter, Lily, a dark-haired beauty around the age of seven, was giggling with her sister, January, and Joss and Braden's daughter, Beth. Seeing her occupied, Nate nodded.

Liv looked at me. "We just got back from a weekend break in Argyll."

"So we're in Dunoon," Nate explained. "Liv's on the docks with January because Jan's still a bit afraid of water. So I take Lily out on a rowing boat on the loch to teach her to fish. And Lily is going through her what-if phase."

"What's a what-if phase?" I asked.

"The what-if phase," Braden said, "is a phase most kids go through. All day, every day, for what feels like months, they ask what-if questions."

I laughed and nodded at Nate to continue.

"So Lily and I are on the boat and she's asking me a ton of questions and I'm trying to answer them as patiently as possible. 'Dad,' she said, 'what if we don't catch any fish?' 'Then there will be one more fish in the loch.' 'Dad, what if we lose an oar?' 'Then I'll use the one we have left to get us back to the docks.' 'Dad, what if we lose both oars?' 'Then we'll paddle back with our hands.' 'Dad, what if a boat came?' 'Then we'd get out of the way.' 'What if it was really close?' 'We'd get out of the way really fast.' 'Dad, what if you didn't see the boat?' And by now I'm losing my patience. 'Lily,' I said, 'I thought you wanted to learn how to fish. Why all the boat questions?' 'Because, Dad, there's a big boat behind you.' I look over my shoulder and the Dunoon ferry is right there!"

We all burst out laughing as Nate starts gesturing with his hands. "I start rowing like hell to get us out of the way and Lily's just sitting there calm as you please."

Shaking with laughter against Cole's side, I could tell the parents at the table totally got the conversation. I didn't think I'd ever gone through a what-if phase as a child. My parents weren't big conversationalists, so I probably didn't even bother to ask.

Olivia was wiping tears of laughter from her eyes, probably having heard the story too many times to count, and still finding it hilarious.

"Well, since you're sitting here today we can safely assume you and Lily made it out of the way," Joss said dryly.

"Just. Alive by the skin of our teeth because my daughter is a smart-arse just like her mother."

Liv shrugged. "I can't help it if she inherited my wonderful sense of humor."

Our chuckles were interrupted by a loud clatter at the end of the table.

Elodie was gripping her arm in pain, her eyes wide with shock, her face sallow and glistening with sweat.

"Elodie." Braden, who was closest to her, pushed out of his chair at the same time Clark started hurrying to get to her from the other side of the room.

A deep unease settled in my gut as we watched on as Braden and Clark questioned her.

She sank into their hold, seeming unable to talk through the pain.

"Call an ambulance," Braden barked, but Marco was already on his phone.

Stunned, I looked up at Cole. He was staring at Elodie with panic in his eyes, his own face pale.

Jo was suddenly at his side, her hand gripping his tightly.

A grim pall hung in the air in Cole's flat. He lay on his bed, staring up at the ceiling while I lay by his side not knowing what to say.

The paramedics had taken Elodie to the hospital; her husband, Hannah, Declan, Ellie, Braden, and their partners and kids took off after them. The kids were crying because they knew something bad had happened, and their parents were trying to keep it together for their sake.

The rest of us were left behind.

Cole was silent.

He was silent when Jo suggested we go home and she'd contact us with any news. He was silent all the way to his flat in the taxi. He'd been silent for the last fifteen minutes.

I'd known he was close to the Nicholses; I just hadn't realized the depth of his attachment until now. He was frightened for Elodie and I knew I couldn't ease those fears even if I tried.

"Can I get you anything?"

He shook his head.

"She'll be okay," I whispered, hoping I was right.

"You don't know that," he replied. "My mum had a heart attack. She didn't make it."

"Elodie's not your mum."

"Yeah," he snorted, sounding bitter. "I know that. That's why this is fucking worse."

Not understanding I whispered his name in question.

His green eyes found mine and I flinched at the pain in them. My hand automatically reached for his. "Elodie Nichols is everything my mother never was. A real mum. A great mum. Kind and compassionate. Loyal. She adds people to her family like it's something everyone does, like it's no big deal to open your home to a stranger."

Seeing the tears in his eyes, I felt a thickness in my throat, and answering tears burned in my own eyes. "What was your mum like?" I wasn't sure I wanted to know, but I definitely knew I *needed* to know.

He exhaled heavily and turned to look back up at the ceiling. "Selfish. Bitter. A drunk."

I squeezed his hand tighter, and his fingers bit into my skin in response.

"Growing up, she was never there for me. Jo always took care of me, making sure I was washed and clothed and fed. Making sure I had everything I needed for school. Mum's drinking got gradually worse, especially when we moved from Glasgow to Edinburgh."

"You're from Glasgow?" I said, surprised.

He nodded. "I don't remember my dad. He was put away for armed robbery when I was about two. I did know he wasn't a nice guy, because as I got older I finally got some attention from my mum. But not good attention."

I felt sick suddenly.

"I was about thirteen, nearly fourteen, and I looked a lot older. I was as tall as Jo by the time I was fourteen." He shot me a sad grin. "I was a total geek. Didn't go anywhere unless it was to my mate's house to play video games or work on the comics we created."

I smiled. "You sound adorable."

"I was really shy." His smile slipped. "I was worried all the time. Jo worked her arse off trying to make ends meet because our mum was a bedridden alcoholic by this point. We were always picking her up off the kitchen floor, cleaning up her vomit . . . Anyway, Jo tried to protect me, but that just made me worry about how much pressure she was under. And she was always dating these men that had money and I knew why. I just felt like shit . . . I wished I was older so I could help, you know."

I reached over and stroked his cheek, fighting tears of compassion.

"We had all this going on and other kids my age just seemed so immature. It made me isolate myself a bit until I was pretty socially awkward."

"I can't even imagine that." I swear my heart clenched in my chest for him.

"It didn't help that Mum had gotten abusive. I tried to hide it from Jo because I didn't want her to have to deal with it . . . and I was ashamed."

I couldn't stop the tears now. "Cole?"

He looked at me, countenance grim. "She said I was like him. My dad. That I was worthless, that I was nothing. And she'd hit me. Not once did I hit her back, though. I wasn't like him. I was never going to be like him."

I swallowed a sob of compassion and guilt. "And I said . . . I said that—"

"Shh." Cole frowned and wrapped his arms around me. I buried my face in his throat and started to cry for everything he'd been through and for what I'd put him through. "Sweetheart, shh, you're killing me here."

"I'm sorry," I hiccupped, desperately attempting to control myself.

He rubbed my back. "Put that out of your mind. For good."

"I didn't mean it."

"I know." He eased me back so I could see the truth in his eyes.

"Shannon, I *know*. It's not the same, but I get what it's like to have someone that's supposed to love you make you feel small and worthless. To have them hurt you with careless violence. I *know*. And that means I know exactly why you have your defenses up so high." He brushed my tears with his thumb. "You're a good person. You are nothing like her. She made it really difficult to love her, and she left me with a whole lot of guilt about that."

I sniffled. "Did Jo find out? About her hitting you."

"Actually Cam did. He was our neighbor. He found out and told Jo. Well, he thought Jo knew and he gave her a rollicking about it and devastated her, so I gave *him* a rollicking and he worked his arse off to make it up to her. He changed everything for us. We owe him a lot."

"And your dad?"

Cole's face darkened. "He used to beat up Jo when she was a kid. Mick found out and beat the shit out of him and he left. Not long after, he ended up in prison." His hand tightened on my waist. "He came back when I fourteen. He was trying to blackmail Jo. Said that if she didn't give him money he would come for me, take me away."

"Oh my God."

"Jo tried to keep him from me, tried so hard he got her alone and attacked her as a warning that time was running out."

There were no words for how shocked I was by all these revelations. I would never have known there was this much darkness in Cole's past. "She really loves you," I whispered, tearing up again but this time with gratitude and respect for Cole's sister.

"Oh yeah." He grinned, but I could see the overwhelming emotion in his eyes. "She's a warrior when it comes to me. Always has been. Belle is the luckiest little girl in the world."

I smiled in agreement before forcing myself to ask, "What happened with your dad?"

"Jo went to Joss and Braden. Braden rounded up Cam and Mick and the three of them took care of it. I didn't ask and I don't want to know what happened. All I know is that they protected us and we've never heard from that man again."

He turned suddenly so he was leaning over me, his eyes blazing with passion that held me rooted, frozen beneath him. With trembling hands he brushed my hair from my face. "That's why you have to know that I won't ever hurt you like that. Ever. You have to believe that, Shannon." He leaned down, his lips hovering over mine, and his next words were whispered across my mouth in a plea. "Please believe that."

Staring up into his gorgeous face and his kind eyes, I felt the memories of the last weeks assaulting me. His patience, his kindness, his compassion, his steadfastness . . . all of it was so much bigger than the hot, cocky, confident tattooist the rest of the world saw.

And like with a hit to the chest, I was winded by the realization that I did believe him.

I believed him.

Scared but needing to reassure him more than I needed to assure myself, I slid my hands around his neck and pressed my mouth against his for a slow, sweet kiss. When I broke it, I stared him straight in the eye and said with a fierceness that surprised even me, "You are not nothing. You are wonderful. Everyone who meets you can't help adoring you—"

"Shannon—"

"You inspire loyalty in people for a reason, Cole, and your mother was the one that lost out here. She missed out on loving a really, really cool kid." I smiled through my tears. "And a smart, good man. Don't feel guilty because you feel more for Elodie Nichols than you did for your mother. Elodie deserves your love. By all accounts your mum never did."

He shuddered against me, burying his face in my neck and wrapping his arms tight around me.

I held on to him, pouring my love into him, despite all my fears screaming at me not to. "I believe you, Cole," I whispered. "I believe you."

Somehow he managed to press his body even closer to me in answer.

CHAPTER 17

I awakened, taking in Cole blearily as he sat up in bed. "Any news?"

The worry in his voice brought me fully into consciousness, the emotional saga of the day hitting me in the chest. The sound of Cole's phone ringing had woken us both. I shuffled into a sitting position, glancing at his bedside clock. It was eleven o'clock at night. After he had confided in me about his family history, I managed to convince him to eat something. Then we'd both curled up on his bed again and fallen asleep.

"But she's okay?" he whispered into his phone. I wrapped my arm around him. Cole slid his free arm around my shoulders and hugged me close. I felt his muscles tense. He was silent as the person on the other end of the line answered. "Okay . . . yeah. Thanks, Jo. Speak soon . . . Yeah, you too." He hung up and glanced down at me.

"That was good news?"

He exhaled. "Elodie had a heart attack."

"Oh God." I gripped his arm tighter.

"It's okay." He clasped my hand. "They did something . . . angioplasty? It removed a blockage. There's not too much damage to her heart, so they think she's going to be okay."

I was relieved for Elodie, and for Cole and the rest of the family. I hadn't been around them all a lot, but it didn't take a genius to realize Elodie was the matriarch of their tribe. "That's good news."

He nodded, but the melancholy that had been entrenched in his gaze earlier that day remained. Staring into his gorgeous, soulful eyes, I was overwhelmed by my need to make him happy.

Easing myself over him until I straddled him, I grasped his face in my hands and pressed a soft kiss to his mouth. "It's moments like these that remind us just how fleeting it all is." My hand dropped to his right arm and I caressed the eagle and the pocket watch with my fingertips. "I grew up listening to music, reading books, and watching films that all kept telling me how much we take time for granted. The warning started to lose meaning. And unfortunately it's only ever when we're faced with our own mortality that we remember that the world is telling us 'life is short' because it's the truth." I looked deep into his eyes and felt that connection between us reach out and plunge straight into my chest. I felt breathless, a little light-headed. Scared. "I can't make promises to you, Cole. Not yet. I really wish I could. But I can try to get there. I want to try to make this work." I smiled, feeling shy and overwhelmed. "I want this to be a relationship."

Something brightened in Cole's eyes, pushing back at the melancholy. He smoothed his hands up my spine, drawing me closer. "Are you saying you want to be my girlfriend?" His voice was gruff, almost teasing.

I leaned into him and whispered against lips, "Are you saying you want me to be your girlfriend?"

"Fuck yeah," he whispered back, and pressed his mouth to mine.

Although Cole said he wanted me to come with him when he visited Elodie in the hospital, I convinced him otherwise. It wasn't because I didn't want to support him or show Elodie I was thinking of her. It was because I didn't feel it was my place yet. I barely knew Elodie, and her heart attack had dredged up so much for Cole. I thought it would be better for him to have some time alone with her.

He visited the hospital the next evening carrying a bouquet of flowers I'd chosen.

Seeing Elodie for himself, getting reassurance that she was going to be all right, took away the grim aspect that had crept into Cole, and as soon as he returned from the hospital to his flat where I was waiting for him, I felt the immediate uplifted change in him. Cole was back to himself again except *more*. He was even happier than before and I was giddy yet equally terrified that this was because I'd promised to try something serious with him.

I didn't intend to let that fear control me, however, and I threw myself with a weird kind of trepidation wholly into this new stage of our relationship. It was in my nature to be openly affectionate with a partner, and so with some difficulty I let that part of me out.

I liked hugs and kisses and holding hands.

Thankfully Cole seemed to like all those things too and he went with the change in my behavior without saying a word.

On Wednesday during lunch break we'd locked ourselves in his room and gotten up to no good on his tattoo chair. I was still all hot and bothered a few hours later when he came out of the room with a customer and approached the desk to pay.

"That's sixty pounds, please," I said to the tall, lanky guy who had so many tattoos I was surprised they'd found space for a new one.

The guy grinned at me and handed me his card.

As I processed the payment Cole said, "I promised Hannah I'd watch Sophia tomorrow, but I want you at my place for dinner at eight p.m."

I quirked an eyebrow. "Was there a question in there?"

He smoldered. "*Please* will you join me for dinner, Shannon?"

Oh boy.

I nodded in acquiescence.

"Dude, she's yours?" the customer asked Cole, who didn't deign to answer. "Dude!" The guy nudged Cole in the elbow in a "you da man" kind of way.

Cole stared at him blankly.

His customer faltered, his cheekiness disappearing as he tried to shrug on some cool. "I mean, I'm just saying." His eyes flicked to me and then back to Cole. "She's hot," he ended on a whisper.

Cole continued to stare at him blankly.

"Right . . . okay." The guy took his card and receipt from me. "I'll just . . ." He gave an awkward wave and scurried out of the studio.

I leaned my elbow on the counter, my chin resting on the heel of my palm. "You deliberately intimidated him."

My boyfriend gave a lazy shrug before bending down to kiss me. "You're not some chick I picked up at an American frat house," he offered as an explanation to his rudeness. I was clearly dating a gentleman.

Pleased, I smiled.

"Tomorrow. Eight o'clock."

"Tomorrow," I promised.

. . .

In hindsight the urgent and sudden need I had to take back some of the control I felt I'd lost to Cole was borne from misunderstanding.

I'd gone shopping for something that I hoped would make Cole lose sense and thus perhaps give me back part of the control I felt I was missing.

"I had plans," Cole said, following me down the hall toward his room. "But if you want to jump right into dessert, I'm good with that."

It was eight o'clock and I definitely wanted to jump straight into dessert.

I turned around and faced him, drinking in the sight of him. I shivered with anticipation of what was to come. Cole was wearing a simple black T-shirt and jeans. He was barefoot. Effortlessly sexy. He just lived and breathed sexiness.

I, however, had to try a little harder.

The tingling began between my legs as soon as I whipped off my shirt and threw it across the room.

Cole's eyes grew hooded at the sight of me in the emerald green silk and lace bra I'd bought just for the occasion.

I grinned wickedly. "There's more."

"Do go on," he said, voice thick.

Slowly I kicked off my heels and then I unzipped my pencil skirt. I shimmied out of it, revealing the matching silk and lace knickers that were cut high across my butt cheeks. The icing on the cake was something I rarely wore.

Black suspenders and stockings.

Cole's lips parted as I stepped out of my skirt and leisurely turned, my hair skimming my lower back just above the black dragon tattoo.

I arched my back so my bottom stuck out in blatant invitation. Glancing over my shoulder, I noted his cock straining against his zipper. I smiled. "Do you like?"

His chest rose and fell quickly. "Do I like?" he said, his voice rough.

I turned back to face him and caressed my breasts. "I got it especially for you."

In answer, Cole tugged his T-shirt off, his muscles rippling with the force of the moment. I gave myself an inward high five in triumph.

"Turn and face the wall." The hard, authoritative words caught me off guard.

"What?" I whispered, uncertain but at the same time turned on by the demand.

"Turn and face the wall."

I did.

"Brace your hands on the wall and arch your back."

My lower belly flipped, hard, and as I leaned over to do as he said, I felt the slickness of my arousal between my legs.

"Cole?"

I heard him approach and then his heat hit me seconds before he touched me. He caressed the skin revealed by the high cut of the underwear and then trailed his fingertips down and under them. They slid inside me and I gasped, pushing back against the wonderful intrusion.

"You're soaked," he said hoarsely.

I moaned and pressed my hands against the wall to push harder against the thrust of his fingers. "Cole, please."

He slipped them out of me and grasped my hips. The coarse roughness of a denim-covered erection rubbed against my bottom. "Is this what you want?"

There went my control. But I didn't feel too badly about that, because I knew Cole was seconds away from losing his grasp on his. "Yes," I whimpered.

The only sounds in the room were heavy breathing and the sound of a zipper. And then the shuffle of his jeans falling to his ankles, followed by the crinkle of a condom wrapper. My inner thighs trembled.

His large hands caressed my bottom, shifting to grab hold of my slender hips. "Spread your legs."

I felt another deep flip in my belly and I did as I was told.

"Oh God!" I threw my head back, my hands slipping on the wall as Cole thrust into me. His hips stilled, but he slid in deeper as he leaned over to readjust my hands on the wall. I bowed my head, my hair falling around my face, and I stared at the floor, aware of nothing but the feel of him surrounding me, pulsing inside me. Callused hands coasted down my arms and around my ribs and gently pushed up my bra.

Cool air tightened my already pebbled nipples, and my breasts swelled into Cole's hands as he cupped me.

He kissed my shoulder, brushing his thumbs over my nipples.

He pulled back and then glided in, sparking heat and sensation down all my limbs.

I trembled, holding on for dear life as he pumped in and out of me in increasingly hurried strokes. Sharp arousal shot down my belly as Cole pinched and played with my nipples.

"Come for me, Shannon," he groaned, his hips jerking harder against me.

I braced my legs and steadied my hands on the wall and I moved back into his thrusts.

"Fuck." He moved one hand to my hip, his fingers bruising the skin there as he increased the speed of his strokes.

It was coming. The tension inside me hit its breaking point and I froze.

"Yes, yes," he grunted, sliding his hand up my spine. "Come, Shannon, come."

On cue the tension split apart and I cried out in release as my sex convulsed around his cock.

"Oh, oh . . . oh . . ." Cole stilled. "F-f-fuck." He shuddered against me as he came.

I slumped against the wall, panting for breath, and Cole pressed in on me, his hands now on the wall beside me. His heavy breaths puffed against my back as he leaned his forehead on my shoulder.

"I guess that means you liked the underwear," I murmured drowsily.

His body shook with gentle laughter. "Good guess."

I realized then that yes, Cole might have more confidence in us as a couple, in our ability to pursue a relationship, but that didn't mean he was taking control from me. If anything we were both at the mercy of each other. That, I could deal with. I think I could deal with anything as long as we were always on equal footing.

CHAPTER 18

"Your next appointment has arrived."

Cole looked up from the folios on his desk. He smiled at the sight of me clinging to the doorframe. "Don't run off." He gestured for me to come inside.

"What is it?" My eyes were drawn to his artwork as I strode into his workroom.

"I want to ask you something." He startled me by hauling me into his arms.

I gripped at his biceps and laughed in surprise. "What are you doing?"

Cole's green eyes glittered. "Kissing you." And then he was.

Reluctantly I pulled back. "We can't do that here," I admonished. "You have a very busy schedule, Cole Walker."

His answer was to run his nose along my jaw and squeeze my

waist. "I know," he groaned. "But I can't get the taste of you off my tongue. It's driving me nuts."

I giggled and pushed him away. "Then stop kissing me."

With a wolfish grin Cole shook his head. "Not a fucking chance."

Pleased, I smiled. "Then at least have some willpower. Come on, your client awaits."

I had to stifle my laughter as he followed me with a comical, petulant twist to his lips. Out in the studio I led him to the waiting area where a tall, slender brunette with lip and eyebrow piercings was waiting for him. She lit up at the sight of Cole and I determinedly squashed my annoyance at her hungry eyes.

"This is Renee. Renee, this is Cole."

"Hi, Renee." Cole held out his hand congenially as the young woman stood up to shake it.

"Well, hello there," she flirted.

I tensed.

At this point I'd usually return to behind my desk and let Cole get on with it, but I was too busy being nosy as well as trying to lock down my possessiveness.

Cole ignored her flirtation, keeping his face perfectly blank. "Do you have any idea what you're after or would you like to look through my portfolio?"

Renee pulled out a folded-up piece of paper and handed it to him. I craned my neck to have a look as Cole unfolded it. A flamingo. Renee shrugged at Cole's curious look. "My friend drew it for me. I've got a thing for *Alice in Wonderland* and I thought this was a subtle way to go." She took a step closer and slid a hand provocatively over her stomach and hipbone. "I want it on my hip. Right here."

Oh, great. So she'd have her trousers half off.

Cole slanted me a look out of the corner of my eye, and he must have caught wind of my annoyance, because his lips twitched as though he thought this was funny.

I turned away in a huff and busied myself behind the reception desk, ignoring them as Cole led her into his room.

I rolled my eyes when I heard her very loud exclamation, "Oh, that's the biggest gun I've ever seen."

Was she kidding with that crap?

Infuriated, I could barely concentrate on my work. This was something I knew I needed to get used to. Cole was good-looking. Women were going to come on to him. I had to learn to deal with it.

"Are you sure you're okay? You look a bit queasy," I heard Simon say as he entered the studio.

I glanced up to see him leading a young woman toward me and she did indeed look very pale. She'd gotten her belly button pierced. Disappearing into the closet behind me where we'd put in a counter with a new coffeemaker we all could operate along with a fridge, I opened the latter and pulled out a piece of chocolate from my stash.

"Shannon, Jen here is ready to pay up."

I smiled at her and handed her some chocolate. "That might help."

Her fingers trembled as she took it from me. "Thanks."

After she paid I watched as Simon, ever the gentleman, walked her to the door. He offered to let her sit in our waiting area until she felt better, but she seemed adamant to get gone. Once the door shut behind her he turned to me with a sigh. "That reaction seemed to come out of nowhere. She's got her nose and ears pierced and never had a problem with it."

"She'll be fine."

Simon leaned over my desk. "Any chance I could nick a bit of chocolate?"

Grinning at the boyish look he gave me, I retrieved chocolate for both of us. Simon finished eating his piece, watching me as I chewed on mine.

Finally he said, "So, any chance you and Cole will be coming out from the lovers' nest to join the rest of the world again? Tony misses you both."

It was true for the last two weeks Cole and I had been a little pre-occupied with each other. We'd moved into a new stage in our relation-ship, though, and admittedly we were both a little addicted. At least, I assumed Cole was as addicted as I was.

I frowned, thinking about the flirty, cocky brunette he was right now putting his ink on. "Drinks this Friday?"

"Not if it's a cause for annoyance." Simon gestured to my frown.

"Oh no, that's not why." I heaved a sigh and lowered my voice. "Cole's customer might as well have stripped naked on the couch and offered herself to him. She's getting a tattoo on her *hip.*"

Simon grimaced. "He gets that sometimes."

"Why are some women so blatant? They don't even think that he might have a girlfriend."

Now my friend was grinning. "And does he . . . I mean are you officially his girlfriend?"

"You know, for someone so alpha you really are a gossip queen."

"Don't avoid the question."

I hadn't actually admitted to anyone other than Cole that we were in fact in a relationship. Announcing it to the world made it seem more real. It would be so much harder to deal with the repercussions if we fell apart knowing that there would be witnesses to my stupidity if I ever turned out to be wrong about Cole.

But I wasn't wrong.

I wasn't.

"Yes, I'm his girlfriend. Happy?"

Simon chuckled. "I'm sure Cole is."

We were silent a moment, Simon scrutinizing me as I chewed my lip in thought. "Simon?"

"*Yes?*" he drawled.

"You're gay."

"You noticed that, did you?"

I smirked at his sarcasm. "Would you say you were particularly perceptive?"

"Because all gay men are clairvoyants?" He was smiling, so I knew he wasn't offended.

"No . . . I just . . . I've always thought most women were more intuitive than most men, and I was just wondering if—"

"Being gay made me more intuitive?"

"It sounds terrible when you say it like that."

"What? Like you're generalizing a whole group of people because of their sexual orientation?" he teased.

I made a face. "Forget it."

Simon tapped my nose with his finger. "Speak up, wee fairy. What's on your mind?"

Glancing over my shoulder at the door to the back hallway, I took a deep breath. "What do you think he sees in me?"

He seemed taken aback by the question, as Simon's inquisitive gaze searched mine. "Really?"

I shrugged. "You said it yourself . . . Cole's hot. Beyond hot. And he's talented and charismatic. He could have his choice of anyone."

"Can I ask you something?"

"Of course."

"Well, Cole told me all about how you two met when you were fifteen."

"Yeah?"

"Can you remember it?"

I smiled softly. "Of course."

"Do you remember feeling insecure then when he was talking to you? Did you ever ask yourself why a good-looking kid like him was interested in you?"

My brow knitted. I slumped toward Simon, my elbows on the counter, my chin resting on the palm of my hand. "No," I said quietly. "I was always a bit self-conscious of my hair and height but . . . no. I was fairly confident when I was younger."

"So why aren't you now?"

Because of Ollie.

My hands curled into fists. "For no good reason at all."

Simon covered one of my hands with his. "Good answer."

I looked up and his expression was tender.

"You know your worth, Shannon. So does Cole. Believe me."

I smiled gratefully. "You're the shit, Simon."

His eyebrows rose and he grinned. "You cursed for me?"

I laughed at how happy a swearword made him. "We really are a weird bunch, aren't we?"

He winked. "Wouldn't want us any other way."

The smell of chlorine hit me as I followed Cole into the sports center and a wave of nostalgia crashed over me. I had loved swimming when I was a kid. Every summer, during the school holidays, Logan would take Amanda and me to our local swimming pool once a week. Sometimes I managed to squeeze two trips a week out of him. My brother never abandoned us if his friends showed up, no matter how much he got teased for hanging out with his little sisters. He was always watching out for us, entertaining us.

"You okay?" Cole glanced back at me as we walked down a cream-colored tiled corridor.

"Yeah. I was just thinking if I wasn't so curious to see you in class I could have gone swimming instead. I haven't swum in ages."

He grinned. "Next time." We stopped outside gray double doors with large half-circle windowpanes. Through them we could see into a good-sized court that was being used as a training room for Cole's judo class. There were a number of people milling around inside—a few guys around Cole's age and older, a number of kids aged eight to about fifteen, and two women who looked just a little older than me. There were two faces I recognized: Cam and Nate. According to Cole this was Nate's class that he taught and it included all different skill levels. Cole's other judo class during the week was one he attended with Nate and Cole held by a sensei higher in rank than them—it was black belts only.

Cole had changed into his suit after work. It was a blue Adidas suit like Nate, Cam, and their companion wore, and Cole's belt was also black. I didn't know what any of the belt colors in the room meant, but I knew black belt was higher than the others in rank. Cole had given me a quick run-through in the car. Although my brain had been a little too preoccupied—with thoughts of Renee and women like her, the fact that my birthday was fast approaching and I still hadn't heard from my family, the fact that I desperately wanted to visit Logan but knew he didn't want to see me, and the fact that I felt guilty because Cole was making me happy while my brother rotted away in jail—to pay enough attention to remember.

It struck me that Logan would like Cole. I knew that without a doubt.

But then I threw Logan out of my thoughts because they were likely to pull me into a dark depression, and instead I looked up at my boyfriend.

Since martial arts were such a big part of Cole's life, I'd gotten a little nosy. I wanted to see what it was all about. Cole became overenthusiastic about my nosiness, assuming that my interest was due to a desire to possibly start taking instruction. He'd suggested I observe a class to see if it was something I might like to try. I was happier with Cole thinking I was curious about martial arts rather than him realizing I was just a little Cole-obsessed right now.

"Ready?"

I nodded and he pushed the door open, holding it for me as I walked into a roomful of strangers who all turned to look curiously at me. Cole dumped his gym bag in the corner and then took my hand, leading me over to Nate and Cam.

They greeted me with smiles of welcome and I relaxed a little.

"So you're here to observe." Nate grinned, giving me his dimples.

"If that's okay?"

"No problem. I'm just surprised Cole's willing to let you watch him get his arse kicked."

Cole laughed. I loved watching him laugh. Loved the way his eyes actually glittered brightly with humor, loved the crinkles around the corners of them, loved the boyish grin that always accompanied his laughter. "You're about to eat your words, old man."

Nate harrumphed. "I'll old-man you. Get in line."

An hour and a half later

"He kicked your butt."

Cole shrugged at me as he approached. Nate had just finished the class and everyone was dispersing to the changing rooms. "I let him. I was feeling charitable."

"Charitable, my arse," Nate said behind him as he grabbed his gym bag off the floor.

Cole smirked at him and turned back to me. He leaned in, smelling of fresh sweat and radiating massive amounts of heat. My lips tingled after he brushed a soft kiss over them. "I'm just going to jump in the shower. I'll meet you in reception."

I nodded and watched him walk out with Nate.

"So, does he know?"

I jerked my gaze from the door where Cole and the rest of his classmates had exited, surprised to find Cameron had stayed behind. He stood in front of me in the now-empty studio, his gym bag tossed over his shoulder. After everything Cole had told me about his past, I couldn't help feeling this strange gratitude and warmth for Cam, even though I barely knew him. "Sorry?"

"Does he know?"

"Know what?"

Cole's brother-in-law took a few steps toward me, his dark blue eyes pinning me to the spot with their intensity. "That you're in love with him."

I think my heart stopped at those words.

Cam gave me a reassuring smile. "If you haven't told him, I won't. But it's pretty obvious to me."

It was? Bizarre . . . since it wasn't to me! "Um . . ."

"It's the way you look at him."

"The way I look at him?"

Cam chuckled at my anxious tone and started walking past me. Before he did he reached out and gave my shoulder a reassuring squeeze. "It's not the end of the world, Shannon. Trust me."

Trust him?

I really wish people would stop asking me to do that.

CHAPTER 19

There was nothing quite like waking up to find that the sky was clear and it was hot outside—*wearing shorts and a T-shirt and buying ice lollies* kind of hot. Those days were a rarity even in summer, and I loved them because it was like being on holiday for a little while. Brisk, bright spring days were good too, when the sun was out but the winter was still clinging to the morning air. Those days always energized me.

Moving to Edinburgh had been like a cold, sunny spring day— here I was, awake for the first time in forever and ready to start over.

Falling for Cole was a hot summer day—like being on holiday and hoping the rain would stay away forever.

Three months ago I'd escaped Glasgow. Almost two months ago I'd started seeing Cole. And it was good. Better than good. It was a hot, hot summer—the best, most heated, and intense distraction from my past I could have asked for.

"You've done a great job," Stu praised me, slapping his hand down on my shoulder so hard I almost winced.

He was covering for Cole, who'd taken a day off because he, Cam, and Nate had tickets to some big judo tournament in Berlin. For the first time in a few weeks, I'd be spending the night alone.

Stu had just finished looking over my completed digitization of his filing system.

"Thanks." I smiled up at him.

"I'm surprised you got it done this fast. Cole can't be distracting you too much from your work," he teased.

Two months ago I would have been worried about what Stu thought of me dating his manager, but Cole had explained everything to Stu and I wasn't surprised to discover that our boss was happy for us.

"I called it as soon as you walked in the door." Stu looked smug. "I said to myself, 'Cole will like this wee fairy, no doubt about that.'"

I snorted. "How could you have known that?"

"Gut instinct. It's never steered me wrong. And then I saw you two together when I came in with Steely and I knew I was right. You can't fake that kind of chemistry. I know. My wife, Rocky, and I have been together for over thirty years. Moment I met her I just knew."

I smiled. "That is some gut instinct."

Stu winked at me before striding off toward the back hallway. "If you need me I'll be in my office."

"Your next appointment is in an hour," I reminded him.

He gave me a wave in acknowledgment and disappeared from sight.

For the next forty minutes or so I sat behind the reception, rereading one of my favorite paranormal books. I'd been interrupted only once by one of Simon's customers. Eating some of the chocolate I kept in the fridge, drinking coffee, and reading my book, I was feeling quite content. How many people had such a cushy job?

But something had to ruin my day.

And that something stepped into the studio in the form of a leggy, attractive brunette.

I jerked up straight in my seat as Tamara sashayed toward me wearing an annoying little smirk on her pretty mouth.

"You're still here," she said with condescension in her voice.

"I am." I put my book down, irritated that her appearance had sent my mood plummeting. "How can I help you?"

"You can help by getting Cole for me."

The heady heat of possessiveness gripped me and I had to give myself a couple of seconds to get a hold on it. "He's not in today."

Disappointment clouded Tamara's large dark brown eyes. "Oh. Is he back in tomorrow?"

"It's his day off tomorrow."

She smiled at that. "Great. I'll just drop by his flat, then."

"He's out of the country," I hurried to say, the thought of her anywhere near Cole's flat giving me palpitations. "He won't be back until Friday."

"Well, luckily I'm here until Saturday."

The urge to mark my territory was unfortunately too great to ignore. "Cole and I are dating," I blurted out.

Tamara's eyes raked down over what she could see of me before she muttered, "There's a surprise." She gave me a pitying look. "Don't get comfortable, sweetie. I've known Cole since he was eighteen and he's a bit of a serial monogamist. He'll get bored of you soon enough."

Uneasiness stirred inside me and I momentarily wondered if she was right. Pushing that uncertainty aside, I shrugged on a confidence I wasn't sure I felt. "You don't know him very well, then."

She curled her lip in annoyance. "I've known him for a lot longer than you. I know when he's done tasting every flavor of woman I'll be the one he ends up with."

I hid my trembling hands beneath the counter. "I thought you two were just friends."

"He's saving the best until last." She guffawed. "Do you really think a guy like Cole will end up with a short, scrawny, talentless redhead whose sole ambition in life is to be a great receptionist? No, sweetie. You're nothing. He'll fuck you until he's had his fill and then he'll dump you."

You're nothing.

Just like that my uncertainty faded away. I laughed. This woman was deluded. She clearly didn't know Cole at all.

You're nothing.

It rang in my head, but it didn't hurt. Now I looked at her with clarity. I had what Tamara wanted and I knew after the bile that had just spilled out of her that she would never have it.

"Something funny?"

"Yes." I smiled and shook my head at her. "Cole's not saving the best until last, Tamara. He doesn't want you, because he knows class when he sees it, and you obviously have none."

Anger glinted in her dark eyes and she had just opened her mouth to retort when loud clapping from the back of the studio drew both our gazes. Stu was leaning against the doorway there, watching us. He stopped clapping and approached us slowly, his blue eyes fixated on Tamara.

I'd never seen Stu with an unfriendly expression on his face before. He was beyond intimidating.

"I've never had the patience for bitches. Get out of my studio."

Tamara flushed. "Stu—"

"Now, Tamara."

There was almost a gust of wind upon Tamara's departure, she moved so fast.

I stared up at Stu wide-eyed. "What was that all about? I felt like I was stuck in some bad fairy tale."

He chuckled and relaxed against the counter. "Tamara has been sniffing after Cole for years. He's told her more than once that nothing was going to happen between them, and I think he thought she understood that." He glanced at the door where she'd just left. "You were right, sweetheart. Cole knows class." He smiled at me now. "You're it. She's not."

I smiled gratefully. "After watching her strut in and then run out of here on the longest legs I've ever seen, I really needed to hear that. Thank you."

Stu threw his head back in deep, bellowing laughter, startling his next customer as she walked in the door.

I was sitting out on the balcony of my flat, my feet up on a stool, my sketch pad balanced on my knees, and I was using charcoals to draw the street below me. In my usual style, I utilized colors that reflected the way I saw the street and its energy, rather than the colors visible to my eyes.

It was close to the back of eight o'clock and I knew I'd be losing the light in an hour or so. I wanted to finish it tonight because I'd be hanging out with Cole tomorrow upon his return from Germany.

The sound of the front door to the flat slamming made me frown. Rae had told me she was hanging out with Simon and Tony tonight.

"Did you forget something?" I yelled, looking into the sitting room, awaiting her appearance.

I nearly fell off my seat when Cole walked into the room.

Delighted to see him, I forgot all about my drawing. I dumped it on the stool and hurried inside to greet him. "You're early." I grinned and launched myself at him.

Cole wrapped his arms around me and I inhaled him, ridiculously glad to see him even though he'd only been gone for two nights.

I was surprised then when he suddenly stopped hugging me, gripped me by the elbows, and pushed me back. My stomach flipped at the sight of his scowl.

"Was there something you forgot to tell me on the phone last night?"

Confused, I shook my head.

This pissed him off more than he already was. "Think," he bit out.

"I'm thinking," I snapped back, jerking my arms from his grip. "Hello to you too!"

"Don't," he warned. "I had to find out from Stu that my so-called friend accosted my girlfriend, rather than hearing that shit from the person who should have told me . . . aka my girlfriend."

"Dammit," I huffed, cursing Stu for telling Cole about Tamara. I hadn't wanted to make a big deal out of it, because in the end it wasn't a big deal. "Cole, it was nothing."

Cole crossed his arms over his chest and I watched his biceps flex. My stomach flipped again—and this flip was much nicer than the previous one. "She verbally attacked you and got in your face about our relationship. Something that has absolutely fuck all to do with her. Something she's now very aware of since I called her half an hour ago and told her to stay out of my life permanently. No one does that to you, especially when I'm not there to protect you."

"Good." I was relieved. More than that I was gratified Cole was taking our relationship so seriously. "Thank you."

"You don't get it."

Why he was still angry with me? "Clearly not."

Suddenly I was pulled into his body as he wrapped his arms around my waist and held me tight to him. He looked down at me, surprisingly intense. "It hasn't been easy to get you to this point, Shannon. I don't need someone coming in and messing with your head and filling it with nonsense about me all over again. And the fact that you hid it from me . . . Well, that tells me you let her get to you. You're letting her mess with your head. You're shutting me out again."

I grinned and then laughed at the immediate annoyance and confusion that sparked in Cole's expressive eyes. His hold loosened and I fisted my hands in his shirt to stop him from stepping away from me. "You're wrong. I didn't tell you because it really was no big deal. Don't get me wrong. At first what with her being all hot and leggy, I was a little worried she might be right. However, that thought was fleeting. She doesn't know either of us well enough to form an opinion. I'm starting to realize my own worth again, Cole. And you're an honest guy. If you wanted to be with Tamara, you would be." I bit my lip, smiling suggestively as I pressed my hips into his body. "Fortunately for me you have a blind spot when it comes to a short redhead with plenty of attitude and an insatiable libido."

Cole's lips twitched. "An insatiable libido?"

"You have no idea." I smoothed my hands over his hard chest, feeling the tingling sensation grow between my legs. "And fortunately for you I have a blind spot when it comes to a tall, hot tattooist who jumps to conclusions."

I let out a little squeal of delight as Cole lifted me into the air. I wrapped my legs around his waist, my hands clinging to his neck as he kissed me. A long, slow, sweet, deep, hot kiss.

I melted into him.

"Now, that is the way to say hello," I murmured.

His hooded eyes were filled with something . . . something I couldn't quite put my finger on, but it was utterly arresting. I stilled in his hold. "You keep surprising me, Shannon MacLeod."

"That's a good thing, right?" I rubbed my nose against his and he nodded, turning his face to catch my lips in another breath-stealing kiss.

When we came up for air, Cole panted, "I have a surprise for you too."

Anticipation rushed through me. "I can feel your surprise."

He shook with laughter. "Not that."

"Ooh, present?" I said, and he laughed even harder at my childish excitement.

Lowering himself to the sofa, he arranged me so I was sitting comfortably on his lap—well, as comfortably as I could with his erection digging into me. I sat patiently as he smoothed his hands down my hair. "Life drawing class wasn't my favorite, but I can't get the idea of drawing you naked out of my mind."

For some reason I found the idea of modeling for Cole both stimulating and embarrassing. "You can draw me if you want to."

He nodded, eyes hot. "I want to. I wonder how long I'll last before I give in to temptation."

I squirmed, my skin heating at the thought of all the ways I could tease Cole while he drew me. "I'm definitely modeling for you," I murmured thickly.

Cole swelled against the apex of my thighs. Hmm, he really liked that idea.

He groaned and pulled my head toward him for a quick kiss. "Before I make love to you I want to give you your surprise."

"Okay."

"I know it's your birthday tomorrow."

Taken completely off guard, I jerked back. "How? I didn't tell anyone."

"I know." He frowned. "And that's really annoying, Shortcake. Luckily you work for me, so I have your birth date on file."

"I didn't want to make a big deal out of it." I shrugged, feeling an unpleasant ache in my chest ruin all my sexy, glowy feelings.

Cole sighed. "Because your family hasn't contacted you?"

I lowered my gaze and nodded. "It's my first birthday without Logan. Without any of them. It was the one day a year my parents actually acted like they gave a crap."

He lifted my chin, forcing me to meet his gaze. His eyes roiled with passion and tenderness. "They don't get to take your birthday away from you. If they don't want that piece of you, then I'll have it. Gladly."

"Cole . . . ," I whispered, folding into him. Some of the ugliness in my chest started to dissipate.

He hugged me tight. "I know you're trying to put together as many different pieces as you can for your portfolio, so I'm taking you somewhere where you can work on your art."

I pulled back, my pulse picking up speed. "Where?"

"Joss and Braden own a private villa in Lake Como. They're letting us stay there in two weeks for seven nights. I've already cleared the time off for us with Stu."

Shocked, I stared at him openmouthed for a few seconds before I squeaked, "You're taking me to Italy for my birthday?"

Cole gave me that boyish, cocky grin of his. "Yes."

"You can't do that."

He raised an eyebrow at me. "I think I can."

"No." I shook my head adamantly. "No one has ever taken me anywhere, let alone a man who's only been dating me for two months."

"Well, it's happening." He laughed.

"No."

"Yes."

"I can't let you take me to Italy, Cole," I argued.

Impatience crackled in his gaze. "Why the fuck not?"

"Because . . . because . . ." I slumped on his lap. "I know I said I know my own worth now, but part of that was just bravado, okay? Don't get me wrong. I'm trying to get there . . . but it's been a while since anyone was good to me and I . . ." I gasped for breath, completely taken aback by how overwhelmed I was by his gift. "I don't know if I can cope."

Fierceness flashed in Cole's gaze and I abruptly found myself in the air as he stood up. "You can cope. You'd better," he declared, carrying me into my bedroom. "Because I don't intend to stop anytime soon."

"I know what will help," I whispered frantically.

"What?"

"Sex. Sex will definitely calm me down."

Cole grinned wickedly seconds before he threw me onto the bed. "Not the way I plan on doing it."

CHAPTER 20

I t was surreal.

I'd never imagined I would ever be surrounded by so much beauty.

Yet there it was all around me.

The lake glistened under the unbending sun, finding pockets of shade only in the shadows cast by the surrounding mountains. Villas and hotels dotted the edges of the lake and mountainsides in bursts of white, yellows, rusts, and red in the tiles of the roofs. Cypress trees framed stunning, luxury homes on the lakeside, and the lush greens and simple, romantic Italian architecture created this Eden of peace and tranquility. Ferries crossed the lake, as did speedboats and Jet Skis in lazy leisure under the heat of the sun.

Sweat and suntan lotion shimmered on my skin, and I found a slight relief from the hot, late-July sun as a small breeze from the lake whispered over me.

The villa Joss and Braden owned on Lake Como was by the water in Menaggio. It was a four-bedroom villa with its own private pool. It wasn't until we arrived at it that I fully grasped how loaded the Carmichaels were. And how differently the other half lived . . .

I smiled out at the water.

For a while I was getting a taste of it.

Water splashed and I looked to my left as Cole climbed out of the pool. It was an understatement to say I enjoyed the way droplets of water rolled down his rock-hard abs. We'd been here only two days and already Cole's skin was turning a gorgeous golden brown. He smiled over at me as he dried himself off with a towel. "If you can tear yourself away from that painting, we could jump on a ferry. See the rest of the lake."

I bit my lip, wanting to do nothing more, but I was anxious to get work done. "I only have a few days to put together a couple of pieces."

"Why don't you put together the bare bones and when we get home you can fill in the rest with that gorgeous imagination of yours?" He stopped where I'd set up my easel and stool. "It looks wonderful."

"Thank you." My eyes traveled up his stomach, taking their time until they reached his face. A small smug smile played on his lips. "Shut up."

He laughed. "I didn't say anything."

"You know you're good-looking and you're using it to distract me."

Cole scratched his brow, appearing to struggle not to laugh again. "All I did was ask you if you wanted to take a break."

"And then you put those in my face." I pointed the end of my paintbrush at his abs.

"Welcome to my world," he said, his voice suddenly gruff. "That bikini . . ."

I glanced down at the white bikini I was wearing. It was a hot bikini. I'd spent the last two weeks shopping for clothes for this holiday and that included a couple of skimpy bikinis. I knew Cole would look good in Saran Wrap, so I was determined to feel sexy at his side.

I felt sexy in this bikini.

It was my turn to smile smugly.

Chuckling, Cole slid his hand across the back of my bare neck and gently squeezed. My hair was piled haphazardly on top of my head. Its length and thickness were a bit of a bother in warm weather. "Come exploring with me?" he said, pressing a sweet kiss to my mouth.

There really was no way to say no to that.

"Okay, we're doing this every day," I said, closing my eyes beneath my sunglasses against the breeze that blew over us. The ferry slowly made its way across the lake. The relief the lake breeze brought from the heat was beyond delightful.

"And you wanted to stay at the villa and paint," Cole teased.

I opened my eyes to look at his smiling, handsome face. I imagined his green eyes were laughing at me underneath his Ray-Ban shades. "I still can't believe you brought me to Italy for my birthday." I gestured across the water. "We can see the Alps."

"And?"

I shrugged, looking away, pretending to peruse the massive villa near the town of Bellagio, which was our destination. "Nothing . . . I just . . . It's a big deal for a couple who have only been dating a few months and yet . . ." I trailed off on another shrug.

"And yet?" Cole prompted.

I glanced back at him, my heart quickening. "It feels like some kind of dream and yet at the same time . . ." The blood beneath my cheeks grew hot despite the breeze. "I don't remember anything ever feeling more real."

Cole was quiet, which only made my heart elevate from a quickening pace to pounding.

"Jesus, Shannon," he finally said, his voice thick, "I wish you would say these things in private."

Hurt and confused, I looked out at the water.

"In private." He grabbed my hand and pulled my body toward his as he leaned down to whisper in my ear, "I can show my appreciation the way I really want to."

Reassured, I sagged into him. "You can always give me a taste of that appreciation. I doubt the Italians will be shocked by a little PDA."

Cole accepted that invitation . . . for the rest of the day. While we walked up the steep, cobbled steps and lanes in Bellagio, while we sauntered along the lakeside in the gardens of the Villa Melzi, and even when I spent most of my time balking at the prices of designer clothes and handbags, Cole showed me his appreciation. Holding me, kissing me, cuddling me—the guy was feeling mighty tactile. I didn't mind a bit.

"You should have bought that dress if you liked it," Cole said, swinging my hand playfully as we walked across the street toward the ferry dock. It was nearing the end of the afternoon and we were all Bellagio-ed out for the day.

"It cost half my monthly wage." I shook my head. "I'd have to be head over heels in love with a dress before I'd spend that kind of money. Even then . . ."

"You don't need it anyway," he assured me, his eyes running the length of me. "What you're wearing is working just fine."

I had on a white cotton sundress over my white bikini.

He let go of my hand to brush his fingers over my shoulder. "You got a lot of color today. We better put after-sun on you when we get back."

Always taking care of me.

I beamed at him and he blinked in surprise.

"What? What did I do?"

I shook my head, my smile turning secretive. Cole shook his head too, amused by my girlishness.

"Looks like the ferry is going to be another five or so minutes," he said as he stopped at the end of a long line of people who were waiting on the dock. He looked over his shoulder and grinned like a little boy. "There's an ice cream parlor."

"Then let's get ice cream."

He tugged on my hand and we hurried across the street before two guys on mopeds hit us. Inside the heavenly air-conditioned ice cream parlor, I studied Cole in growing delight as he bit down on his thumb and stared at all the ice cream flavors with this studious pinch between his eyebrows.

I struggled not to laugh at his adorableness. "Having trouble choosing?"

Expression still serious, he nodded, eyes not leaving the ice cream for one second. "Do you know what you want?"

You, you, you!

I choked back the desire to yell that and throw my arms around him. "I'm thinking chocolate and caramel."

"Hmm . . . why don't we get a three-scoop cone?"

My lips twitched. "Okay. What would you like?" My eyes rose to the older woman behind the counter, who was smiling at Cole like she found him just as charming as I did. The endearing guy who was excited about eating ice cream on a hot day was so at odds with his looks. He was wearing a white T-shirt that showed off his muscular, tattooed arms and neck, and a pair of long shorts with flip-flops. For once he was clean-shaven, but his hair was as messy as ever. He looked less bad boy than he normally did, but still . . .

"I'm thinking lemon and lime, watermelon, and strawberry."

"You keep your fruits." I nudged him with my hip. "I'll have the chocolate and caramel, the mint chocolate chip, and the double chocolate chip."

Once we had our cones we dug into them right away, moaning at the creamy flavors that cooled us down temporarily.

"Here." Cole tipped his cone down to me. "Try the strawberry."

I took a lick and instantly wished I'd chosen it. "Gorgeous." I held my cone up to him and he bent down to take a lick and ended up getting chocolate all over his nose. I giggled and gestured with my free hand for him to bend his head. As soon as he did I licked his nose, laughing while he tried to take another taste of my cone and got more around his lips rather than in his mouth.

We stood on the pavement, laughing and kissing ice cream off each other, uncaring we were acting like teenagers in public. We had such a carry-on with those cones we almost missed the ferry.

Running down the gangway, we caught up with the rest of the tourists and residents who were shuffling across the iron plank to get onto the ferry.

"I wish we could stay here forever," I said, filled with longing.

Cole squeezed my hand in answer and I realized as I looked up at him standing next to me that I'd never been so happy in my whole entire life.

Somehow I managed to swallow the sound of my indrawn breath at that startling revelation. Dazed, I absentmindedly held out my ticket to a guy dressed in a crisp white ferry uniform.

"*Inglese*, yes?" he suddenly said.

I blinked up at him, distantly taking in his handsome dark looks. "Scottish."

"*Scozzese*." He grinned, his dark eyes glittering appreciatively. "All such beautiful women, yes?"

Cole's hand tightened on mine and I was tugged none too gently into his side. The ferry worker gave Cole a taunting smile and waved us onto the ferry. I could feel the Italian's eyes burning into my back while the hand Cole was gripping was almost numb from his fierce hold.

"You can ease up there," I said as we took our seat in the back of the ferry. Unfortunately all the seats outside were taken, so we were trapped inside. It was like an oven.

"Fucking Italians," Cole muttered under his breath.

"Tony's Italian," I reminded him. "He's always coming on to me."

The muscle in his jaw ticked. "Yeah, with no intention of ever trying to fuck you. If that prick could have fucked you with his eyes, he would have."

"It's not a big deal." I frowned, surprised by how pissed off he was.

At my placating tone, Cole shoved his sunglasses up onto his head and glowered at me. "It's always a big deal when a man comes on to a woman in front of the man she's clearly with. It's like asking for a fist in his face."

"Which we all know you could land quite easily." I brushed my fingers over the fist he'd made subconsciously. "But there wouldn't be any point since a million men could come on to me and I'd still only want you." I rubbed his hand soothingly. "It's not like you to take these things to heart."

It was Cole's turn to frown as he realized the truth in my words. It wasn't like him to get worked up over something that was really trivial at the end of the day. He looked away from me, but not before I saw the muscle in his jaw flex.

The ferry had begun moving away from the dock when Cole said so softly I almost didn't hear him, "It's because it was you." He turned to meet my gaze, his heated. "What are you doing to me, Shannon?"

My breath caught.

Finally I whispered, "Exactly what you're doing to me."

That evening we returned to the villa to shower and dress for the evening. Joss and Braden had recommended a restaurant up in the hills of the neighboring town of Tremezzo. They knew the owners and had booked a table for us in advance. They'd also left us with the number of a taxi driver since they were few and far between in the area.

Dressed in a cool, flowing turquoise blue maxi dress that contrasted nicely against my hair, I felt that feeling of utter contentment come over me as I clasped Cole's hand and let him lead me up the stone slab steps to the restaurant. He was dressed in a white dress shirt and black trousers—effortlessly stylish. He also smelled amazing. The restaurant was beautiful, built in the style of a Swiss chalet, and as the friendly owner led us out into the garden to a table that had the most breathtaking view of the lake, I almost felt like crying.

This place, with this man at my side, was all too good to be true.

In the romantic setting, as I watched the sun slowly lower behind the mountains, my skin prickled—and not with growing chill. The air around Cole and me was electric, and I knew he was feeling all that I'd been feeling today. Despite the headiness between us, we managed to have a fun—and thick with innuendos—conversation while we indulged in the most astounding food I'd ever eaten. Everything just tasted so much more delicious here than it did back home. The vegetables, the fruit . . . all of it was bursting with flavor.

Allowing our food to settle, we sipped at our wine and looked out over the lake.

"Thank you for bringing me here. It's beyond anything I've ever experienced before."

Cole reached for my hand. "Thank you for coming with me."

Our eyes met and the electricity that had been sparking between us all night crackled.

"Let's go back to the villa," I said, the words coming out thick.

On the return trip I forced myself to try to find my equilibrium. I was likely to explode into a million different pieces if I didn't try to control what I was feeling for Cole.

As soon as we walked into the villa, my gaze locked on the pool glittering in the moonlight outside the sitting room. "Let's go for a swim," I suggested, thinking it might cool me down. I half suspected it was the heat that was making me feel so discombobulated.

"A swim?" Cole sounded confused, but I was already heading into the bedroom to grab a bikini. Cole had disappeared while I changed and I was out in the pool by the time he appeared in his swim shorts, carrying two cold beers.

I smiled at him as he lowered himself into the pool. "Good thinking," I said, taking the proffered beer.

We sipped in silence for a while, gazing up at the starry sky.

"Why are we in the pool?" Cole asked, amusement in his voice.

I swallowed hard, unable to look at him. "Because I needed to cool down before I injured either you or myself tackling you to the ground."

"Huh. A relaxing dip in the pool or tackled by a gorgeous redhead." He slanted me a mock-confused look. "Are you sure you understand men?"

I laughed and nudged him with my elbow.

In response Cole took the beer out of my hand and put it on the flagstone bordering the pool. "What are you doing?" I asked.

He answered me by turning to me with a determination in his gaze I recognized. My pulse started to race and I—

Cole pushed me back against the edge of the pool, his mouth devouring mine as he lifted my legs around his waist and ground his hips into me. I clung to his neck, pressing into him, kissing him back just as voraciously. Our tongues licked and tangled and tasted as the normally placid water sloshed against the sides of the pool.

Cold air covered my breasts as Cole deftly untied the string behind my neck and pulled it loose. I felt him swell against me as my nipples puckered up for him. He groaned deep in his throat moments before he bent down to suck my left nipple into his hot mouth, playing the right with his thumb. Heat began to build between my legs as he tormented me with his mouth and fingers until I was writhing against him.

The entire day had been leading toward this, and any control or patience I had was gone. I smoothed my hands down his back until I reached the waistline of his shorts and tugged.

Panting, Cole lifted his head from my chest to meet my gaze. His voice was hoarse. "I don't have a condom."

I smiled, my eyes bright with emotion. "We don't need one."

Cole froze against me, processing my words, the expression on my face, and what it all meant.

I trusted him.

He let out the gust of air he'd been holding and sank against me, his mouth slamming down on mine. If I'd thought our kiss before had been wild, it had nothing on this one. Kissing him and panting for breath at the same time, I gripped Cole tight with my legs while he quickly removed his shorts. I loosened my hold so he could take off my bikini bottoms. They floated off into the water as Cole smoothed his hands along my thighs, my hips, and around to my bottom. He lifted me easily in the water, his cock prodding against my entrance.

My inner thighs trembled and my fingers dug into Cole's biceps with the fierceness of my anticipation.

The cry of exultation from both our lips flew up into the night sky as Cole slid inside me. Those cries, like birds, were followed by the feathers of softer, broken cries that fluttered up in their wake upon his slow, excruciatingly wonderful thrusts inside me. He teased and tortured us both.

"Cole," I begged against his lips. "Please."

"What do you want?" he panted. "Tell me what you want."

I kissed him. "Harder," I whispered, giving him everything.

His arms tightened around my waist and as he slid back inside me it was with more force than before.

"Oh God." My head dropped back as he pumped faster and harder into me. I felt the heat inside me build toward a blaze. "I'm close."

I barely even felt the hard edge of the pool as Cole lost the last remnants of his control and pushed me back against it so he could increase the force of his thrusts.

"Cole!" I screamed, exploding around him.

He grunted in surprise when my inner muscles clenched and unclenched around him powerfully as my orgasm rippled over me. "Shannon." He choked out my name and tensed. A second later he groaned through gritted teeth as his hips jerked against mine.

A little while later as our senses returned, Cole pressed a sweet kiss to my lips. "Thank you," he murmured.

I didn't need to ask him what he was thanking me for. Instead I joked, "We'll need to have this pool cleaned before we leave."

His body shook against mine in the most wonderful way as his deep laughter filled the air around us.

CHAPTER 21

"Where do you think you're going?" Ollie stared at my suitcases with a sneer.

Despite the fear snaking through my body, I jutted my chin out defiantly. "I'm leaving. We're done. Get out of the way."

I heard this inhuman growl, just before a blur of color streaked across my line of sight and a sudden pain slammed into my head.

Agony ripped through my right shoulder. I was dazed, and my vision kept blinking out, but I could still feel the pinching pain around my upper arms and the hot breath on my face.

Somehow I was on the floor. Ollie had me pinned there, his grip bruising my skin.

I shrieked in outrage, ignoring the throbbing ache on the left side of my head. I tried to push back against him, kicking with my legs, but my struggles were temporarily paused when he punched me in the gut.

The wind was knocked right out of me and I could do nothing but try to breathe.

Fire spread out across my cheeks from the almighty burning sting in my nose where his fist had just landed.

He pressed the right side of my face into the carpet—another kind of fire from the carpet burn streaking down my cheek. Then his weight was off me, but I took too long to realize it, turning my head to stare up at him as his foot swung into my gut.

I grunted, curling in on myself, gritting my teeth against the pain in my shoulder and the burst of pain that lit up my ribs every time he swung his boot into them.

"Mine, Shannon!" he roared. "Fucking mine!"

I felt the crack and the resultant agony, and the scream tore out of me before I could stop it.

There was nothing beyond the pain. I was barely cognizant of the crazy stuff pouring out of his mouth, about how it was us forever, only us.

It was only when I felt the cold air across my chest and the push of his hand between my legs that my survival instinct kicked in. Panic and terror rushed over me, the adrenaline kicking in, numbing the pain.

I fought. I clawed. I scratched and bit . . . but he wouldn't get off me.

I felt him push against me. Ready to steal everything from me.

"No," I sobbed. This wasn't how it really ended. I had gotten away.

"You'll never get away," he panted in my face, his eyes turning black like a demon's. "This is where you belong. No one wants you but me, Shannon. No one's here but me. Not your family, not your brother. They hate you. They'll never forgive you." He kissed my lips gently. "But you'll always have me." His grip on my wrists tightened and he surged—

"No!" I cried out, my eyes slamming open in the dark.

I panted for breath as my eyes adjusted and I looked around. I was in Cole's flat, in his bed.

"Shortcake?" his sleep-roughened voice queried from beside me.

The nightmare had been so real.

So goddamn real.

I sobbed in relief, drawing my arms up around my knees.

"What the fuck?" Cole muttered, and the bed moved as he sat up.

The light came on and he cursed again seconds before he pulled me into his arms. I fell against his chest, unable to control the sobs that felt like they were being ripped out of me.

"Shh," he soothed, rubbing my back in comfort. "It was just a dream. You're okay. You're safe. You're safe, Shannon."

I was still feeling a little shaken as Cole returned to the bedroom carrying two mugs of tea. His hair stood up in all different directions, his lids were droopy with sleep, and he was half-naked. That was because it was only four o'clock in the morning.

But he didn't seem to care.

He handed me a mug and climbed back into bed. He slid his free arm around my shoulders to pull me into his side while we sipped the chamomile tea I'd added to his kitchen along with a variety of other stuff a few weeks ago when he told me to make myself at home.

"A nightmare?" he said, his voice still hoarse with tiredness. "Do you get those a lot?"

"Sometimes," I admitted. "But I haven't had one in a while."

I was frustrated I was having them again. Especially after our trip to Lake Como. Cole and I had reached new levels of intimacy in Italy—if anything I felt safer now than before we'd left for our trip. However, we'd returned two days ago and I'd spent most of those two days trying to shove the fact that I still hadn't heard anything from my family out of my head despite my birthday having passed three weeks ago. And the reason I couldn't get them out of my head was my guilt. I was so happy with Cole that it just made my remorse that much more insistent. It was plaguing me. My family was plaguing me.

"What are the dreams about?"

I sucked in a trembling breath. "Ollie's attack. Except in the dream I don't get away."

The air around us crackled with Cole's anger.

"I'm okay," I promised.

"You're not okay." He put his mug down none too gently on the bedside cabinet and turned me to face him. His green eyes were more alert. Anger had bled into them. "You're in my bed having nightmares."

I gave him a shaky smile. "It's not because we're not good. You know we are. We're so good in fact that I feel guilty all the time."

Realization dawned. "Because of Logan."

I nodded. "I know they told me to stay away from him, from them . . . but I thought . . . They're my family. I thought they'd call at least."

"Not going to lie, Shortcake. I really hope they don't. With the exception of Logan." He shook his head. "Why did they even bother having kids?"

I laughed bitterly. "You sound like Logan. He used to say that all the time." I sank into Cole's embrace and sipped on my tea. "My parents just don't have enough love to go around. They're not capable of it. They gave most of it to each other and we get the scraps whenever they feel like it. Logan was the only one of us they ever showed genuine interest in. Amanda and I were just a second thought." I looked up at him, saddened by the distance in my family. "Amanda's always hated me. I was close to Logan because we were more alike. Also, I look like Mum and Amanda doesn't, which means my somewhat narcissistic mum spent more time with me when I was little, trying to turn me into her little duplicate. That changed when I became a teenager and started developing my own opinions and interests. Still, Amanda never really forgave me for those mother-daughter bonding moments I got and she didn't. When I got into the clueless pattern of dating losers, Amanda loved it. It was something she could bond with my parents over."

"I'm sorry it was like that for you," he said softly, sincerely.

"Don't feel sorry for me, Cole. I had my grandparents." I grinned remembering them. "They were everything my parents were supposed to be, so I never really felt like I missed out on much. But they're gone." My lips quivered as my eyes filled with tears. "Logan's gone. And for once . . . I just really want my family to care."

"I get it," he murmured, kissing my head. "I do. And I know it's not the same, but you have me now. I'm not going anywhere."

I sniffled and turned my cheek to press a kiss to his chest. "I know."

We were quiet a moment as I sipped on my tea and attempted to calm my nerves.

"I found something that might cheer you up."

I pulled back from him. "Oh."

"One second." He gently eased away and got out of bed, striding from the room. He returned a minute later holding a folded-up piece of paper in his hand. He climbed back into bed and, giving me that boyish grin of his, handed it to me.

It was a piece of cartridge paper. On it was a drawing of a comic book superheroine and a zombie. She had her hands braced on her curvy hips and she was wearing a sexy black-and-blue costume. An abundance of red wavy hair blew back from her face as she faced off against the zombie. There was a speech bubble above her: *I'll destroy you with my razor-sharp disinterest and lack of fear, slow, stupid zombie guy.*

I laughed, covering my mouth in shock.

Cole tugged the drawing out of my hand. "I drew this the night after we met when we were kids. I was big into comics at the time."

I stared at him in wonder. "You saw me as a superhero."

He waved the paper. "Correction. A hot superhero."

"Cole . . . you still have it?"

"Yes. And here's the cool part." He settled on his side, gazing at me with so much tenderness I felt full to bursting. "Jo and I were living in Cam's apartment at that point in my life, but my mum still lived in the flat above us. We used the extra rooms in our old flat for storage. I had a lot of artwork in my old bedroom. My mum never really let up on me even after we moved out. In fact, she blamed me—said I'd turned Jo against her."

I glowered, my blood turning instantly hot with anger. "Does Jo know that?"

"Nah. I didn't see the point. Jo was happy and she deserved to be. I could handle Mum."

"So she was continuing to be a bitch to you?"

"Yeah. And one day I went into the flat to pick up something, a hoodie or jacket . . . and I walked into my old bedroom and it was a wreck. Mum followed me in, looked me in the eye, nothing in her expression, and said, 'We'll never be even.' She left me to go through the destruction she'd caused. She left clothes and stuff like that alone"—he curled his lip in disgust—"and she went straight for the stuff that mattered. Photographs and all my artwork."

"All of it?" I gasped.

"Everything . . . except . . ." He lifted the comic drawing and gave me a small smile. "I found it tucked behind the radiator. It must have whipped up into the air during her frenzy and hid out there." He shrugged, running his fingertips over it. "It felt important that it was the one thing that had escaped her. So I kept it."

I couldn't stop the tears that spilled down my cheeks. There was so much going on inside me. I hurt for him and what his mother had put him through. I hurt for him in a way I didn't think was possible to hurt for another person. The thought of anyone being cruel to him tore me up inside. At the same time I was overwhelmed by the drawing and the story behind it. There was a stunning reassurance in believing that something bigger than me had always planned to give me a life as beautiful as the one I'd found with Cole Walker.

Cole sat up to brush my tears from my cheeks and he dipped his head toward mine. His lips inches from my lips, he confessed, "I love you, Shannon. I want to protect you and keep you safe. I want to be your family and to give you mine so that you never have to feel sad about anyone who is too stupid to realize they've let go of something so special their lives will always be a little darker for it."

I choked back more tears, feeling too much—much too much— all of it building in my chest. I pressed my mouth against his and clung to him, pulling the calm I needed out of him. Finally, when I felt able to speak, I broke the kiss and clasped his face. I stared straight into his eyes and fought every single fear inside me. "I love you too."

CHAPTER 22

Rae was smirking at Cole and me as we walked over to the table hand in hand. Tony and Simon were wearing similar expressions.

"Managed to drag yourselves out of the love shack, did you?" Rae had practically yelled, and I could feel the curious and amused gazes of the other restaurant patrons burning into me.

"Remind me that I kind of love her," I said, gritting my teeth.

Cole grunted. "Hard to do when I'm busy trying to remind myself."

"No!" Rae continued to speak much too loudly as Cole pulled out the seat next to her. "Switch with Simon and Tony. If I sit next to you two I'll look like someone has rolled me in flour."

Assuming she was referring to the tans we'd gotten in Italy, I took the seat Cole had offered. "Suck it up."

She pursed her lips in annoyance. Finally, as Cole settled into the seat next to mine, she said, "There's something different about you. And I'm not talking about your smarter-than-usual mouth."

I shrugged. "It's called happiness."

Rae's attention flicked between Cole and me. She gave us a huge beaming, genuine smile at odds with her next words. "Cheesy buggers."

"So, okay, I really want to find out what you think of my home country." Tony smiled lazily, but I could see a glitter of excitement in his eyes. "But first I want to tell you something."

"Tony." Simon groaned.

"No, no." His partner narrowed his gaze. "I want to know what they think."

"About what?" Cole said.

"I want to adopt a child," Tony announced, his usual air of insouciance gone. "Simon, he no want to because he think I'm crazy. Convince him otherwise."

Cole relaxed back in his chair, seeming to be unperturbed by what I considered to be huge news. "Okay, well, I will but it all depends."

"On what?"

"On if you're crazy or not."

Simon snorted.

Tony did not look amused. "I am ready to be a papa. I think Sy and I would make wonderful parents."

"I think you would too," I found myself opining before I could stop myself. From the moment he'd announced the news, sounding almost as casual as if he'd decided he needed a new car, I'd felt the irritation heating in my blood. I tried to temper it, knowing Tony had a good heart. He smiled at my words, but I cut him off. "But only if you both want it and have thought long and hard about it. A kid isn't an accessory—something to have because it fits your mood and it's what people expect. You can't just return it, Tony, and you can't ignore it because a child isn't all you'd hoped it would be for you, and you certainly can't raise a child in a household where one parent may possibly resent it."

Everyone sat in stunned silence at my outburst.

Cole reached for my hand under the table and gave it a squeeze at the exact same time Simon lifted his glass of water in a toast to me. "Thank you. A voice of reason in the madness."

Tony shot him a hurt look. "I don't think it's an accessory. I want a child."

"And I'm not ready. I also don't want to discuss this shit in front of our friends."

Squirming uncomfortably, I held Cole's hand tighter as the tension mounted around the dining table.

"Is everyone ready to order?" A waiter suddenly appeared beside us.

Rae snapped open her menu. "Unfortunately we've been too busy participating in really fucking awkward dinner table conversation, so we're not quite ready yet. Give us a couple of minutes."

The waiter scurried off as quickly as possible.

I shot Cole a look of concern. "I don't think he's coming back."

Cole's lips twitched. "Would you?"

I looked down at my menu, avoiding eye contact with the warring couple opposite us. "Absolutely not."

Tony sighed wearily. "I'm sorry, okay? I didn't mean to make anyone uncomfortable. I got excited about the idea." He leaned in closer, trying to smile away the troubled look in his eyes. "So, tell me, how you find Lago di Como?"

Before I could answer, Cole's ringtone sounded from his pocket. He pulled it out and glanced down at the caller ID. He frowned apologetically. "Sorry. I have to take this." He tapped the screen and held the phone to his ear. "Marco?" Cole tensed.

So did I.

"Shannon and I are on our way."

We were? Where?

Cole shoved his phone in his pocket and pushed back from the table. "To make this more awkward than it already is, Shannon and I have to leave." He winced. "Hannah just went into labor."

"I would never have guessed any of that. Hannah seemed so cool and together about the pregnancy."

I was snuggled up next to Cole in the hospital waiting room and he'd just finished telling me a little bit about Hannah's history. Everyone had turned up at the hospital when she went into labor, but five hours later most of the family had to leave to get sleepy children home to their beds. Marco was with Hannah, who'd finally dilated enough centimeters to be sent to the delivery room. The clock on the wall told me Cole and I had been there for over ten hours. As for Clark and a much-recovered Elodie, they were looking after Sophia, and Dylan was with his mum.

That left an exhausted Cole and me. To stay awake we'd been drinking coffee and chatting until we were hoarse. I discovered why Cole wanted to stay after he told me about his best friend's history.

Apparently when Hannah was seventeen she'd been on a day out with Cole and Jo when she suddenly collapsed.

"It was awful," he said, eyes bleak with the memories. "There was all this blood and I didn't know what it meant. I had my suspicions because what else could it be? But this was Hannah . . . Anyway, she was unconscious, deathly pale, and still as Jo and I waited for the ambulance to come. When they lifted her into the ambulance, I just knew . . ." His eyes were suddenly bright. "She was dying. I felt it in my gut."

"Oh my God, Cole." I gripped his arm, shocked.

"They rushed her into surgery. Her heart stopped on the table, but they brought her back. By this point her whole family was at the hospital and they kept asking us questions. I was numb with shock. Hannah and I weren't really close, but I thought she seemed like a cool girl, a quiet girl who wouldn't get into trouble, and all I kept thinking was if she came out of it I'd be a better friend. A friend who would have known something was going on with her in the first place. Thankfully she came out of it. She'd been pregnant and didn't know it. There was a complication and one of her tubes burst, so she was bleeding internally. They performed surgery, she made it through, and they told her that she could still have children. However, the whole thing marked her." His expression hardened a little. "The kid had been Marco's. I didn't discover that little nugget of information until just after he and Hannah rekindled things. She wouldn't tell anyone in her attempt to protect him. After it happened, things were bad for her at school, she was depressed . . . and I wanted her to have someone. So we grew close. I became her best friend. She still didn't tell me the truth. I put two and two together much, much later."

"Did Marco know?"

Cole shook his head. "Nah. I confronted him, violently," he admitted ruefully. "Until Hannah arrived to break it up, and she explained that Marco didn't know about it. That's why he's still living."

I burrowed a little closer to my wonderfully overprotective boyfriend. "So Hannah has issues about being pregnant?"

"Yeah. She was terrified to have kids. She even thought about walking away from Marco because she was convinced she wouldn't be able to get past it." He sighed, playing with the hem of my T-shirt. "Sophia was an accident. Hannah was petrified but she stayed strong. This time around she's been okay, but she's had her moments. Knowing she's anxious makes me anxious, so I just want to be here until that kid comes popping out."

I kissed him, a soft brush of my lips against his. "You are such a good friend."

He slipped his hand under my shirt, running his knuckles over the flat of my stomach. "It really doesn't bother you, does it? My friendship with Hannah."

"No." I tilted my head, trying to think how I could explain it so he'd really believe me. And then it hit me. My gaze dropped from the stark white ceiling to his eyes. "There are moments when you're talking or laughing together that I see this look on both your faces . . . this really familiar look.". My throat was suddenly thick with emotion. "It's familiar because it's the same look Logan always gave me."

Cole's expression softened. "Shortcake, you need to go to him."

The door to the waiting room suddenly blew open and Marco was standing there, exhausted but beyond happy. "It's a boy." He grinned.

Laughing, Cole got up off the hard, uncomfortable chair and walked over to shake hands with Marco. "Congrats, man. Mum and baby are all okay?"

He nodded, rubbing a hand over his close-shaven hair. "They're perfect, Cole. I mean my wife just told me we're never having sex again, but other than that we're perfect."

It wasn't long before the whole tribe descended on the hospital in the wee hours of the early morning to come and meet the newest member. I'd never met a group of people so closely tied, and as I stood on the fringes of their lives, watching them take turns to hold baby boy Jarrod D'Alessandro and kiss his mother's cheek, I felt a pain in my heart so sharp I couldn't breathe.

And I couldn't stand to watch anymore.

Retreating from the room, I hugged myself as I blew down the corridor, desperate to find somewhere I could take a minute to find that momentary peace I was always seeking these days.

I wasn't even halfway down the corridor before I found myself stopped and yanked back around by a concerned Cole.

He took one look at me and he didn't even have to ask. He pulled me against his hard chest for a hug. "I mean it, Shannon. You need to speak with your brother. He's a big part of you. You have to face what he has to say to you, no matter what that might be."

I wrapped my arms around him, holding on tight. I knew he was right. "This is my third favorite thing about you."

I heard the amusement in his voice. "And what's that?"

"You give the best hugs in the world."

He squeezed me tighter and chuckled. "What's number one and two?"

"Two is your ability to bring me to orgasm every single time we do it."

Cole laughed outright at that, and I heard the masculine pleasure in his voice. "And one?"

I shook my head. "One is too cheesy. Just know it's a good one." I pulled out of his embrace and sighed. "I'll visit my brother this Thursday." I pressed my hand to my stomach and blew air out between my lips on a shaky exhale. "Oh hell, I feel like upchucking just at the thought of it."

Cole took my hand and began leading me back to Hannah's room. "Upchuck if you need to. Just give me some warning first."

We were about to enter the room when Cole halted me with a look. I lifted a hand to stop him from saying what I knew he was about to say. "I'll tell you number one when I'm drunk. I'm mushy when I'm drunk."

He grinned and nudged me inside. "Good to know."

. . .

Cole and I were lying in bed. He'd just made love to me in that slow, tender way of his that melted all my insides. Afterward he'd curled me into his side, my head resting on his chest, our legs tangled together. Cole didn't like to sleep without some part of me touching him.

I knew he was close to drifting off, because the rhythm of his breathing had changed, but I didn't think I could hold it in until morning.

Butterflies flurried in my stomach. "I contacted my brother."

Just like that, Cole was instantly alert, his body tensing against mine. "And?"

"He's only allowed four visits a month. He was supposed to be catching up with a friend, but he said I can come instead."

"You spoke to him?"

"Not him directly. It's all arranged. Visiting hours on Thursday at quarter to three."

He caressed my arm gently, making soothing circles on my skin with his fingertips. "How do you feel?"

"Like I want to cry every five seconds."

"Then cry, Shortcake."

Instead of letting go of the tears, I whispered, "I've decided I don't need to be drunk to tell you what number one is."

He waited silently.

"It's your ability to make me a better me. I want to be the person you see in me."

"Shortcake," he breathed, pulling me closer.

"You should also know I'll never be able to look at shortcake the same way again."

I felt his body shake with laughter—and for a little while the anxiety over seeing my brother was diminished.

. . .

I stared at the redbrick visitor center.

I was close to losing my breakfast.

Cole had made me shove down some toast and eggs this morning, but I'd refused to eat lunch. Good thing too or I think I'd definitely be losing it outside the prison.

My supportive and anxious boyfriend had really wanted to join me in Glasgow. He was going to wait outside in the car park while I visited with Logan, but I'd declined his offer. It wasn't that I didn't want him there, but I needed to do this myself.

There was a huge possibility I was going to walk into that visitor room and have the only other person on the whole planet that I adored tell me he hated me and he'd never forgive me. I'd been running from that fear, that consequence, since the judge passed down his sentence. It was time to be brave and face it, even if it meant losing my big brother forever.

However, it was much, much harder than even I'd anticipated.

I knew I had Cole waiting back in Edinburgh for me and with him the promise of this beautiful family who were there for one another like families should be. Yet that promise, no matter how much it wanted to offer itself to me as a balm against the possibility of losing Logan, was never going to do that. Gaining them didn't mean losing Logan wouldn't break my heart.

I had so many cracks in my heart . . . I wasn't sure it would handle another without shattering into a million unglueable pieces.

A child's laughter jerked me out of my maudlin thoughts, and I watched as a young mother carried her happy child inside the building.

It was time to suck it up.

"And you have no more than ten pounds in cash on you?" the prison officer asked me at security check-in.

I pulled out my purse, my hands shaking. "Uh, yes."

"I'll need to take your purse along with your phone." He took it and gave me a ticket to retrieve my things when I was leaving.

Before I stepped into the visitor room, I had to pause. The chaotic fluttering in my stomach swarmed into a panic in my chest and I felt a rush of breathless dizziness. I braced my hands on my knees and bowed my head, taking in air through my nose and releasing it slowly through my mouth.

"Miss, are you okay?"

I glanced up through my hair at the prison officer standing at the entrance of the room. I straightened and smoothed trembling fingers over my dry lips. I let out another puff of air. "Yeah. I'll be fine."

His look of concern told me he wasn't convinced, so I threw back my shoulders with more determination and assurance than I felt and took those first steps into the large room.

There were about forty tables and a small play area near the entrance where kids were supervised. Three seats were placed in front of each table, and only one opposite them for the prisoner.

My eyes swept the room, coming to a stop along with my heart at the sight of my brother. He stared across the room, his expression hard.

Somehow my jellified limbs took me over to him and I slipped into the seat opposite him, just staring at him, drinking everything in.

He looked different.

His dark hair, which had always been wavy like mine, was shorn close to his head, accentuating the sharp cheekbones and cut jawline he'd inherited from Dad. Once clean-shaven, he now looked rugged and older with the short beard he'd grown. Violet eyes, just like mine, pierced into me beneath his dark lashes. Although he'd always been fit, I could see in the breadth of his shoulders and chest that he'd packed on quite a bit of muscle since he went inside.

He looked tired; he looked grim.

He looked hardened.

I couldn't even begin to imagine the things he'd seen and the people he'd been forced to be around.

"Logan," I whispered, shrugging uncertainly. "I don't even . . ."

His eyes roamed over me. "You look well."

I leaned in closer at the sound of his voice. "I—"

"Where the fuck have you been, Shannon?" he hissed, the hardness in his eyes shoved aside momentarily to make room for the hurt.

It felt as if someone had just thrown a brick at my chest.

I smoothed a hand over my hair, and the motion drew Logan's attention. His eyes narrowed. "You're shaking." He sat back, shocked and wounded. "Are you afraid of me?"

"Of course not," I snapped, and then lowered my voice when I realized I'd drawn attention to us. "But I *am* afraid of what you think of me. I didn't think you'd want me here. Mum, Dad, and Amanda said you wouldn't either. They told me to stay away."

"What are you talking about? They said you just took off and you haven't been in touch." Anger flared in his eyes like purple sparks. "Do you have any idea how goddamn relieved I was to hear from you? You've had us worried sick, Shannon."

"No." I shook my head in denial, my heart pounding. "Mum, Dad, and Amanda . . . they told me this was my fault, that you all thought it was my fault. They told me they'd never forgive me. I thought it was best to just . . . leave. For everyone's sake."

"They said what?"

I tensed at the surprise on his face. "You never thought that?"

"No," he spat. "And you should have known better."

"How? Logan, I put you in prison."

"*I* put me in prison." He thumped his fist against his chest. "I did.

I'd do it over again if it meant getting to put that fucking animal in the hospital."

Suddenly I was flooded by the memories of that day, of the following days and weeks . . . My chest felt tight and the flashbacks turned to hard lumps in my throat. Although the pain and humiliation of that day had diminished since striking up a relationship with Cole, it hadn't completely disappeared. As evident by the way I was feeling upon seeing Logan for the first time. Tears burned in my eyes. "If I hadn't been such an idiot. If I hadn't been with him . . . if I hadn't run to you, you—"

"Don't." Logan grabbed my hand. "If you hadn't spent every day after you got out of the hospital avoiding me when I was out on bail, then I would have told you then what I'm telling you now—none of this is your fault. None of it."

I started to cry, bowing my head so my hair would hide my tears from the strangers around me. "I've been a coward. I should have come sooner. I . . ." I stared up at him, curling my fingers tighter around his and begging him with my gaze to believe me. "I know our family has never been close, but when they turned their back on me I felt really alone and I just couldn't face that they might be telling me the truth, that the one person . . . that you wouldn't want me to be your sister anymore."

"You're a fucking idiot," he said softly. "But fear makes us stupid." His lips twisted and that hardness was back in his eyes. "Believe me. I've seen plenty of that in here."

"Logan, I am so sorry. I never meant for any of this."

He shook his head in the way he did whenever he was flabbergasted. "Shannon MacLeod, you are the kindest person I've ever known. You're my blood. And someone thought he could hurt you. I don't regret *advising* him otherwise."

"There's not a single day I haven't thought about you."

He glanced away and I caught the sadness in his eyes. Logan had always been a bit like Cole—hotheaded with a quick temper that died down as quickly as it flared. But that was the extent of any kind of "darkness" in him. Logan was light. He was protective and hardworking, but he also knew how to have a good time. He was a joker with constant humor in his eyes.

That was when I realized what was so different about him.

That spark of mischief, of easy humor . . . it was gone.

Guilt gnawed at me despite my best efforts to soak in his words of reassurance. "Do Mum and Dad visit you often?"

Logan turned back to me and nodded. "They visit twice a month. Amanda does too. The other two visits I keep open for friends."

"You haven't lost any, then?" That was something I'd worried about too.

"No. They understand why I did what I did. I have good friends, Shannon. And, believe it or not, Mum and Dad have really been there for me."

I was confused and angry and yet thankful at the same time for that. "I'm glad."

"I'll be having a word with them, though, about how they treated you."

"Don't."

His eyes flashed. "You were in the hospital because you were beaten and almost raped, and rather than being there for you, they chased you off. I mean, what the fuck have you been doing these last few months? Where have you been?"

"Edinburgh."

Understanding lit up his eyes. "Running to Gran like always."

"Except—" My lips trembled.

"She wasn't there." He squeezed my hand again. "Have you been alone all this time?"

"No." I took a deep breath and told my brother everything. From being homeless and jobless to fate's twisted sense of humor landing me a job at INKarnate, to meeting Rae and being taken into her weird but wonderful fold, to Cole, to the antagonism between us and why, to learning all I did from his family, to our relationship changing, to how supportive he'd been, to how I'd fallen for him, and how he was the one who convinced me to face Logan.

When I was done, Logan sat back in his chair, his brow puckered in contemplation.

"Say something," I pleaded quietly. "I need you to believe I'm not making another mistake. You have to know after everything that I would *never* make that mistake again."

Logan nodded. "He sounds like a decent guy and I'm glad you've had people around you." He gave me his no-nonsense big-brother look, and warmth exploded in my chest at the familiar sight of it. "But I will have to meet him."

"Of course," I readily agreed.

He snorted. "You got a tattoo?"

"Yup."

"Think I'd get a free tattoo when I get out of here? From the legendary Stu Motherwell himself?"

I grinned. "Definitely."

"Good because I'll have plenty of inspiration by the time I do."

My stomach dropped at the reminder of where we were sitting. "How have you been? You're . . . okay . . . right?"

"I'm not sunshine and roses, but I can handle myself. Don't worry about me."

"But what's it been—"

"I'm not telling you that shit, so you can forget about it."

I could feel my eyes bug out at his snapping, and raised my hands in surrender. "All right, all right."

He smirked. "I've missed you, Shay."

I almost burst out crying at him using the nickname he hadn't called me since we were kids. "I've missed you too," I choked out.

"Ah, don't get all watery on me again. We have stuff to sort out." He leaned forward, his stare direct. "Neither of us should have listened to Mum, Dad, and Amanda's bullshit, but we did. That's over now. What's not over is this family. I know we're not perfect, Shannon. But they are our family and they have stepped it up and been there for me. I want you to reconcile with them so we can try to be a real family. Promise me."

Panic fluttered in my chest. After everything, no matter his protestations, I owed Logan. If he wanted this from me I had to figure out a way to give him it. But it was going to be difficult bringing my family around to the idea of forgiving me.

Moreover, it meant I'd have to forgive them.

I ignored the deep-seated uncertainty and gave my brother a reassuring smile. "I'll try."

CHAPTER 23

The sight of your childhood home wasn't supposed to fill your mouth with the taste of ash and your stomach with dread. Yet, staring at the prewar bungalow I'd grown up in on a quiet street in a wee town outside Glasgow, I felt just that.

What I really wanted to do was jump on a bus back to Edinburgh, but I'd made a promise to my brother. I just hoped Amanda was still living with our parents so I could kill three birds with one stone.

On the back of that thought, the door to the house opened and my pretty sister stepped outside in house shoes, ratty jeans, and an oversized T-shirt. Her dark hair was piled on top of her head and she was staring at me with the dark brown eyes she'd inherited from Dad. To my surprise I saw a flicker of relief in them that was at odds with her dry "You're alive, then."

"You would have known that if you'd called."

She rolled her eyes. "Works both ways." On that note she slipped inside, leaving the door open for me.

The familiar smell of my dad's tobacco hit me as soon as I entered. Gran had hated Dad's smoking, but no matter how much she nagged she couldn't get her son to quit. Mum never nagged him about it. She said Dad was always going to do what he wanted to do and she loved him enough to leave him alone to do it in peace.

I thought that was a copout, but then, she was always like that with Dad. He won every argument because she didn't want him to see her as anything less than the perfect, supportive wife she tried to be. Personally I thought they were living in the freaking fifties. I shuddered when I remembered how similar I'd acted with Ollie until near the end. Of course, Ollie was a violent woman beater. Dad was just a stubborn pain in the arse.

Full of trepidation, I followed Amanda into the large sitting room where my dad was watching TV while Mum sat at the dining table, typing on a laptop. They looked up at my entrance and Dad pressed the mute button on the remote.

Our eyes met and I could see that familiar stubbornness in his dark gaze fighting an emotion I couldn't quite name.

He stood up abruptly, drawing his hand across his mouth before sagging on a loud exhale. "Thank fuck."

I was abruptly pulled against him, his arms tight around me as he hugged me.

It took me a minute to get over my shock and hug him back.

"You should have bloody called," he bit out, and then pushed me back from him. He gripped my biceps so hard I winced.

"Dad, you could have called me," I said, trying to keep the hurt and annoyance out of my own voice, unsuccessfully. "You were the one that told me this was all my fault and that I should stay away from Logan. I thought you'd be happy to see the back of me."

He let me go, that stubborn chin of his jutting out. "I didn't say it was *all* your fault."

"So why didn't you call?"

"Why didn't you?"

I sighed. Typical Dad. His pride would never allow him to admit he'd handled this badly. I shot a look at my mum, who'd come to stand in the middle of the room beside Amanda. Amanda was taller than her. I'd gotten my lack of height from Mum along with her hair and eyes and figure. She was young looking—so young looking we could probably pass for sisters. But that was where the similarities between us ended. I was like neither of my parents.

I was all Gran, through and through.

Thankfully.

"A lot of things were said and done," Mum said. "But that was no excuse for what you've put us through."

My hands fisted at my sides. "It hasn't exactly been easy for me either."

Mum sighed. "I imagine not. But it isn't always about you, Shannon."

"I didn't come here to fight," I replied through gritted teeth. "I've just been to see Logan. He asked me to try to work things out with you and I promised I would."

"Fine." Amanda crossed her arms over her chest, eyes narrowed. "You can start with where you've been for the last few months and why there's a tattoo on your back that wasn't there before."

Damn. My shirt must have ridden up when I hugged Dad. "Okay. Let's sit down."

· · ·

"I cannot believe this!" Amanda shot to her feet once I was done telling them the story of my life in Edinburgh. "This just takes the biscuit."

"It's not like that." I glowered up at her. "You can't possibly believe I'd be so stupid again. Not after everything we've all been through."

"Yes, yes, I can!"

"Amanda," Dad said gruffly. "Calm down."

"Look." I drew her annoyed gaze from Dad to me. "I explained about me and Cole. I was just as suspicious and wary of him as anyone who has been through what I've been through would be. But he's a good guy. He's the one that's believed in me. He's gotten me here. He's gotten me to face Logan."

The panic gripping my chest was unbearable. I wanted to run from the house—and from that feeling—but I couldn't because I'd bloody well promised. So I had to face my family's response and I had to convince them I wasn't making a mistake in dating Cole.

"I want to meet him." Amanda glared at me. "I can come to Edinburgh and I'll decide."

"You'll decide what?"

"If he's a decent guy or another one of your losers."

"And what the hell would you know about a decent guy, Amanda? You're twenty-eight years old and you've never been in a serious relationship."

She sucked in her breath, hurt flaring in her eyes.

"Shannon," Mum warned. "If you want us to start over we need to know you aren't going to bring a whole new load of trouble into your life and, subsequently, ours. We're not going through this again. Your brother hasn't finished dealing with the consequences of your last disastrous romance."

"It's not up to you to judge Cole," I continued to argue, hating the idea of anyone believing he somehow had to prove himself. "He deserves better than that."

Amanda grunted. "No offense, but you're not exactly known for being able to distinguish a good guy from a loser. You want us to mend fences. Then you'll introduce us."

Reconnecting with Logan ended up burning out something inside me that I'd gotten so used to I hadn't even realized it shouldn't be there. Until it was gone.

It was this emptiness in my gut. A horrible space that couldn't be filled no matter how happy Cole and my new life in Edinburgh made me. It was a feeling that had grown to become a part of me, so much so I'd grown resigned to the idea of it always being there.

It had disappeared. With such sweet, sweet relief, that emptiness was gone.

The remorse was a different story. That might never go away and it certainly wouldn't be going anywhere anytime soon. Not as long as my brother was in prison. Maybe once he got out I'd have a fighting chance at battling that guilt, but for now it was a part of me, and yes, I was reconciled to that no matter my brother or anyone else's reassurances.

After talking round in circles with my family, I'd left them with my contact details and told them that we could talk once we'd all slept on it. Then I went straight to Cole and cried in his arms until I fell asleep.

The next day I told him everything that had gone down and he listened without interruption. But I could feel the tension mounting around him.

He was pissed off at my family.

"You don't have to deal with that shit," he had said. "Not after the way they've treated you."

"But I do," I'd insisted. "I have to do this for Logan."

For now we were agreeing to disagree. As were Rae and I. I'd told her everything too and she was of the same mind as Cole. And although Cole did agree to meet Logan (I'd already arranged for us to go in a couple of weeks on our day off), I discovered upon my arrival at work that not only was Cole being a little distant, but Rae was too.

"This is going to be a fun day," I muttered after having had the coffee I'd handed each of them snatched out of my hands without even a thank-you. With Cole I knew it was because he'd gone inside his own head to brood over the matter. With Rae it was because she was just really annoyed at me.

Thankfully, as always, we were busy on a Saturday and I could pretend Cole's quietness was due to his professionalism.

However, I knew with sinking dread in my stomach that all the pretending was about to fly out of the shop door when my sister opened it and stepped inside.

Frozen to the spot in surprise, I watched as her eyes roamed the tattoo studio, her upper lip curled in distaste. Amanda was pretty much my opposite. She hated tattoos, piercings, hair dye, or anything that modified your body from its natural state. She didn't have a creative bone in her body and she'd never felt the need to enhance or change anything about herself or express who she was through her appearance.

She equated body modification with a deficiency of character.

Amanda finally caught sight of me standing behind the reception desk, and, ignoring the people sitting in the waiting area, she strode over to me with her eyebrow quirked. "This is the famous INKarnate?"

Feeling defensive, I stiffened. "Yes."

She rolled her eyes. "Only you would think working at a place like this was cool."

"No, actually hundreds of people would. It's well respected for its art and it pays well because it gets a lot of business."

She harrumphed and waved my comment away. "Look, I'm here because we all agree we want you back in our lives. You may have it in your silly little noggin that we could give a shit, but that's not true, Shannon. We love you. We just . . . We know what you're like. You have bad judgment. I'm here to make you see some sense."

I'd gone from being amazed that she'd said the L-word to being indignant at her condescension. "I told you we'd discuss this. You can't just walk in here, expecting to pass judgment on Cole. One, you just can't. And two, he's working. It's a Saturday. We're really busy."

"I just want to meet him. I'm not going anywhere until I do." She smirked. "Or don't you want to make good on that promise to Logan?"

I gritted my teeth in frustration. Sometimes my sister was just pure evil. "Wait there."

I hurried into the back, knocking on Cole's door.

"Come in," he called over the buzz of the needle.

I opened the door to find him tattooing a very detailed Minotaur onto a wannabe biker chick's arm. Her name was Vik and she was a regular. She'd come in for a tattoo way back when I first started working at the studio, and she'd been three other times since then.

Cole looked up at me and stilled at the sight of my expression. "What's wrong?"

"My sister is here." I grimaced. "I'm so sorry. I didn't know. And she won't leave until she meets you."

Cole's features hardened. "I'll be out when I'm finished with this tat. She can park her arse in the waiting area."

I nodded and moved to hurry out when he called my name.

"Yeah?" I asked over my shoulder.

"Don't offer her coffee, water, anything. She's not welcome here, and the only reason I'm not throwing her out on her arse is you and your brother."

Uneasiness moved through me, but I gave him a quick jerk of my chin in agreement and hurried out. I had a feeling this meeting wasn't going to go too well.

Amanda made a face as I introduced Cole. I'd taken her into his room for some privacy. Cole hadn't offered her his hand. He'd just given her a nod of his head and pulled me protectively into his side.

I scowled. "Amanda, you two haven't even exchanged a word yet."

"Look at him." She waved her hand at me. "Like he's going to stick around *you* for long."

"What the fuck is that supposed to mean?" Cole snapped.

Amanda snorted and shot me a pointed look. "Charming."

Impatience sizzled in my blood. I stepped forward. "Amanda, quit it. You're supposed to give him a fair chance."

"I don't need to. Look at him. I think your first instincts were right on this one, Shannon."

Realization hit me. "You were never going to give him a chance. You like this. You like me being the black sheep."

She rolled her eyes at me again. "You did that to yourself. You pick these losers. These big nothings—"

I shot toward her so fast she stumbled back in fright. "Don't you ever call him that," I hissed, fists clenched at my sides.

"Shannon," Cole murmured, but I ignored the placation in his tone.

"You don't know anything about him or me. Why?" I pleaded.

"Why are you being like this? I'm trying to fix things because Logan wants his family back, and you're playing your petty games."

"I'm not playing. This is serious. *This* doesn't look like trying to me."

I shook my head, feeling immensely sad all of a sudden. "You said you love me, but I'm not sure I believe that. You and me . . . we've never gotten along and I still don't know why you've always had it out for me—"

"Oh, for God's sake! If only you'd been this paranoid about your boyfriends, maybe Logan wouldn't be in prison."

I felt Cole's heat at my back and I pressed a hand out behind me to stop him from saying or doing anything in retaliation. "Cole does not need to prove himself to you or to anyone. Now, you've insulted him enough. I want you to leave."

Face red, eyes suddenly filled with a surprising amount of emotion, Amanda whispered, "I don't know what you think or why you think it, but I do care about you. I just don't trust you and I'm trying to save you from making another huge mistake. I'll never forget what you did to Logan, but I was willing to try to forgive. Please, Shannon. You let me walk out that door, then you're cut off from this family."

As I was almost paralyzed by her words, it was only the touch of Cole's hands on my hips that reached me. Fear of disappointing Logan again kept me from saying anything.

Amanda took my silence as rejection and with wounded eyes and a disapproving grimace she hurried out of the studio before I could figure out how to make it all work.

CHAPTER 24

I felt sick.

Logan wanted one thing from me, *one thing*, and I'd already mucked it up.

I spent the next few hours trying to push past my emotions and think rationally. I needed to come up with some way of making this situation work out for everyone.

I just didn't know how.

"Are you going to speak ever again?" Cole said.

He sat across from me at Rae's kitchen table. Rae was out. After having heard the commotion at work, she'd decided we probably wouldn't be great company that night. Why she couldn't just say she was giving us some space, I didn't know, but that was Rae's way. You would think being thoughtful was something to be ashamed of the way she tried so hard to hide her considerate side.

"I'm sorry." I pushed my plate of egg noodles and red Thai chicken away. "I just keep thinking things over and over and I still don't know what to do." I bit my lip and then suggested softly, "Perhaps we should take a step back."

Cole froze for a second before his fork clattered to his plate. "Excuse me?"

I continued thinking out loud. "Just until I breach the distance with my parents. You know . . . ease myself back into the fold, show them I'm trying, and then when they see that, you and I can pick up speed again and they'll see for themselves what a good guy you are."

The air in the room turned arctic. I knew immediately I'd made a huge error in judgment by thinking out loud. Anger, incredulity . . . and hurt blazed in Cole's eyes as he shoved back from the table to tower over it and me. His voice was almost a whisper, it was so choked with emotion. "After everything, after the way they've treated you, neglected you, you want to put *us* on hold to appease *them*?"

I slid back from my chair, desperately trying to think of a way to calm the situation, to articulate this correctly, because clearly I was messing it up. "No! I mean, just temporarily."

Wrong thing to say! My eyes widened as his whole being seemed to expand with anger. "You cannot be serious?" he said.

"Cole, please. Try to see it from my perspective. This is my family. And yes, they're not a great one, but they're still my family. They're hurt and scared and I've been running from them, it all, for too long. It's time to fix things. It's what Logan wants and what I think I need." I took a step toward him, placation in my eyes. He flinched back from me. I was royally screwing this explanation up. "Cole . . . you of all people have to understand. Your mum was a crap mum, but you never abandoned her. Not completely."

A muscle flexed in his jaw as he nodded with teeth gritted. Finally he expelled his breath in a hoarse voice. "But I would never have chosen her over you."

"I'm not choosing anyone over—"

"I can't do this right now." He held up a hand to interrupt me. "I need to walk out of here before I say shit I'll regret."

Wondering how the conversation could have taken such a bad turn, I pleaded with him. "Don't. I'm not trying to hurt you. I'm just trying to think of—"

"Not trying to hurt me?" He pushed the chair he'd been sitting in hard against the table. It was my turn to flinch back. "You're asking me to fucking prove myself. If anyone has to prove themselves it's them!"

I pressed my lips closed, realizing with a heaviness in my gut that that was exactly what I'd just asked him to do. After telling my family that I would never do that to him, I'd done it without thinking. "I didn't mean that," I promised. "I really didn't. I just don't know what else to do."

But my apology didn't even penetrate his anger. He leaned forward, eyes narrowed, and hissed, "Here's a hint: You should never have said you wanted to take a break. You should never have asked *me* to prove myself after all the shit you've put me through." He cut me another disgusted look and strode out of the room while I recovered from his furious attack.

Hearing the front door open, I snapped out of my stupor and raced down the hallway. "Cole!"

He spun around. "And to think I was going to ask you to move in with me. What a huge fucking mistake that would have been."

Oh heck, this was not happening. "Cole, please—"

The door slammed shut on my face.

I stumbled forward, about to chase after him, when his words started ringing in my ears. He was furious. My continued attempts to rectify the situation weren't going to change how he felt at the moment.

I leaned my forehead against the door. "Fuck, fuck, fuck, fuck," I whimpered.

My suitcase lay open on my bed, my clothes scattered all over my bedroom, and I was staring at my artwork wondering how I was going to pack it up when the front door slammed.

"Shannon fucking MacLeod, you and I need to have a word!" Rae shouted through the flat. "I've just been consoling your very pissed-off and hurt man and I've got to say . . ." Her voice trailed off as she entered my bedroom. I watched as she took in the suitcase and the clothes that were in the progress of being packed into it. "Okay." She swallowed hard. "You should know that Cole is really hotheaded. He doesn't seem it because he's so laid-back all the time, but when something pisses him off, I mean, he just lets fly without thinking." She was rambling now. "Did you know that when he found out Marco was the guy that knocked Hannah up when she was seventeen, he didn't even give her a chance to explain shit? He just flew off the handle and went after Marco. He tried to beat the crap out of him on a construction site. Got a few good punches in too."

I opened my mouth to explain, but my phone rang before I could. Glancing over at it on the bedside cabinet, I recognized the number. "Oh, I have to take this." I snatched it up and answered, all the while waving at Rae to get out of my room to give me some privacy.

She stared at me stubbornly for a second but finally edged out of the room.

By the time I got off the phone with my dad to arrange everything, it was late and Rae was lying across her bed fully clothed. Her snores filled the entire flat.

Rae was already up and gone by the time I woke up. It was puzzling because Rae was never out of bed before me. I'd lain awake for most of the night worrying myself sick about Cole and forcing myself not to call him. There wouldn't be any point trying to talk to him when he was still riled up.

Exhausted, I walked into INKarnate, heading straight for the coffee machine. I was feeling a little breathless, anticipating seeing Cole after our first huge argument as a couple. Technically I think maybe he'd broken up with me, but I couldn't even process that right then without wanting to burst into tears, so I concentrated on the coffee.

I chewed on my lower lip, trying to decide if I should take Cole a cup.

"There you are."

I looked over my shoulder at Rae standing behind my desk. "Morning."

She scowled at me. "Whatever. Cole called in sick. You need to phone and reschedule his appointments for today."

My heart took a swan dive out of my chest. "Sick?" Cole never called in sick.

"Like you care," she snapped.

"Rae." I stomped my foot in exasperation. "Why did Cole—"

"I can't hear you!" she yelled childishly, and strode away from me.

I hurried out of the closet onto the main floor. "Rae!"

"Don't push me." She stopped and glared at me over her shoulder. "You're my friend, Shannon. I care about you, but if I have to choose, I choose Cole. So back the fuck off before I slap the fucking stupidity out of you."

Aghast, I stood there, stunned, as she disappeared into the back.

I was still standing there when Simon ventured out of his room. From the look on his face he had heard everything. Whatever he saw on *my* face made him hold up his hands in surrender. "I don't want to know. I'm sorry, babe, but I've got my own shit going on with Tony."

I crushed my rising panic. "Are you okay?"

He shrugged glumly and walked past me to get a coffee. "We're trying to work through this baby thing."

"I'm sorry." I slumped against my desk, wishing relationships didn't have to be so bloody heartbreaking.

Simon gave me a sad smile. "I'm sorry too."

Frozen out by Rae for the rest of the day, I'd lost strands of hair from tugging it in frustration so much. I couldn't believe what she'd said to me. I didn't even know what I'd done to deserve it.

Finally, after locking everything up for the day, I reached for my phone. I felt so sick I thought I might actually vomit, and the only way to get rid of that sensation was to call Cole.

It went straight to voice mail.

Rae came out of the back wearing her jacket and bag. Simon had already left. I reached for my own jacket. "Don't even think about walking me out," she said, sneering, as she strode by my desk.

"Where the heck is Cole?" I called after her.

"With Hannah." She shook her head at me, all childishness gone and replaced with disappointment. "Don't bother them. He's visiting the baby."

I slumped. "I didn't mean to hurt him, Rae."

"You gave up on him. How was that not hurtful?"

"I never gave up on him. I'm just trying to keep a promise to someone."

"The wrong someone, apparently." She shook her head. "Cole's really been there for you, and you've gotten in deep with him, which means somewhere along the line you've made promises to him too. Maybe you should work out whose promise is the one you should concentrate on keeping."

"Why does it have to be an either-or situation?"

"Because someone is making it that way . . . and again, maybe that's the someone you should be taking time off from. Not Cole." She slammed out of the studio, leaving me alone to lock up and ponder the many ways I'd somehow managed to let everyone in my life down in less than seventy-two hours.

CHAPTER 25

There's nothing quite like the feeling of fear you get in your gut when you know you've hurt someone you care about. The fear turns into a flurry of nerves the more time passes with everything unresolved.

I was scared sick.

That night I tried calling and texting Cole, but he didn't answer. Desperate to talk everything through, to fix it, I took a taxi to his place, hoping he'd cooled down enough so we could talk.

However, Cole wouldn't answer his door.

I returned home that night with this heavy, thick, swelling sickness in my gut.

That feeling only worsened when I walked into work on Monday to find myself face-to-face with Stu. "Cole needs a break, so he's off on some photography trip with his friend Nate for the next couple of days. I'll be covering his appointments."

I was a little breathless at the news that my boyfriend had up and left town without informing me. "Trip? Where?"

Stu shrugged, not meeting my gaze. "Not sure."

"Stu—"

"Look, Shannon." Stu shrugged at me, sympathy mixed with hardness in his eyes. "You're good at your job, but if your presence here is going to be a problem for my best artist, I will have to let you go."

"Let me go?" I stumbled forward, shocked to my core. "Cole and I had an argument. We'll sort it out."

That darn sympathy melted the hardness completely. "Cole seems awfully upset."

"I suggested something, he took it the wrong way, but that's hardly . . ." I touched my forehead as the room started to wobble. "He's hotheaded and he said things, but I thought . . ." I trailed off as I searched my bag for my phone. Cole and I needed to talk. He couldn't just run away.

It wasn't like him.

"This isn't like him," I muttered, fumbling for the phone. This time it rang, but I got no answer. I winced at the sound of his voice asking me to leave a message. "Cole, it's me. Answer your phone. This is ridiculous. We need to talk."

Stu grimaced. "I hope you're good at groveling, wee fairy."

I sighed. "I have a feeling that by the time this week is over, I'll have made an art form out of it."

"I miss it here." Dad smiled, taking in the view of the castle out the coffee shop window. "Your mum is pure Glasgow through and through, but this place never stopped feeling like home."

I nodded. "It's in my blood too."

"Yeah, you have a lot of my mum in you. Might be for the best considering your sister has a lot of your mum's side in her and look how neurotic she turned out."

I wrinkled my nose. "Dad."

He just chuckled and sipped his coffee.

"Thanks for meeting me." I'd decided after my argument with Cole that perhaps it would be better to try to have a rational discussion with a member of my family. Dad had been the one who'd seemed most receptive to me, so I'd called him to arrange meeting up. He could only meet me at the weekend, which meant I'd had to ask Rae to cover me—something she'd done begrudgingly. Although she was still pissed at me for upsetting Cole, she could see how much of a toll it was taking on me that he hadn't returned my phone calls all week. So, despite the fact that my roommate was barely speaking to me, she *had* agreed to cover my shift.

"It would be nice to have some peace in the family again." Dad shrugged. "If we can find a way to do that, then great."

"I don't want to have to compromise my relationship with Cole in order to maintain one with you. It's not fair."

He threw me a disapproving look. Frankly I was weary of seeing that look on the faces of the people I knew. "Amanda told us about him."

I bit back my frustration. "She barely let him say two words. She walked into the studio and just started insulting him. She had no intention of giving him a chance."

"She says he looks and acts exactly like all your ex-boyfriends."

"He's nothing like them." I leaned forward, infusing every word with my conviction. "He's the best person I know."

"Why can't you just be single for a while, Shannon? Take time to figure things out. Our family needs a break from the drama."

"There was no drama between me and Cole." I could taste bitterness on my tongue. "Until my family came back into the equation."

Dad frowned.

"That's not what I meant." I waved off my last comment, but I wasn't sure I hadn't meant it. "I'm just trying to do the right thing by everyone. Logan wants us to be a family again, but to do that you want me to break up with a guy you know nothing about."

"Look at it from our point of view. The last time you were in a relationship with some tattooed . . . anyway, you let it get so bad your brother got put away for protecting you. That's beyond normal." He clasped my hand. "Kid, you need time to sort out your head. There's no way you could have had time to do that since you left Glasgow, not after jumping into another relationship with another idiot."

I wrenched my hand out from under his. "Cole's not an idiot. And I keep trying to tell you he's the reason my head *is* sorted out. He's helped me. He's done so much to make me feel valued again, and more than that he got me back to Logan. You know, I kept having these nightmares. I'd think they were gone and then they'd come back. I've not had a single one since I visited Logan. Not a single one. And Cole did that."

To my growing annoyance, Dad still looked unconvinced.

"Why did you come here if you weren't going to hear me out?"

"I came here in the hopes that you'd hear *me* out." He stood up and threw money on the table to cover his coffee. "We'll be there for you, sweetheart, as long as you leave the baggage behind. Come home and start over again. Not just for us, but for yourself."

"I'm guessing from that look on your face the meeting with dear old Dad didn't go well." Rae kicked off her shoes, only to pull on her boots. "So much for the packed bags, huh?"

286

I glowered at her, confused by her comment, but too focused on one thing to question it. "I just tried calling Cole again. Did you tell him I've been trying to contact him?"

"We were kind of busy at work today. He was getting back into the swing of things after his week off."

Chest aching, I couldn't hold back my tears. "I didn't mean to hurt him. Why won't he let me explain?"

Her eyes flared with anger. "Because after everything, you chose your family over him. You chose people who turned their backs on a daughter who'd just been sexually assaulted and hospitalized. What the fuck does it say about how you feel about Cole that you'd choose *them*?"

Horror shot through me. "Is that what he thinks? That I chose them? I didn't choose them. I was trying to come up with a way to appease them. I never had any intention of giving Cole up. I just thought we could take some time—"

"A break," she interrupted. "A break from him. The guy can barely to stand to be away from you for a few days and you were willing to go home to Glasgow for God knows how long. And he was what . . . just supposed to sit around and wait for your call for however long it would take for your parents to approve of him? And again, parents who gave a crap about you when Cole would move the heavens to protect you." She stood up and grabbed her purse. "What was a silly argument to you was a huge deal for him. For reasons I get and reasons I don't. But I'm guessing you do. I'm guessing he's told you everything about himself. And I'm guessing you know that even suggesting taking a break from him cut him deeply for a reason, and you know exactly what that reason is."

She turned to leave.

"Wait." I shot up from my chair. "I need to see him, Rae. Are you going to meet him?"

"No. I don't know where he is tonight."

I narrowed my eyes on her back as she walked out. Rae was lying. She never lied.

Grabbing my own purse and keys, I hurried after her at a discreet distance. I followed her and felt nervous anticipation when I saw her head inside the Walk. Cole was there. I'd bet everything I had on it.

The pub was pretty crowded. It always was on a Saturday evening. I pushed past people standing around the bar near the door and craned my neck as I struggled out of the small crowd to the main floor. Every table was filled.

I caught sight of Rae winding her way through the tables, and my gaze zeroed past her.

That sick feeling in my stomach intensified.

Cole was sitting with the twins and Karen, a pint of lager in hand. He had other company too. A pretty blond woman was sitting with her thigh pressed against his, and Cole had his head bent so she could whisper in his ear.

My cheeks grew hot, my skin prickling.

Letting the burn of jealousy rush through me and flare out, I took a deep breath. Cole would never cheat. I knew that. I knew that the picture in front of me was innocent.

But I'd spent the whole week agonizing over our relationship and feeling guilty, and he'd spent the whole week avoiding me. Now he was allowing some woman to chat him up.

I felt the prickle of tears in my eyes.

I couldn't handle this. Not with everything else that was going on. I needed coolheaded Cole back, because hurt, hotheaded Cole was tapping in to all the insecurities I'd been fighting the last few months.

On that thought I whirled around and started pushing back through the crowds. I was almost at the door when something stopped me.

This wasn't like Cole.

This wasn't like him at all.

Hadn't that been my mantra this whole week?

I sucked in a breath and spun around.

There was something more going on here that I didn't understand.

Praying I wasn't acting like a too-trusting lovesick fool, I forced my way back through a now-annoyed crowd. The blonde remained, but Cole's attention was on Rae. He was frowning at whatever she had to say.

That was when he seemed to feel my gaze.

Ignoring the raging swarm of angry nerves in my stomach, I wound my way through the tables while Cole broodily watched me approach. When I came to a stop the twins and Karen said hello. I gave them a distracted nod.

Cole and I stared at each other and the longer we did, the deeper I felt the wound of his avoidance. I'd missed him so much. A whole week without him had felt like forever. It had been painful and frankly unnecessary. I was mad at him as much as he was mad at me and I couldn't hide it. I flicked a hand to the blonde. "Why?"

He frowned. "We're just talking."

"But why are you talking to her and not to me? Why haven't you answered my calls? Why did you leave? Why can't we be grown-ups and discuss last Saturday?"

"Not here," Cole said softly.

"I don't care," I snapped, and I didn't care if we had an audience. "This isn't you. I came in here, after one of the most awful weeks of my life, and I could have just walked back out again . . . but *this* isn't you. I don't understand what's going on with you."

The stark hurt in his eyes made me gasp. "You don't understand?" He stood up abruptly, slamming his pint on the table. "You don't understand I'm upset you're packing your shit and taking off for Glasgow to be with that fucking family—choosing them over us? You don't understand that might upset me?"

The people around us stopped talking.

I didn't care. I was too confused to care. "What the heck are you talking about?"

"Rae told me." He raked his eyes over me, seeming to flinch in pain at the sight of me. "Just go, Shannon. All these months trying to get you to trust me . . . what a waste of my time."

"I do trust you." I pushed him—hard—and he stumbled back against the bench seat in surprise. "That's why I'm giving you the benefit of the doubt. Now, what the heck"—I threw a glare at Rae—"did she say?"

"I told him the truth." She returned my glower. "That you're leaving us. You were packing last weekend. Or you were before you failed with your dad today."

"You silly cow," I hissed, not sure if I was calling myself that or Rae. My gaze swung back to Cole. Now *I* was pissed. "I was packing my stuff because you said you were going to ask me to move in with you. I was under the impression once you cooled down and realized I was sorry that the offer would still be open."

Cole blinked, stunned.

I shook my head in exasperation. "It's you and me. This." I gestured between us. "This is how we started out and this probably won't be the last time we have an argument. I have a tendency to think out loud, and sometimes my thought process involves really crap ideas before I get to the good ones. That's what happened last week. You blew up and I get why, but I never believed we'd stay mad at each other or broken up." I took a step toward him. I was relieved to see his expression soften. "I trust you, Cole. I trust you because I know you. I love you because I know you. All this time we've talked about my trust issues and never about yours. Clearly this proves you have them." I braced. "So decide, Cole . . . Do you trust me?"

"I don't know." His eyes flared at the sound of my hurt gasp and he leaned into me. "You know," he said, voice low with emotion. "You know everything. You know how she made me feel my whole life, and still you sat there and suggested putting me to one side so you could work on me gaining your family's approval. She was unworthy of me and still she made me feel like nothing, like I had something to prove. *They're* unworthy of you and still somehow you made me feel like the nothing, like *I* have something to prove. *You*, of all people."

"No," I pleaded, tears blurring my vision. "I never meant for you to feel that way. Not ever again."

"But I did. And I don't know what that means for us."

"You look like hell."

I lifted my gaze to meet Logan's and he winced at whatever he saw in my eyes.

"What happened?"

I ran a trembling hand through my hair. "I've messed up. Again."

"Messed up how?"

"I wanted to make this right for you." Feeling the burn of tears in the backs of my eyes, I fought them. I was sick of crying. It felt like I'd spent the last four nights crying. "You wanted our family back, and I wanted to give that to you. I owe you that. But I don't think I can, Logan." I shook my head, anger stinging in my blood. "They gave me an ultimatum. Them or Cole. *Them?* They've never once asked me how I've coped with Ollie's attack. Not once. They act like I was asking for it or something."

Logan's violet eyes darkened with anger and I knew it wasn't directed at me. I knew because the anger mingled with disappointment. I'd seen that look on his face many times over the years when he was thinking about our parents.

I took a shuddering breath. "Because I hesitated I've lost the only guy who's ever really loved me." Losing the battle with my tears, I swiped at them in frustration, unable to meet Logan's gaze. "Cole broke up with me because of them."

"Shay, I don't understand . . ."

So I told him everything.

"I was happy, Logan," I concluded. "I felt guilty for being happy while you're in here and I wanted to do something for you, but I can't do this. I've screwed it up with you, with them, and with Cole." I tugged on my hair. "Ugh, maybe it's not unsalvageable. I mean Cole's gone, so Mum, Dad, and Amanda will accept me back into their lives. Maybe we *can* be a family again." *I'll just bury my resentment.*

"Shannon." Logan grabbed for my hand and my full attention. Concern was written all over his face. "You're looking and acting like you haven't slept in days."

I pulled gently on his hand. "I've only ever had two people in my life that I adore . . . and I've hurt them both. I put you in prison and I broke Cole's heart." I swatted at my tears. "And I can't stop crying. It's ridiculous. Even Rae's being nice to me. That's when you know you're pathetic." I shrugged. "Stu's probably going to fire me anyway. The atmosphere between me and Cole at work is horrendous and Stu warned me he'd get rid of me if I was causing problems wi—"

"Can you please shut up for two minutes?" Logan interrupted, scowling at me. "One: I'm not going to repeat this again. You did not put me here. *I* put me here. Two: Shannon, I would never have asked you to do anything that would make you unhappy to make *them* happy. As long as you and I are good, what does it matter?"

"But you said—"

"You didn't have to take it so much to heart. I didn't realize how guilty you've been feeling. I mean, I knew you felt guilty for some fucked-up reason, but I didn't realize it was this deep-seated. Sweetheart." He shook his head. "You've got to let that go."

I was silent. There was no point replying, because I couldn't give him the assurance he was looking for. I felt remorseful. That feeling wasn't going anywhere anytime soon.

"As to Cole . . . I've never seen you this bad before. I'd never seen you as happy as I had last time either, so I can tell this guy is different. Forget everyone else, Shannon. Go back to Edinburgh and make it right with him. And when you do, come back here and let me thank the guy who's been taking care of my wee sister while I can't."

I smiled tremulously. "Were you always this awesome?"

Deadpan, he said, "Wise since birth, wee ane. Wise since birth."

I laughed softly and then stopped at a sudden, terrible thought. "He's not going to take me back. I don't know how to make him see how much he means to me."

Logan winked. "Go big . . . or go home."

CHAPTER 26

The Georgian town house on Dublin Street was stunning. Beyond stunning. I couldn't stop gawping at the gleaming dark hardwood floors and the expensive but simple furnishings.

The gorgeous property belonged to Joss and Braden and was currently filled with the couple's closest friends and family, who were there to celebrate the birth of baby Jarrod. I'd gate-crashed and was incredibly worried I was about to vomit all over their hardwood floors.

Joss didn't seem too concerned I'd gate-crashed. In fact, she got this almost satisfied sparkle in her gaze when she opened her front door and found me on the stoop.

"I'm here to go big or go home," I said without preamble.

She grinned and stepped aside. "Then by all means come in."

The noise from the sitting room jolted me as I followed the hostess into it. Light streamed in from the huge floor-to-ceiling windows situated on opposite ends of the long room. Nate, Liv, Mick, and his wife, Dee, were chatting to Cole and Cam, who was holding Belle in his arms by the old Georgian fireplace. Dylan led Elodie across the room toward Luke, William, and Bray, who were huddled around toys on the floor. Clark, Declan, and Marco stood laughing by the nearest window at whatever Braden was telling them, while Jo sat perched on the armchair Ellie was sitting on as they ate finger food. Squeals of laughter sounded from the back of the room where Beth, Lily, and January were watching a Disney movie on the large television. Beth had little Sophia in her arms.

As if he sensed me, Cole glanced over. He stiffened at the sight of me and I braced myself. A hush fell over the room as the adults noted my presence.

"Cole, Shannon is here to see you." Joss stared him down on my behalf until his feet started moving toward me.

"What are you doing here?" he asked, appearing a little shell-shocked to see me.

The dark circles that had been under his eyes all week hadn't gone anywhere and his usual scruff was turning into a beard. It was selfish of me, but I was relieved he wasn't dealing well with our separation either.

I licked my dry lips, glancing around at everyone staring at us. Finally I looked up into Cole's handsome face. "I'm here because I love you, and I need to ask you something." I took a deep breath. It was time to go big.

I lowered myself to one knee.

Cole's eyes grew round and I heard a few female gasps behind him. "Shannon, what—"

"Cole Walker, I once told you in fear that you were nothing, but there has never been a day of your life that that was true and there has never been a day I've ever really thought that. You've been extraordinary to me since we were fifteen." I smiled shakily, feeling vulnerable and frightened but hopeful too as he stared down at me with growing tenderness in his expression. "Apart from Logan I've never had a *real* family. The kind you can count on through everything. The kind that gives you second, third, fourth chances because the other option is no option at all. Because they love you and they're there for you. Unconditionally. Logan was the only one who ever gave me that. Until you. You're my family, Cole. I want you to be my family forever." I laughed hoarsely. "I don't have a ring or anything. I just have me. And I know I'm not perfect and I know you deserve perfect . . . but I love you more than anyone else in this world and I promise you I'll never let you forget that again." My heart slowed its rapid beating as a sense of calm came over me. A sense of rightness. It was as if I'd found the balance I'd been missing ever since I got in that car and left Cole behind on that stoop on Scotland Street all those years ago. "It's always been you, and I always want it to be . . . Marry me, Cole."

Everything seemed to freeze around us as Cole's glittering gaze stayed locked on mine. He lowered himself to his knees and slid his hand over my leg while his other cupped my cheek. I leaned into his touch. "You really know how to get a guy's attention . . . between that hair and the proposal . . ." He grinned.

I curled my fingers around his wrist. "Was that a yes?"

He tugged me toward him and I braced my hands on his chest. "Even though you stole my thunder . . ." He nodded and pressed a soft kiss to my lips. "Yes, Shannon."

Euphoria swept over me as Cole kissed me again, this time long and hard. I kissed him back with abandon, barely even aware of the laughter and celebration of his family all around us.

. . .

My fingers curled into the bedsheet and I gasped, my head falling back against Cole's shoulder as he moved inside me. We lay on our sides, my back to Cole's chest.

It was intoxicating—like he was all around me, inside me, a part of me. His scent was everywhere, his heart beat at my back, and his hand caressed my breast. I was aware of everything—the roughness of the hair on his legs brushing against the soft skin of mine, the sound of his breathing as it quickened, the thick, all-encompassing sensation of him inside me.

Overwhelming.

Pure.

True.

In a way nothing ever had been before.

When I came around him my pulse throbbed so hard it reverberated in the base of my throat.

"Shannon," Cole panted. "Oh, f-fuck," he stuttered out as he tensed seconds before he climaxed.

Damp from sweat, I found it a small kind of relief when Cole bunched my hair in his hand and lifted it off my neck so he could kiss me there. Since our return from Joss and Braden's and our reconciliation/engagement, we'd gone at each other like lust-starved teenagers. First he pinned me against the wall of his hallway; then he carried me to his bed, where we'd screwed each other's brains out.

Finally our urgency eased as we silently reassured each other. We'd made love slowly, leisurely, and somehow it was the most erotic part of the whole evening.

Cole shifted as if to pull out of me and I put my hand on his hip to stop him. "Stay," I whispered.

"Inside you?"

I nodded, grabbing his arm and tugging it around my waist.

Catching on, Cole took me with him as he moved to switch off the light. He then settled, spooning me.

My eyes were just drifting closed when he spoke into the dark. "You were right. What you said about me trusting you. I didn't even realize it until you said it."

Fully alert, I ran the tips of my fingers along his forearm. "It's okay."

"I need you to understand something. I need you to understand why I reacted the way I did, why I didn't give myself time to think. See . . ." His voice grew low. "All those years ago on Scotland Street when I stepped out of Ellie's door and you turned around, I thought—" He cut off abruptly, subconsciously tightening his hold on me.

"You thought?"

"I don't know how to say it without sounding like a cheesy idiot."

"I just proposed to you without a ring or an actual plan in front of your whole family. There's no judgment here."

He laughed, his breath puffing against my neck. "True." He kissed me again. "When you turned around, it was like you'd . . . I don't know, like, you'd been conjured from air or something just for me. I can't explain it. I just knew that you were meant for me," he confessed. "To me it was like you were there to make up for all the bad stuff that had come before you. But then just like that you went away and I guess I believed that made more sense than anything good ever could. At the time anyway. I grew up and grew out of that broody shit." He gave me a squeeze and I wondered if he could hear how hard and fast my heart was pumping in my chest.

"And then you walked back into my life and I wanted you. Because I felt drawn to you still. It was, and is, powerful, Shannon. I've never felt like that with any woman.

"Jo, Hannah, Liv, all of them are special to me and I've always had reasons to trust them. But you . . . Someone tried to break you, take you away from yourself, and in a way take you away from me. I guess I've just been waiting for you to stop trusting me because it doesn't seem possible that I get to keep this dream." He leaned over and I turned my head to meet his gaze, feeling so much more for this man than I'd known it was possible to feel. "I'm sorry if I let you down lately."

"No." The tears came and I let them fall. "Cole, you could never let me down. Do you know what it means to me that you see me that way? Don't you get it? You're the most beautiful man I've ever met—you're kind and smart, loyal and compassionate, and strong and talented and brave and forgiving. You're everything I ever wanted from life, and that you feel the same way back . . . All my life I've been scared and I never knew why." I smiled through my tears. "I'm not scared anymore."

He crushed my lips beneath his, his groans of joy surrounding me like everything else about him.

Once he was finished showing his appreciation for my words, my confession, I settled back, clasping his arm tight to my breasts, and I promised him, "I meant what I said. I'll never choose anyone over you. My family should care enough not to put me in that position. I'm going to see them next week and that's exactly what I'm going to tell them."

I felt Cole's hesitation and he didn't even have to say what he was thinking. I just knew.

"Don't worry. This is what I want. Logan wants this for me too. The contention between me and my family doesn't need to affect my relationship with my brother." I relaxed deeper against my pillow. "Cole . . . they've never given me what you've given me. Not once. You're worth it." I smiled into the dark of our bedroom. "You're worth every bad thing that's ever happened to me, because going through them led me to you."

"Shannon." He pulled me closer, his voice gruff, thick with emotion.

I decided to stop there. Cole finally got it.

I wasn't going anywhere.

Why would I when I had the best seat in the house?

"I guess this means I need to start being nice to you again?" Rae wrinkled her nose.

Cole and I had just been ambushed. We broke the news of our engagement to Rae and Simon that morning before clients started appearing, and it had been received with enthusiastic congratulations, followed by whispering and secretive, mischievous glances.

Their behavior started to make sense ten minutes after our last client left and the bell over the door rang. In walked Stu, followed by Tony. Rae and Simon had called to tell them about our news. Stu set off party poppers around us. I got bear hugs from all the guys and finally a tentative embrace from Rae.

"Being nice would be appreciated. If you can manage it."

"I can try."

I sighed and offered her a small smile. "Look, I understand you were just being loyal to Cole."

"Don't." She held up a hand to stop me. "I fucked up, Shannon. I stuck my nose in your business and I made it worse. I'm sorry."

I raised an eyebrow but decided not to tease her for admitting she was wrong. "It's in the past. It all worked out, right?"

"Yeah." She smirked and shot a look at Cole. "Although you did kind of steal his moment proposing to him. He's the most bloody romantic guy I know, and he didn't get to propose to his girlfriend."

I bit my lip, staring at him as he laughed at something Stu said. "Do you think he minds?"

"I think he gets to marry you . . . so no. I don't think he minds."

A couple of hours later we were joined by the twins and Karen, Mike, and a few of Tony and Rae's friends. People brought beer, food, and champagne, turning the get-together into a full-blown engagement party.

A little tipsy on champagne and wanting the whole world to be as happy as I was, I found myself sidling up to Simon, who was standing brooding in the corner of the studio with a beer in hand. He smiled at my approach. I slid an arm around him and cuddled into his side.

"Are you okay, friend?"

Simon looked down at me. I'd been a little too preoccupied lately with my own stuff to notice the weariness in his eyes. "I will be."

"The baby thing?"

"Shannon, this is your engagement party. Let's not talk about it."

"I want to. I want my friend to be happy."

He smiled and bent his head to press a kiss to my forehead. "I'm okay."

"Is Tony?"

Realizing I wasn't going to stop pestering him until he gave me something, Simon replied, "He loves me. He's not leaving me."

"I sense a but."

"I just don't want him to end up resenting me."

"Do you never want to have kids?"

He shrugged. "I don't know. I just know I don't right now."

"That's why he's staying." I squeezed his arm and pulled away. "Who knows what you'll want in the future? No one ever does. Tony doesn't want to walk away from you on a maybe. He loves you, Simon. And you love him. So stop brooding about the future and just enjoy what you have right now."

Simon pushed away from the wall, his gaze fixed on his partner, who was laughing with Rae and looking exceptionally handsome in a black open-collared shirt and black trousers. Simon couldn't hide the way he felt about Tony. It emanated from him. He shot me a smile of thanks. "I think I'll do that."

I watched as he strode across the room with purpose, coming up behind Tony and placing a hand on his shoulder. He leaned in and pressed his lips to Tony's jaw. Tony's eyelids grew heavy and lazy as he turned to meet Simon's mouth with his own.

"Playing matchmaker?" Cole murmured, wrapping his arms around me and drawing me back against his chest.

I relaxed against him. "Just passing along a very important lesson you taught me."

"Hmm." He brushed his lips over my ear. "How about we go home and I teach you a little something else?"

I shivered in anticipation. "Like?"

"Life drawing skills. If I remember correctly you promised you'd let me draw you naked."

Grinning, I turned around in his arms. "I did, didn't I?" I pressed closer. "Let's make it more interesting."

"More interesting than drawing you naked?"

"Uh-huh. Let's make a bet."

"A bet?"

"I bet you that you'll give in to temptation and score with your nude model within ten minutes."

Cole gave me an "oh, please" look. "I'll take that bet. I'll last at least thirty minutes."

"So cocky." I was so going to win this bet. "Terms?"

"If I win I get your mouth first." He winked.

I laughed. "Dirty boy. Fine. If I win I get your mouth first."

"Deal."

I shook the hand he held out. "Deal."

I didn't play fair as a nude model. Let's just say I was never very good at sitting completely still.

Cole lasted three minutes.

CHAPTER 27

A week later we found ourselves back at Joss and Braden's home. Ellie wanted us to celebrate our engagement in style. I don't know how they managed to pull off another get-together so quickly, but the dining table was covered in buffet food, and there were decorations and cake. Everyone had carved time out of their busy schedules. They'd also brought gifts that were now piled in the hallway.

"There you are." Hannah smiled at us. She approached carrying the tiny bundle that was Jarrod.

Cole's family and friends lounged in the sitting room in much the same way as they had the week before. I was a little nervous being around them again after they'd witnessed my emotional proposal, but after having dinner with Jo and Cam this week, I at least felt more comfortable around Cole's big sister.

And of course Hannah always put me at ease.

Taking in Jarrod's beautiful little face and the blue vest that had the words "I'm so cute I must be Scottish" printed on them, I immediately let go of Cole's hand. "Can I hold him?"

She chuckled and nodded, passing Jarrod over to me.

I took his solid, warm little weight, beaming into his now-inquiring eyes as he squirmed a little. He settled as I secured him in my arms. "Well, aren't you the most gorgeous little thing on the planet?" He had Marco's coloring, although his eyes were dark blue, but that might, and probably would, change as he got older. "Look at you, charming the pants off women already."

Cole smoothed his large hand over Jarrod's head and I swear to God my brooding levels hit an all-time high. "Learning from the best, buddy, eh?"

I stared stupidly up at my fiancé. "What?"

Hannah snorted. "She's having a moment. Leave her."

Cole quirked an eyebrow. "A moment? A—no." His eyes grew comically round. "One thing at time, Shortcake. Now, hand the child over slowly."

I giggled and passed Jarrod back to an amused Hannah. "You'd make a great dad."

"I'm sure I will," he said confidently. "And I look forward to it . . . in at least five years' time."

I was delighted he'd even thought about it. I didn't want kids right away either. I had so much I still wanted to do. But it was nice to know Cole and I were on the same page about something so huge.

I gestured to Jarrod. "I don't know how you get anything done with all that adorableness around you."

"Actually, despite the distracting adorableness, Jarrod has been great. Sophia cried most nights, but Jarrod sleeps a lot. He's an absolute angel."

Seeing the loving look on his friend's face, Cole said cautiously, "Not looking forward to returning to work, then?"

Hannah shrugged. "I'm looking forward to getting back into the classroom, but I'll miss this. I'm only going back part-time to begin with. I still need more time with this little guy." She suddenly grinned at me and stepped closer, lowering her voice. "Cole tells us you're a talented artist and have a particular talent at landscapes."

"Oh." Surprised by the change in subject and the compliment, I found myself stuttering, "I'm all ri— Okay, I mean, I guess I—I'm okay."

Cole wrapped an arm around me and jerked me into his side. "What she meant to say was 'Yes, I'm a bloody fantastic artist, thank you.'"

I rolled my eyes. "What he said."

Hannah laughed. "Well, good, because we were all trying to come up with the perfect gift to give the couple who have everything." She gestured to the room around us, so I gathered she meant Joss and Braden. "And then we thought it might be a lovely idea to commission a cityscape of Edinburgh."

"Commission?" I put my free hand to my chest. "Commission *me?*"

"Well, yes. We trust Cole's eye, and if he says you're good, then you're good."

Amazed, humbled, excited, all of the above, I nodded enthusiastically. "I'd love to. What are they celebrating?"

"Joss's pregnancy, of course."

More surprise shot through me and I looked up at Cole in question.

He winced. "With everything we had going on I forgot to tell you."

"Tell her what?" Joss's familiar voice queried behind us.

We turned and she, Jo, and Ellie closed in on us so we created a small circle.

"That you're pregnant." I smiled. "Congratulations."

Her gunmetal eyes softened. "Thank you. This is the last one, so Braden has everyone making a huge deal out of it."

"It is a big deal." Her husband sidled up to her, inserting himself in beside her and Ellie so he could press a kiss to Joss's neck. Joss leaned into him and sighed.

"Fine, it's a big deal, but can we please stop talking about it? This is Cole and Shannon's engagement party."

"Oh, please," Hannah snorted as her big sister took Jarrod from her. "This is *Ellie's* party."

Ellie grinned unashamedly. "Any excuse, eh, baby boy," she cooed, pressing a kiss to Jarrod's forehead.

"Oh, give him here." Elodie appeared at her side, reaching for her grandchild.

"You're not playing pass the parcel," Hannah huffed.

"Shush." Elodie waved her off and pressed Jarrod to her body. "I haven't held him in fifteen minutes. I'm having withdrawals."

"How are you feeling?" I felt the need to ask. During all the excitement last weekend, I hadn't inquired. "You look well."

Her cheeks were flushed, her eyes bright, and she had lost that haggard tiredness she'd worn after the attack.

"I'm fine, sweetheart," she assured me, giving me a kind smile. "I've had plenty of rest and I'm feeling strong. Especially now that I have another beautiful grandchild to keep me busy, and a wedding to look forward to."

"Shannon, before I forget," Braden suddenly said, drawing my attention from the matriarch of the family. "I have an offer for your brother."

"An offer?" I said, puzzled.

Out of the corner of my eye, I saw Marco appear. He pulled Hannah into his side.

"I shared," Cole explained, looking concerned. "Not about everything but about why Logan was in prison. I thought they could help. I'm sorry. I should—"

"It's fine." I cut him off and pressed a hand to his arm in reassurance. "I trust them." I glanced back at Braden. "What kind of offer?"

"I imagine he'll find it hard to get work when he gets out of prison, but Cole explained matters and a man shouldn't have to bear those kinds of consequences for protecting his family. When your brother gets out send him to me and I'll find a job for him wherever he feels he wants to start over. I have a number of opportunities for him."

"Same here," Marco said. "I'm site manager for a construction company. If he doesn't find anything to suit him with Braden, I'd be happy to set him up somewhere suitable to his skill set."

Overwhelmed by their generosity, I was struck completely dumb for a few seconds.

The silence only broke when Cole sought to close my mouth by pressing a finger under my chin. Everyone chuckled and I swatted playfully at his hand.

"Thank you," I managed. "That really means a lot. It'll mean a lot to Logan too."

"You're Cole's family now. That makes you our family." Elodie smiled.

"And on that note." Cole stepped away from me and lowered himself to one knee.

"Cole, what are—"

"Stealing my thunder back." He grinned and took my hand. "Here in this room are the people who mean the most to me. A family that embraced my family and made us stronger for it. It was the best gift I'd ever been given until the moment you told me you loved me."

My breath hitched.

"You offered me everything last week, and I want my chance to offer everything back to you. I'm offering you what they once offered me. I'm offering you a family who will love and protect you not only because *I* love and protect you, but because you're an amazing woman who deserves every sweet thing life has to give. We're going to spend the rest of our lives happier and stronger because we have each other, and because we finally have the kind of family behind us we both always dreamed of having."

The tears were pouring so fast down my cheeks I could barely see through the blur as he produced a narrow-pointed marquise diamond perched on a platinum band. His own eyes were bright with emotion as he slid the ring onto my finger.

Seconds later I was lifted into his arms. I wrapped my legs around his waist as I kissed the life out of him. When I finally managed to pry myself from him, a teary-eyed Jo, Liv, and Elodie hugged me, followed by a grinning Joss, Ellie, and Hannah. I received more congratulatory hugs from the men and even from the kids, and I stood there in Cole's arms, staring every five seconds at the beautiful ring on my finger, thinking how strange life could be.

How a person could go from feeling so lonely and broken to so cherished and hopeful in only a few short months.

As I gazed around at the colorful characters who surrounded me, I decided it was *them*. They had a kind of magic about them, a magic they'd gifted to Cole, who in turn had gifted it to me.

It had been two weeks since our engagement. In that time I'd moved all of my things into Cole's, where he surprised me once more. He'd had a sofa bed put in the guest bedroom to replace the bed that had been in there. He did this to provide more room . . . more room for all of my art stuff. It was also a great space away from the studio for him to concentrate on his own artwork.

Living with Cole was pretty easy overall. I'd be lying if I didn't say it was scary and heady and exciting too.

Before I got to do the fun moving-in stuff, I went back to Glasgow to meet with my family. They were pissed, but I was done trying to prove myself to them. Only time would tell whether or not we'd get past our issues.

I had Cole now.

And I'd always had Logan.

My eyes were drawn to my brother as soon as Cole and I walked into the visitor room at the prison. Logan sat waiting for us, looking alert, scrutinizing Cole as he led me by the hand through the room.

I smiled at my brother as we took our seats opposite him. "Logan, it's good to see you again."

"You too, Shay." His eyes flicked to Cole. "I take it you went big, not home."

I laughed and nodded.

Cole looked confused.

"My brother encouraged me to propose."

My fiancé raised an eyebrow at that. "Without having met me?"

Logan shrugged. "I went with my instincts on this one."

Feeling giddy for many reasons, I leaned toward him. "I'll let you two chat and get to know each other in a minute, but first I have great news."

"Greater than that big bloody diamond on your finger?" Logan took my hand and then smirked at Cole. "Nice."

"Focus." I jerked on Logan's hand, bringing his attention back to me. "Look, you remember I mentioned Cole's family are involved in quite a bit of business in Edinburgh?"

"Yeah."

I grinned. "Logan, Braden's offered you a job. So did Marco. When you get out . . . they'll have something waiting for you."

Logan stared at me dumbly for a second and then at Cole. When he returned his gaze to me, he said softly, "Are you kidding me?"

"Nope. They know everything and they get it. They want to help you out."

"That's . . ." He shook his head. "Why would they? They don't know me."

"They know me." I squeezed his hand. "And they're good people."

Logan rubbed a hand over his short hair. "I'm a bit speechless. I've been . . . I've been worrying about what would happen once I get back out there . . . This . . ." He looked at Cole. "Thanks, mate. This means a lot. Tell them thanks."

Cole nodded. "It's not a problem."

Logan gripped my hand harder. "Thanks, Shannon."

"No." I smiled, fighting tears of happiness. "Thank you."

EPILOGUE

Eighteen months later

Light flooded the room. The smell of flowers and paint fumes had already become so familiar to me it was like being home. I was so comfortable there I lost myself in the art. Sometimes I had no idea how much time had passed.

Stepping back from the large piece of canvas, I contemplated the scene. It was a dystopian New York painted in gouache. It was my first time using the paint and so far I was enjoying the velvety effect of it.

"Shannon."

"Hmm?"

"Shannon, what are you still doing here? It's six o'clock."

That penetrated my fog. "What?" I glanced over my shoulder at my friend and classmate Bernice. Bernie and I were both older freshman at Edinburgh College of Art and had gravitated to each other almost immediately when we started a few short months ago. I stared around at the empty classroom. "Damn." I put my brush down. "I'm supposed to be at Joss's book launch in an hour."

"You can make it if you hurry."

I nodded, grabbed my bag, and rushed past her. "Thank you! See you tomorrow."

"You're covered in paint," Cole said without preamble as soon as I stumbled into our apartment. He grabbed my hand. "Shower."

I felt a rush of anticipation but tried to squash it considering we didn't have a whole lot of time. "I can't shower with you. We'll be really, really, really late."

He pushed open the door and shrugged out of his shirt, revealing the stylized "S" he'd had tattooed on his chest. Just like Stu had predicted, Cole had not heeded Steely's warning about getting a woman's name tattooed on him. I'd talked him out of getting my entire name scripted onto his skin, and we'd agreed on the initial. "Then we'll be really, really, really late."

Laughing, I followed him, tugging off my own shirt and leaving it behind on the floor beside his. "If anyone asks, I'll blame you."

"You're late," Hannah whispered as Cole and I pushed through the small crowd in the bookstore to stand with our family.

"Cole's fault," I whispered back.

"What was it this time?" Marco muttered. "Testing the weight of the kitchen table?"

I grinned, staring straight ahead at Joss, who was talking about the inspiration behind her latest character. "Nope. The effectiveness of our showerhead."

"I think I'm going to be sick."

I laughed softly at the familiar grumble and looked over my shoulder. Logan stood behind me, dressed smartly in a dark blue shirt and black jeans.

He grimaced at me. "Do me a favor—look around the room before you share those kinds of details."

Trying to stem my giggling, I nodded and turned back to listen to Joss.

A few minutes later she'd finished her introduction, signed some books, and was now heading toward us. She took in my still-damp curls and the high color on my cheeks. "First you're late and then you talk through my intro. You owe me another painting."

"Sorry. It was all Cole's fault."

"Stop." Logan held up a hand. "What did I say?"

"What did you say?" Braden came to a stop beside him.

Logan frowned at his boss. "I can't discuss it."

"It involves me, Cole, and a shower."

Braden winced. "Oh, don't go there."

My brother groaned. "I need a drink." He wandered off toward the drinks table and I watched him lift a glass of champagne. A pretty brunette reached for one at the same time and smiled flirtatiously at him. Logan gave her a cocky smile and leaned in to speak quietly to her. I knew not to get my hopes up about anything serious happening there. My brother had made it clear he was not interested in developing any kind of meaningful relationship with a woman anytime soon. I thought that was a shame. I was convinced the right woman would help rid him of the hard aspect prison had put in his eyes.

"He's doing well." Braden drew my attention back to him

Logan had gotten out of prison a couple of months ago and Braden, true to his word, had given him a job as security at his nightclub,

Fire. In a few short weeks Logan's natural air of authority and leadership became quickly apparent. Braden was impressed with the changes he'd suggested for the club's security, as well as creative ideas he had for the club itself.

"I'm really proud of him for starting over." *And as for my guilt . . . it's nearly all gone.*

"You should be."

"Shannon!"

I turned around and caught sight of Elodie waving at me. She was standing with Jo, Hannah, and Liv and there was a very obvious pile of wedding magazines in her arms.

"Seriously?" I shot a look at Joss. "It's your night."

Joss laughed. "Hey, wedding trumps book launch, and this long engagement is starting to kill Elodie and Ellie."

"We haven't even set a date yet."

"Exactly. If I were you, I would. The faster you get it over with, the quicker your life will return to normal."

"No more bridal magazines, dress samples, and venue selections," I mused, and then, mind made up, I whipped around, searching the room for Cole. I found him standing in the corner with Marco, Cam, and Nate. "Cole!"

He raised an eyebrow at my shouting.

"We're setting a date!"

"Finally!" we heard Ellie cry happily from the other side of the bookstore.

Cole and I burst out laughing along with the rest of our family.

Later that night as we lay snuggled together in bed, Cole murmured, "How was school today?"

"Good. Work?"

"Good. I miss you during the week, though."

Since I started art school, Stu had hired someone to work part-time during the week, and I worked the weekends. "I miss you too."

"So we're setting a date?"

I smiled and pressed my lips to his chest. "It's time, don't you think?"

"I'll marry you whenever you want, Shortcake. You know that."

Warmth spread through my whole being as I curled up against him. "I spoke to Dad yesterday and he said Mum wants us over for dinner at the end of the month."

"Another dinner?" he teased. "I think she's starting to like me."

I chuckled. "It's killing Amanda."

"Good."

Smiling at his dry reply, I closed my eyes.

For the last few months it really felt like my life was finally finding balance. What with Cole, school, Logan, and now my parents coming around to the idea of my fiancé, I felt more at peace than I'd ever felt before.

Suddenly our conversation all those years ago on Scotland Street came to me.

"So, are you a hero, Cole Walker?"

"What is a hero, really?"

"I suppose it's someone that saves people."

"Yeah, I suppose it is."

"So, do you save people?"

"I'm only fifteen. Give me a chance."

"I'm so glad I did," I murmured drowsily as Cole's arm tightened around me.

ACKNOWLEDGMENTS

Ever since Cole first appeared in the *On Dublin Street* series, readers wanted him to grow up so I could share his love story with them. I want to thank all those readers for being so passionate about this series and its characters, and I really hope Cole is the kind of man you all hoped he'd grow up to become. I know I'm proud of him.

I want to also say a massive thank-you to the team of people around me who help make each book develop into the best story it can be: my agent, Lauren Abramo; my editor, Kerry Donovan; the entire team at NAL; my readers; the passionate bloggers I speak to on a daily basis; my friends and family; all the musicians on the *On Dublin Street* series playlist that inspire me; the delivery woman from Domino's who sees way too much of me when I'm nearing the end of a manuscript; and my author buds, Tammy B and the Indie Hellcats.

All of you support me and encourage me and challenge me in the best way possible and there's not a day that passes when I don't appreciate every single one of you.

ABOUT THE AUTHOR

Samantha Young is the *New York Times* and *USA Today* bestselling author of the *On Dublin Street* series. She resides in Scotland.

CONNECT ONLINE

samanthayoungbooks.com

Grace Farquhar came to Edinburgh to escape the rarified world of privilege and deceit in which she was raised. There, away from the power games of the family she was born to, she can build her own life, work, and the family of her choosing. Her life would be perfect if a) she could find Mr. Right, and b) her annoying, womanizing ruffian of a neighbor would find himself a new flat in an apartment on the other side of the planet.

Logan and Grace are total opposites. She spends her nights working; he fills his nights with women. He's ready to dive into his life now that he's out of jail; she's trying to play it safe. She's sure he's an uneducated, selfish brute; he's sure she's a prissy snob. Their arguments become as routine as their lives—until a fifteen-year-old girl changes everything. She claims to be Logan's daughter, and her arrival gives Logan a sudden dose of responsibility, and Grace a dose of perspective, as she watches Logan shoulder his new burdens with grace and some terror.

Despite the past antagonism between them Grace wants to help Logan, and soon neither of them can deny the sparks that start to fly when anger is transformed into friendship. Throw in conniving friends, a plotting teenager, and families digging up pasts best left forgotten, and Grace and Logan find that while chemistry may be simple, nothing else is.